WILL TANNER, U.S. DEP

DIG
OWN

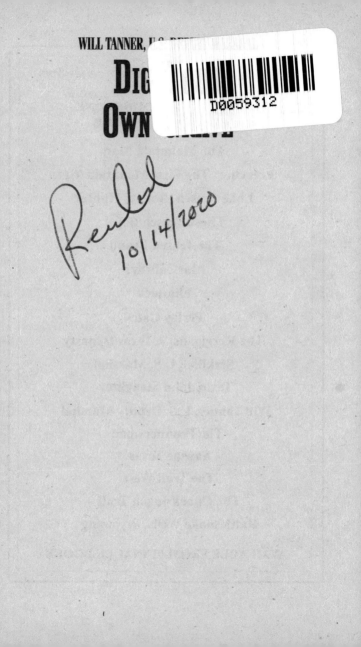

D0059312

Renfold
10/14/2020

WILL TANNER, U.S. DEPUTY MARSHAL

DIG YOUR OWN GRAVE

William W. Johnstone
with J. A. Johnstone

PINNACLE BOOK
Kensington Publishing Corp.
www.kensingtonbooks.com

PINNACLE BOOKS are published by

Kensington Publishing Corp.
119 West 40th Street
New York, NY 10018

PUBLISHER'S NOTE
Following the death of William W. Johnstone, the Johnstone family is working with a carefully selected writer to organize and complete Mr. Johnstone's outlines and many unfinished manuscripts to create additional novels in all of his series like The Last Gunfighter, Mountain Man, and Eagles, among others. This novel was inspired by Mr. Johnstone's superb storytelling.

All Kensington titles, imprints, and distributed lines are available at special quantity discounts for bulk purchases for sales promotions, premiums, fund-raising, educational, or institutional use. Special book excerpts or customized printings can also be created to fit specific needs. For details, write or phone the office of the Kensington sales manager: Kensington Publishing Corp., 119 West 40th Street, New York, NY 10018, attn: Sales Department; phone 1-800-221-2647.

PINNACLE BOOKS, the Pinnacle logo, and the WWJ steer head logo are Reg. U.S. Pat. & TM Off.

ISBN-13: 978-0-7860-4362-0
ISBN-10: 0-7860-4362-8

First printing: April 2019

10 9 8 7 6 5 4 3 2 1

Printed in the United States of America

Electronic edition: April 2019

ISBN-13: 978-0-7860-4363-7 (e-book)
ISBN-10: 0-7860-4363-6 (e-book)

Chapter 1

Looks like Tom Spotted Horse was right, he thought. He dismounted and dropped Buster's reins to the ground, then proceeded on foot to get a better look at the camp by the water's edge. The Chickasaw policeman had told him Ike Skinner had passed through Tishomingo, headed toward Blue River. Will wasn't surprised. He figured Ike was on his way to Texas after a series of train station robberies south along the MKT. So when Dan Stone had sent him to arrest Ike, he had headed down the line to Atoka in hopes of cutting him off before he reached that town. Unfortunately, he was too late by half a day to intercept him in Atoka, but he had an idea that Ike might cut over to Tishomingo. He was sweet on a Chickasaw woman named Lyla Birdsong, who lived there, and that was where Will had arrested him before. Ike was never a man to use good judgment, and it looked like the two years he had spent in prison had done little to teach him any common sense.

Will had also been too late to catch him at Lyla Birdsong's father's cabin in Tishomingo, but he hadn't been hard to track from there. Ike had not waited long to camp for the night, which didn't surprise Will, since he hadn't seen Lyla in two years. *He should have waited at least until he crossed the Red and celebrated their reunion in Texas,* Will thought. He almost felt sorry for him. Ike was not a cruel criminal by any standard. He just wasn't smart enough to make a living from anything but stealing. *Better get my mind back on business,* Will reminded himself, and made his way carefully through the stand of oaks on the banks of the river. Close enough to see the two people seated by the fire clearly now, he took a moment to verify what he had suspected. The other person with Ike was, indeed, Lyla Birdsong. He had hesitated because Lyla had apparently grown some in the two years since Ike was away, not so much up, but out. Will had seen her before on only one brief occasion, and she was a husky woman then. Looking at her now, she looked to be more woman than Ike could handle. He could only assume that she had come with Ike willingly, so he wouldn't have to be charged with abduction on top of the armed robbery charges.

Will moved a few yards closer before suddenly stepping out from behind a tree and calling out a warning. "Don't make a move, Ike, and we'll make this as easy as possible!" As he expected, the warning was wasted as Ike, startled, tried to scramble to his feet. Ready for just such a possibility, Will had his Winchester in position to fire. He placed a shot that kicked up dirt at Ike's feet and stopped him from running. Then he quickly cranked another round into the chamber and placed a second shot in the dirt on the other side of Ike when he started to run in the opposite direction. "I ain't gonna waste any more ammunition in the dirt," Will threatened. "The next one's gonna stop you for good." The warning served its purpose. Ike hesitated a moment, but gave up on the idea of running for cover.

"Will Tanner," Ike moaned plaintively, "I shoulda known it would be you." He stood by the fire, feeling helpless as Will approached, his rifle cocked and still trained on him. "Dadgum it, how'd you find me so quick?"

"You're a creature of habit, Ike," Will replied. "You need to change your old ways, if you're plannin' to be an armed robber the rest of your life. Now, with your left hand, unbuckle that gun belt and let it drop." While Ike dutifully complied, Will kept an eye on the Chickasaw woman, who had so far shown no reaction to his intrusion. Sitting calmly, her stoic expression registering no sign of alarm, she prompted Will to be extra cautious, lest she might suddenly explode.

"Whaddaya botherin' me for, Tanner?" Ike implored. "I ain't done nothin' to get the law on my tail."

"You held up the train depot in McAlester and again in Atoka," Will answered. "Both stationmasters identified you as the bandit."

"How can they be sure it was me?" Ike blurted. "I was wearin' a bandanna on my face." A pregnant moment of silence followed immediately after he said it. "Uh . . ." he stumbled, an expression of utter frustration cramping his whiskered face. "I mean, he was most likely wearin' a mask, weren't he?"

"Yeah, he was wearin' a red bandanna, like the one you're wearin' around your neck," Will said. "Now, you've rode with me before, so you know I don't give you any trouble as long as you don't cause me any." He turned to the somber woman still sitting there, watching impassively. "How 'bout you, Miss Birdsong? There weren't any reports that Ike had anybody with him when he held up the railroad offices. I'm guessin' Ike just picked you up last night. Is that right?" She looked up to meet his gaze, but did not answer his question. "I'm gonna take that as a *yes*," Will said, "so you're free to go on back home." He watched her carefully while she considered what he had just said. "Ike's gonna be gone for a long spell," he added.

"I go," she spoke finally, and got to her feet. It would have been hard to miss the reluctance in her tone. Will could easily understand why. Lyla had an ugly scar on her nose that testified to her having been marked with a knife for entertaining too many men. Almost certainly, she saw Ike Skinner as her only chance to escape her father's cabin, for no men of her tribe would have anything to do with her. No doubt her father would be disappointed to see her return home just as much as she would be.

When she started toward her horse, Ike pleaded, "Lyla, honey, don't leave me. I came to get you as soon as I got outta prison. We was gonna make it down in Texas."

"You not go to Texas," Lyla said. "You go to jail. I not go to jail with you. I go home."

"I reckon this just ain't your day, Ike," Will said. "She wouldn't have stayed with you for very long, anyway." He pointed to a small tree close by. "You know how this works." Ike knew it was useless to balk, so he walked over and put his arms around the tree. Will clamped his wrists together with his handcuffs, then went to help Lyla saddle her horse and get her things together. When she had packed up her few belongings and ridden away, he saddled Ike's horse, then went to retrieve Buster. In a short time, he rode up from the river, leading Ike and his packhorse behind him. Ike didn't have a packhorse. Will suspected that was Ike's packhorse that Lyla was now riding. The makeshift Indian saddle had led him to believe that to be the case. Her father might not have gotten rid of her, but at least he gained a horse.

Will figured three and a half to four days to make the trip to Fort Smith, barring any interruptions along the way, and he didn't expect much trouble from Ike. When he was working in this part of the Nations, and headed home, he usually camped overnight at Jim Little Eagle's cabin on Muddy Boggy Creek near Atoka. He decided there was enough daylight left to make it to Jim's before dark, and the horses were already rested. Jim, the Choctaw policeman, was a good friend of Will's, and his wife, Mary Light Walker, was always a gracious hostess. With that in mind, he started out with thoughts of maybe a couple of biscuits from Mary's oven for him and his prisoner.

They rode for only about thirty minutes before striking a trail that ran between Atoka and the Arbuckle Mountains, a trail that Will had ridden many times before. Following the familiar trail, they approached a low line of hills and a stream that ran through a shallow pass between them. Will usually paused there to let the horses drink and that was his intention on this day. Sensing the water ahead, Buster quickened his pace in anticipation of a drink. Will leaned forward on the big buckskin's neck to give him a playful pat, instantly hearing the snap of a rifle slug passing directly over his back. It was followed almost at the same time by the report of the rifle that fired it. Acting on instinct, he didn't wait to hear the next shot. Hugging Buster's neck, he shifted to the side as much as possible while giving the buckskin his heels. There was no time to worry about Ike following behind him. His reins were tied to a lead rope behind Will's saddle. His first thought was to find cover, so he drove Buster into the trees beside the stream as a second shot whined through the leaves of the trees. He pulled up only when he felt he had put enough trees between himself and the shooter, who he figured was on the other side of the stream.

That was mighty damn careless of me, he thought as he told Ike to dismount. He had a pretty good idea who the shooter was. "Hug that tree!" he ordered.

"You tryin' to get us both kilt?" Ike complained. "You can't leave me locked to a damn tree with somebody tryin' to shoot us!"

"Hurry up and get down off that horse," Will demanded. "I don't wanna have to shoot you outta that saddle." He waited just a moment to make sure Ike did as he ordered. "I don't think you've got much to worry about. I'm pretty sure I'm the target." Once he was satisfied that Ike was secured to a tall pine tree, he made his way back toward the bank of the stream, where he could scan the other side. There had been no more shots fired after the first two, so all he could do was try to guess where the sniper was hiding. As he shifted his eyes back and forth along the stream, he decided that the best place for the shooter to hide was a narrow ravine that led up the slope. He figured the sniper, having missed the kill shot, might be inclined to depart, so he decided to try to keep that from happening. "You just sit tight," he said to Ike when he came back into the trees and started trotting downstream.

"Where the hell are you goin'?" Ike blurted.

"Just sit tight," Will repeated without turning his head. "I'll be back to get you."

In a matter of seconds, he was lost from Ike's sight, and when he decided he was far enough downstream not to be seen, he crossed over the stream and climbed up the hill on the other side. With his Winchester in hand, he hurried along the top of the hill, back toward the ravine he had spotted. He paused briefly when he suddenly heard a wailing from the trees he had just left across the stream. "Lyla, honey!" Ike's mournful voice called out. "Is that you? Be careful, he's comin' to get you!"

"I shoulda stuffed a rag in his mouth," Will mumbled, and started running along the crest of the hill, thinking he'd have to hurry to catch her before she ran. Then he spotted Lyla's horse still tied behind the hill. More careful now, he slowed down as he approached the top of the ravine, expecting to meet her climbing up out of it. There was no sign of her, however, so with his rifle at the ready, he started making his way down the narrow ravine. He had not gone halfway down when he saw her. She had not run at all, but had remained sitting behind a low shoulder of the ravine, her old Spencer carbine still aimed at the trees across from her.

Taking pains to be as quiet as possible, he inched down the ravine until he was no more than thirty feet from the unsuspecting woman. "Make a move and you're dead," he suddenly announced, causing her to freeze for a few moments, afraid to turn around. "Lyla, forget about it," Will warned when she hesitated, as if trying to decide to act or not. "I'll cut you down before you have a chance to turn around. Now, drop that rifle and raise your hands in the air." She hesitated a few moments more, painfully reluctant to admit defeat, then she finally realized she had no chance and did as he instructed. "Doggone it, Lyla, I let you go before, because you hadn't committed any crime. Now you've gone and tried to shoot me, and all to free that worthless saddle tramp, Ike Skinner. So I'm gonna have to arrest you, and I reckon I oughta warn you, white, Indian, man, or woman, it doesn't matter to me. If you don't do like I tell you, or try to run away, I won't hesitate to shoot you. You understand?" She did not reply, as was her custom, so he asked her again, this time a little more forcefully.

"I understand," she said. "I no run."

"Good," he said. "Now we'll go get your horse. Start climbin' up outta this ravine." He followed her up, carrying her old Spencer as well as his Winchester. Once out of the ravine, they went down the backside of the hill and got her horse. She went along without protest, knowing she had been arrested for trying to kill a U.S. Deputy Marshal and would most likely go to jail for it. She had failed in her attempt to free Ike Skinner, but she had managed to complicate the deputy's job of transporting his prisoner. He didn't want to bother with Lyla, even if she did take a shot at him. *I'll decide what to do with her after I get to Atoka*, he told himself.

Upon approaching the spot where he had left Ike and the horses, Will stopped short and dropped the carbine to free both hands to fire his rifle. He was looking at the tree where he had handcuffed Ike, but Ike was gone. Then he noticed a few broken limbs and branches at the base of the tree. They prompted him to look up to discover Ike about fifteen feet up the trunk, clinging to a limb that was obviously too big to break off. Will was frankly amazed. Ike had climbed up the trunk like a telegraph lineman until reaching the limb that stopped him. As insane as it was, Will had to ask, "What the hell were you tryin' to do? Did you think you could climb right up over the top of the tree?"

Ike didn't answer at once. He had to rethink his failed attempt to escape. Still clinging to the limb fifteen feet up the trunk, he finally replied, "I weren't sure it would work, but I figured I'd give it a try."

Will shook his head and shrugged. "Well, shinny back down. I brought you some company, and I'm plannin' to ride awhile before we stop for the night, so hurry up." He figured he had enough time to make it to Jim Little Eagle's cabin before darkness really set in. He was sure he could count on Jim for some help with his prisoners. Since he had brought only one set of handcuffs with him, he had to tie Lyla's hands with his rope. So he busied himself with getting her in the saddle to the accompaniment of little yelps of pain behind him as Ike descended the rough trunk of the pine. Having arrested the simple man before, Will was inclined not to be surprised by any harebrained plan Ike came up with. Lyla, on the other hand, could not be taken lightly. She had already proven to be more dangerous.

The Chickasaw woman's attempt to shoot a lawman

in order to free her lover was a notable boost to the slow-witted outlaw's confidence. "I knew you'd try to get me back, darlin'," he said when they were both in the saddle. "I'm sorry we wound up in this fix after you waited so long for me."

The stoic woman replied with nothing more than a grunt. It was Will's opinion that Lyla's decision to take a shot at him was not an act of devotion toward Ike. It was more an attempt to avoid growing old in her father's cabin. In view of her past indiscretions and unfortunate physical appearance, she was desperate to go with any male who would have her. In spite of what she had done, he felt sorry for her.

The sun was already about to drop below the far hills west of Atoka when Will and his prisoners entered the clearing on Muddy Boggy Creek where Jim Little Eagle had built his cabin. Will called out and identified himself before approaching the cabin. A moment later, Jim, carrying a lantern and his rifle, walked out of the barn. "That you, Will? I wondered who was coming to call this late in the day. Who's that with you?"

Will rode on in and reined Buster to a halt beside the Choctaw policeman. "I've got a couple of prisoners I'm transportin' to jail. Sorry to be ridin' in on you so late, but if you don't mind, I'll camp here on the creek tonight."

Jim walked back, holding his lantern up to get a better look at the prisoners. When he got to Lyla, he held the lantern up a little longer. Walking back beside

Will's horse, he commented, "One of them is a woman. One of our people?"

"Chickasaw," Will replied. "I was thinkin' about turnin' her over to you, her being an Indian. Figured it was more under your jurisdiction. I'll take Ike back to Fort Smith for trial."

"What did she do?" Jim asked, and took a second look at the sullen woman.

"Not much, really," Will said. "Took a shot at me and that's really the only reason I arrested her." He went on then to tell Jim the whole story.

Jim turned his gaze back on Ike then. "So this is the man that stuck a .44 in Sam Barnet's face and rode off with twenty-two dollars."

"That's the man," Will replied. "Twenty-two dollars, huh? Is that all he got?"

They both looked at Ike then, and Jim said, "Yeah, Sam just gave him the little bit in the cash drawer. He said the safe was sitting there with the door open and about twenty-five hundred dollars in it, but your man was in a hurry to run." Ike hung his head, embarrassed upon hearing of his folly. Back to the other issue, Jim said he could put Lyla in jail, since there was no one presently occupying the small building that passed for the Atoka jail. She would be held there until the council could meet to decide her sentence. "Are you charging her with attempted murder?" Jim asked Will.

Lowering his voice to keep Ike and Lyla from hearing, Will said, "I really don't wanna charge her with anything. I'd just like you to keep her till I can get away from here in the mornin' and not worry about her maybe taking another shot at me. Keep her a day, then turn her loose and tell her to go on home."

Jim nodded slowly. "I can do that." He smiled and said, "You're getting a little softhearted. Maybe you've been in this business too long." That reminded him of another subject. "Ed Pine was over here a week ago. He said you were going to get married. Any truth to that?"

"That's a fact," Will answered. "I finally got up the nerve to ask her and damned if she didn't say she would."

"Good for you," Jim said, beaming at Will's sudden blush. "Mary will want to know this. She said you'd never get married. You're gone all the time. Not many women like that." When Will shrugged, Jim went on, "Maybe you hang up your guns and settle down on that ranch you own in Texas."

"Maybe. At least I'm thinkin' about it. I ain't even sure she'd like it there in Texas."

"When's the wedding?" Jim asked.

"To tell you the truth, I don't know. She and her mama are makin' a lotta fuss about planning a big weddin'. Her mama wants to have it around Christmas. I don't care, myself. I'd just as soon jump a broom and be done with it."

"Christmas?" Jim responded. "That's almost five months away."

"Yeah," Will acknowledged with a chuckle. "I think her mama's hopin' Sophie will change her mind before Christmas." He shrugged and said, "I'd best get my prisoners camped and comfortable. I'll bed 'em down in that same spot I used before."

"Who are you talking to out here?" The voice came from the cabin, followed a few seconds later by the appearance of Mary Light Walker. Seeing Will, she answered her own question. "I thought it must be you, Will, so I mixed up some more biscuits. I just put them in the oven. They oughta be ready by the time you set up your camp."

"Howdy, Mary," Will greeted her. "I apologize for showin' up so late in the evenin'. I didn't expect to bother you with fixin' any food for me and my prisoners."

"You never were a good liar, Will Tanner," Mary replied. "Go ahead and take care of your prisoners. Hurry up, or those biscuits will be cold." As her husband had done, she took a second look at Lyla, but made no comment.

"We can lock the woman up in the smokehouse," Jim volunteered. Will had hoped he would. It would not be the first time they had used the smokehouse this way, and it would make it a lot easier on Will. It was a great deal more trouble to take care of a female prisoner, and even greater trouble to have to tend to a male and female. As they had done before, a blanket and a pallet were placed in the smokehouse for Lyla's comfort, as well as a bucket for her convenience. After she was locked inside the smokehouse, Will made his camp by the creek, secured Ike to a tree, and took care of the horses. Even though Will insisted he would take care of feeding his prisoners, Mary fixed extra ham and biscuits for them. She was happy to do it because, during the time she and Jim had known Will, they had always been the recipients of his generous sharing of any spoils confiscated as a result of arrests and captures.

After everyone had finished supper, Will said good night to his friends and returned to his camp and his prisoner. "I'm damn glad you showed up again," Ike greeted him when he returned. "I gotta get rid of that coffee I drank, and I can't do nothin' with my hands locked around this tree." After that was taken care of, Will sat him down at the tree again, locked his hands, and tied his feet around the tree as well.

When Jim Little Eagle got up the next morning, Will had already gone. He checked on his prisoner in the smokehouse and decided the Chickasaw woman had passed the night peacefully, for she was fast asleep. She was awake when he returned with Mary and her breakfast. "What will you do with me?" Lyla asked.

"Will said he wouldn't make any charges if you promise to go back home and behave yourself," Jim told her. She promptly agreed to do so, but Jim kept her in the smokehouse until afternoon before releasing her.

Chapter 2

As he had figured, it took three days to ride from Atoka to Fort Smith and Will rode straight to the courthouse with his prisoner. Ron Horner, the night jailer, met him at the jail under the courthouse. "Whatcha got there, Will?" Ron greeted him.

"Got another guest for your hotel," Will answered. "This is Mr. Ike Skinner. He's stayed here before. I hope he ain't too late for supper."

"He's just in time," Ron said. "They're just gettin' ready to serve it. I'll go ahead and check him in. What's he in for?"

"Robbery," Will answered. "He won't cause you any trouble. He ain't mean, he just makes some bad decisions." He stood there until Ron led Ike inside and closed the door behind him. He shook his head and sighed. He couldn't help feeling a measure of compassion for the simple soul who was Ike Skinner. *He's probably better off locked up*, he thought. Then he rode down to Vern Tuttle's stable to leave the horses, and he left his saddle and packsaddle there as well. After a short conversation with Vern, he took his rifle and saddlebags and headed back to the courthouse to see if he could catch his boss before he went home for supper.

"You're just the man I want to see right now," U.S. Marshal Daniel Stone declared when Will walked into his office. "When did you get in?"

"About a half hour ago," Will said. "I brought Ike Skinner in."

"Good," Stone said, then quickly changed the subject, obviously not interested in details of the arrest of Ike. "I might need to send you out again right away, but I won't be sure till I hear something more from the marshal's office in Missouri. How soon can you be ready to ride? I know you just got in and you'd probably like to catch a few days in town."

"Well, I'd like to rest my horse," Will said. "In the mornin', I reckon."

Stone couldn't help but laugh. "That long, huh? Tell you what, come back tomorrow morning and maybe I'll know if we're gonna be called on to help the Missouri office out."

There were a lot of thoughts running through Will's mind as he walked toward Bennett House, as Ruth liked to call her boardinghouse. Most of these thoughts circled around Ruth's daughter, Sophie, and the fact that he never seemed to be in town for any length of time. He had not been around for any of the wedding plans, a fact that made him just as happy, but it seemed to irritate Sophie more and more. He had always thought that planning a wedding was usually the bride's job, with little or no help from the groom. He figured he was like most men, preferring to just have a preacher tie the knot and be done with it.

Walking past the Morning Glory Saloon, he paused and looked at his watch. They would most likely be finished with supper at the boardinghouse by now and probably cleaning up the dishes. If he went home now, he was sure Sophie would insist that he should eat, and he didn't want to cause her the trouble of fixing anything. He hesitated a moment longer, then decided to get something in the Morning Glory.

"Well, howdy, Will," Gus Johnson greeted him from behind the bar. "I see you're back in town."

"You don't miss a trick, do ya, Gus?" Will japed. "You think Mammy might have anything left for supper?"

"She usually does when she knows it's you that's wantin' it," a voice declared over his shoulder.

Recognizing the husky tone of Lucy Tyler, Will turned to say hello. "How you doin', Lucy?"

"I've been better," the prostitute replied. "Ain't seen you in a while. You been outta town, or have you just given up associatin' with the common folk?"

"I've been outta town," he answered.

"Will's wantin' some supper," Gus said, and winked at Lucy. "I'll go see." He walked over to the kitchen door and stood just outside it. "Hey, Mammy, somebody's wantin' some supper. Is it too late to get a plate?" He turned back toward Will and Lucy, a wide grin plastered across his face, and waited for the expected response.

"Hell, yes, it's too damn late!" the scrawny little woman screamed back. "I'm already cleanin' up my kitchen." Gus remained by the door and waited, still grinning. After a long moment, another screech came from the kitchen. "Who is it wantin' to eat?"

"Will Tanner," Gus answered, trying to keep from chuckling. "I'll tell him it's too late." He walked back to the bar.

In a moment, Mammy appeared in the doorway and craned her skinny neck toward them to make sure it was Will. When she saw him, she stuck her lower lip out and blew a thin strand of gray hair from in front of her eyes. "I've still got some soup beans and a chunk of ham. There's a couple of biscuits to go with it. It'll keep you from starvin', I reckon."

"Yes, ma'am," Will said. "I surely would appreciate it."

When Mammy went back inside, Gus shook his head and marveled, "Ain't nobody else in this town Mammy would do that for. Beats all I've ever seen."

"Maybe that's the reason you don't ever wanna go upstairs with me," Lucy joked. "Maybe it ain't that little gal at the boardin'house who's got you buffaloed. Maybe all this time it was Mammy."

"Could be, at that," Will pretended to admit. "Most likely I remind her of her son, if she ever had one." He hesitated to continue with what he started to admit, but decided they would know sooner or later. "You might as well know, I'm supposed to get married around Christmastime."

They were both surprised, Lucy more so than Gus. "Well, I'll be damned . . ." she drew out. "That little gal at the boardin'house, right?" She didn't wait for Will to answer. "I knew that was bound to happen. Did you ask her, or was it her idea?"

"Of course I asked her," Will replied. "At least, I

think I did." When confronted with the question, he wasn't sure now.

Lucy continued to stare at him in surprise, finding it hard to believe. She somehow never expected Will Tanner to get married. He seemed to have been bred a loner. Finally, she congratulated him and wished him a long and happy marriage. Then she returned to her teasing. "Christmas, huh? Well, I reckon me and Gus are gonna be invited to the wedding."

"Right now, I ain't sure *I'm* on the invitation list," Will said. The japing was cut short when Mammy came from the kitchen and placed a plate of food on one of the tables. Already sorry he had confessed to his impending trip to the altar, he quickly retreated to eat his supper. It failed to save him further embarrassment, however, for Lucy followed him to the table.

When she saw him place his saddlebags on a chair and prop his rifle against the wall before sitting down, it occurred to her that he was on his way home. It prompted her to ask to be sure. "Are you on your way home?" He nodded. "And you stopped here first?"

"I didn't wanna put her to any trouble," he explained.

"Well, she ain't likely to be very happy if she finds out you stopped at a saloon before you came home to her. I swear, Will, I'm tellin' you as a friend, you'd better eat that food quick and get your ass home. You gonna be in town for a while now?"

"I don't know for sure till I see my boss again in the mornin'," he answered, choking his food down as fast as he could chew it.

Gus laughed when he heard Will's answer, and

Lucy remarked, "Damn! You might be one helluva lawman, but you don't know the first thing about women."

"Well, it ain't like I've got a choice," Will said in his defense.

He paused at the gate in front of the rambling two-story house Ruth Bennett's late husband had built shortly before he died of consumption some twenty years ago. Two of Ruth's longtime borders were sitting on the porch, enjoying their usual after-supper smoke. "How do, Will?" Leonard Dickens greeted him. "Glad to see you got back all right again."

"You were gone for a good while," Ron Sample said. "You'd best hurry inside before the women clean up the kitchen."

"No hurry," Will replied. "I figured I was a little late, so I grabbed a bite at the Mornin' Glory on my way back."

"Just as well," Leonard said. "Margaret fixed her special chicken and dumplin's. I swear, that woman sure ruined a good chicken. She's a pretty good cook with most things, but she don't know a real dumplin' from a lump of clabber dough. My late wife made the best dumplin's I ever et."

Will opened the front door when Ron took his cue from Leonard and began a testimonial on his late grandmother's dumplings. Will found Sophie standing in the parlor, talking to her mother. "Will!" Sophie exclaimed, and moved quickly to greet him. He dropped his saddlebags and rifle when she stepped into his arms, ignoring his embarrassment when her mother witnessed her embrace. When she stepped back, she held him by his shoulders at arm's length as if to examine a wayward child. "No new wounds," she declared. "Thank goodness for that. You must be starving. I wish you could have gotten here when we had supper on the table, but I'll fix you something."

He took a moment to say hello to Ruth before telling Sophie it wasn't necessary. "I knew I was too late for supper, so I got somethin' at the Morning Glory on my way home."

"You stopped at a saloon before you came home?" Sophie responded. He realized then that it would have been best left unsaid. He should have listened to Lucy Tyler's comment. "Gone as long as you were, I would have thought you'd want to come to see me before anything else," Sophie started, then reconsidered. "But never mind, at least you're finally home. For a good while, I hope, because we've got a lot to discuss, a lot of planning for our wedding." She glanced at her mother, and Ruth nodded to confirm it.

That was not particularly good news to him, but he supposed he was going to have to get involved with the wedding plans, so he tried to put on a good face for his bride-to-be. "Let me take a few minutes to clean up a little bit, and we'll talk about it," he said.

"Well, I must say you look a little better," Sophie commented when Will walked into the kitchen to join her. "You were a little scruffy-looking when you came in the door. I wasn't sure that was you under all those whiskers and dirt."

He smiled and rubbed his clean-shaven chin thoughtfully before responding. "I reckon I did, at that, but a man doesn't get a chance to take a bath when he's transportin' a prisoner across Indian Territory." He pulled a chair back and sat down at the table, prompting her to get up and go quickly to get a cup of coffee for him.

"If you had come straight home to supper, instead of stopping at that broken-down saloon, you could have had a piece of apple pie with this coffee," she chided, "but it's all gone now."

"I know," he interrupted, "but I told you I didn't want to cause you any extra work." He had already been scolded for his stop in the saloon before coming home—he didn't need more chiding.

She was about to continue, but Ron Sample came into the kitchen at that moment. "Excuse me for interruptin', Will, but Jimmy Bradley's out there on the porch lookin' for you—says it's important."

Surprised, Will asked, "Did he say what it's about?" Jimmy was Clyde Bradley's son. Clyde was the owner of the Morning Glory Saloon, and Jimmy liked to hang around the saloon doing odd jobs for Gus Johnson. Will had just seen Jimmy sweeping the floor behind the bar when he had stopped in earlier.

"No, he didn't," Ron answered, "just said it was important."

Will looked apologetically at Sophie, who returned the look with one of exasperation. He shrugged as if helpless. "I'll go see what he wants. I'll be right back." He pushed his chair back and followed Ron to the front porch. Sophie sighed and put his saucer on top of his cup to keep the coffee from cooling too fast.

"Jimmy," Will said when he found him waiting by the bottom porch step. "What is it, boy? You lookin' for me?"

"Yes, sir," Jimmy replied, speaking almost in a whisper. "Gus sent me to get you. There's some trouble at the Morning Glory."

"What kinda trouble?" Will asked. Ron and Leonard Dickens, their conversation having stopped, leaned forward, straining to hear Jimmy's message.

"That feller, Maurice, he was there when you came by this evenin'." When this drew a blank expression from Will, Jimmy continued, "He was settin' at a table with Lucy when you came in."

"All right," Will replied. "What about him?"

"He's raisin' hell in the saloon, throwin' glasses at the wall and breakin' chairs and I don't know what all," Jimmy reported, his eyes getting wider by the moment. "He pulled his pistol and shot a hole in the front window."

"Gus sent you here?" Will asked. "Didn't he tell you to go to the sheriff's office?" He was somewhat puzzled. Gus would normally send for the sheriff and one of the sheriff's deputies would handle a roughneck drunk.

"He said to go get you," Jimmy maintained firmly. "Maurice dragged Lucy upstairs and said he was gonna kill her. He hit her, hard, busted her lip pretty bad, said he was gonna beat her to death. Now he's holed up in her room with her and says he'll shoot anybody who tries to come in."

Will didn't have to be told why Gus sent for him, then. This type of trouble in the city of Fort Smith was supposed to be handled by the Fort Smith sheriff's office. Sometimes, however, the sheriff, as well as his deputies, was satisfied to let the saloons take care of their altercations themselves. And this time, the life of Lucy Tyler was involved. Gus knew that Lucy was a friend of Will's and Will would come to her aid. "Tell Gus I'm on my way," he said to Jimmy, and went back to the kitchen to tell Sophie.

Reading the look of concern on his face, Sophie asked at once, "What's wrong?"

"There's been some trouble I've gotta take care of," Will answered.

"Right now?" she asked. "Where?"

"In town," he answered. "I hope I won't be long, but it's important. I'll see you when I get back." With no desire to give her any details, he turned then and hurried out the door.

"Will?" she called after him, at first baffled by his behavior. Seconds later, exasperated by the infuriating habit he had of darting in and out of her life, she spat, "Your damn coffee! It's getting cold!" Resisting the urge to throw the cup against the wall, she stood there until she heard his footsteps as he bounded down the back stairs. She ran to the kitchen window in time to see him run past outside. Seriously concerned now, she hurried out to the front porch, where Ron Sample and Leonard Dickens were still sitting. "What was that all about? Where's he going?" she demanded.

"Gone to the Mornin' Glory," Leonard replied. "There's a feller up there gone crazy drunk, threatenin' to shoot the place up. They sent for Will."

"The saloon?" Sophie exclaimed. "He's going to the saloon to arrest a drunk? That's not Will's job! That's not the job of a U.S. Deputy Marshal."

"I expect that's right," Ron said, "but this is different. This feller has got Lucy Tyler locked up in the room with him, and he says he's gonna kill her."

Sophie was struck speechless. She knew who Lucy Tyler was, a common whore who preyed on the drunken drifters that frequented the Morning Glory Saloon. Gradually at first, but steadily picking up speed, the anger deep inside her began forcing its way to the surface of her emotions until she could no longer contain it. "Damn him!" she cursed. "He just left that hellhole of a saloon and now he's running back to save a whore!" She looked around at the two men in the rocking chairs, staring at her, and realized she had lost her temper, so she spun on her heel and went back in the house.

Ron looked at Leonard, his eyebrows raised, and shrugged. "I don't think she took that too well," he remarked.

"Didn't seem to," Leonard agreed.

Will covered the short distance to the Morning Glory at a trot. In his haste to respond, his rifle was the only weapon he'd taken. As he trotted, he checked to make sure the magazine was fully loaded. He stopped before the two swinging doors that Clyde Bradley had installed at the beginning of summer and peered over them before stepping inside. The barroom was empty of customers, all having fled when the shooting started. Only Gus Johnson remained and he stood behind the bar, his shotgun on the bar by his hand. Will didn't see Lucy or her captor, so he pushed on through the doors. Gus turned when he heard Will come in and came at once to meet him. "I'm sorry as I can be to bother you, Will, but that crazy fool is gonna kill Lucy. I'da sent Jimmy to fetch the sheriff, but he mighta sent one of those two deputies workin' for him, or he might notta sent nobody. I knew you'd come when you heard it was Lucy."

"Where are they?" Will asked. "Up in Lucy's room?"

"Yeah, he's got her up there and the door locked," Gus replied.

"Which room is it?" Will asked.

"I forgot, you ain't ever been up to Lucy's room with her." Remembering then, he said, "That was what she was always complainin' to you about." He paused for a brief moment until he saw Will's look of impatience. "Top of the stairs, first room on the right," he blurted. When Will started toward the stairs, Gus caught his arm to stop him. "There's somethin' else, Will. He said he's gonna kill her, but he said after he done for her, he was gonna kill you." That was a surprise, and Will had to ask why. "Lucy was settin' at the table with Maurice when you came in," Gus said. "When she saw you, she left him settin' there and went to say hello to you, so Maurice thinks he's got to kill you to make sure she don't run to you again."

"Why the hell didn't somebody explain it to him?" Will replied. "Lucy and I are just friends. Somebody coulda told him that."

"You ever try explainin' somethin' like that to a damn drunk?" Gus responded. "Especially when he thinks he's in love and you're standin' between him and his lady."

"I reckon you're right," Will said. "You don't think

this fellow's just another loudmouth drunk with his whiskey doin' the talkin'?"

"I don't know for sure." Gus shook his head slowly as he thought about him. "He fetched Lucy a pretty stout fist in the mouth when she told him to go to hell. Then he pulls his handgun and starts shootin' the place up—ran all my customers out and shot a hole in the front window. I tell you, it's a wonder there ain't nobody got shot."

"And now he's locked himself up in Lucy's room," Will declared with a tired sigh. "I'll go upstairs and see if I can talk to him." He started up the steps, not certain what he could do to defuse the situation. If this Maurice fellow refused to open the door, he'd likely have to kick it in, and then he'd have to worry about what would happen to Lucy, once he did. Maurice might be the kind to take it out on Lucy, in the form of a bullet in the head.

When he reached the top of the stairs, he paused a moment to listen for any sounds coming from inside the room. All he could hear was a constant series of guttural mumbling, typical of a rambling drunk running his mouth. He decided that Maurice was in the bragging phase of his drunk, probably telling Lucy what a big man he was. This might be a good time to give him a chance to prove it to her, so he rapped sharply on the bedroom door. "All right, Maurice!" Will bellowed. "Let's see if you've got the guts to back up your big talk!" The rambling voice stopped and Will challenged again. "That's what I thought, all talk!" In a few seconds, he heard a piece of furniture crash when it hit the floor, and the shuffling of unsteady boots on the other side of the door.

Will heard the bolt slide open on the door and it opened to reveal the unsteady form of Maurice Cowart, a six-gun in hand. He stood there for a fraction of a second, snarling his drunken defiance, before Will planted his fist on the bridge of his nose. Maurice went down like a felled tree, his head slamming against the edge of the bedside table he had knocked over on his way to the door. He was out cold, stopped so suddenly that he had not had the time to pull the trigger in reaction to the blow from Will's fist.

Will kicked the pistol that dropped from Maurice's hand across the floor before looking at Lucy, huddled in the corner of the room. Her mouth and nose were swollen and her clothes were torn from her captor's abusive attempts to conquer her. She didn't get up at once, just gazed at him until slowly, huge tears welled in her eyes. After a moment, she spoke when he walked over and extended his hand to help her up. "I'm glad he didn't get to see me cry," she said, defiantly. Then she looked up at Will. "I thought he was gonna kill me." She put her arms around him and gave him a tight squeeze, like a mother hugs her child. "Thanks, Will, thanks for coming."

He didn't know what to say, so he held her by the shoulders while he took a look at her damaged face. "We might better get Doc Peters to take a look at those bruises," he said. "First, I reckon I'd better take care of ol' Maurice, here, before he takes a notion to wake up."

"I don't know," Lucy said, already beginning to regain some of her confidence. "He went down pretty hard, and he cracked his head on my good side table. I was hopin' he was gonna talk himself to sleep before you came, 'cause he drank almost all of a quart of whiskey."

"I'll haul him outta here," Will said. He grabbed Maurice's boots and dragged him out the door into the hallway. "I swear, he weighs a ton." He dragged him to the top of the stairs and then down several steps before he managed to take his arms and, using the angle of the steps, pulled the limp body over to settle on his shoulder. Gus ran up the steps to help him turn around and steady him as he carried his burden downstairs. "I reckon that's his horse at the rail," Will said. "It was the only one there when I came in."

"Stop just a second," Gus said. "Lemme look in his pockets to see if he's got any money to pay for some of the damage he did."

"Well, hurry up," Will said. "He ain't gettin' any lighter."

He carried the unconscious man outside, and with Gus's help, plopped him across his saddle, just as Deputy Johnny Sikes walked up. Sikes watched silently until the body was resting on the horse. "Will," he said, and nodded. "A feller came in the office and said he thought there was some trouble down here."

"There was," Gus answered. "There ain't now."

"His name's Maurice Cowart," Will said, and told Sikes what had happened, what Maurice had done to Lucy, and the damage he had done to the saloon. "So I reckon you might wanna put him in your jail for a while till he sobers up. Then you might wanna warn him not to come near the Mornin' Glory or Lucy Tyler again."

"I expect so," Johnny replied. "I'll take care of him, and much obliged."

Gus stood with Will for a few moments, watching Johnny untie Maurice's reins from the rail and lead the horse back up the street toward the jail. Then they went back inside to help Lucy. "I'll walk you down to Doc Peters's to let him take a look at you," Will offered when he saw Mammy cleaning the blood from Lucy's face.

"No need for that," Lucy said. "Mammy's took care of me before. This ain't the first time I've been punched by a loudmouth drunk, besides, Doc Peters has already gone home by now."

"Suit yourself," Will said. "You're in pretty good hands with Mammy, especially if she's half as good a doctor as she is a cook," he added, primarily to please Mammy. The only acknowledgment he received from the scrawny little woman was a snort of indifference. "I reckon I'll say good evenin', then." He nodded to Gus, then looked at Lucy again when she called his name.

"Thank you again, Will," she said. "When you come back, I'll owe you a drink, or supper. And anything else you might want," she added wistfully.

"'Preciate it, Lucy, but you don't owe me anything. I'm just glad I could help a friend."

He found Sophie waiting for him in the parlor when he returned and he knew without asking that he was in trouble. The frown she greeted him with seemed to be permanently etched on her face. "Trouble at the Mornin' Glory," he offered weakly. "I don't know why Gus didn't call the sheriff instead of me."

She said nothing, but continued to stare at him with eyes as cold as ice. "Fellow named Maurice," he continued bravely, "shot a hole in the window and mighta killed somebody, if he wasn't stopped. Had to put him in jail—got back as soon as I could."

When he paused, finished with his explanation, she continued to stare icily at him for a long moment before asking, "Is Lucy Tyler all right?"

"What? Oh . . . yeah, she's all right, got roughed up a little, but she's all right." He had hoped Lucy's name wouldn't come up, but evidently Ron or Leonard had told Sophie what they had overheard on the porch. He would have preferred that she not know that he had been summoned primarily because Lucy was in danger, but now that he was facing her cold accusation, he decided it was time to stop acting like he was guilty of something. "Look, Sophie, Lucy Tyler's a friend of mine, that's all. I ain't one of her customers, I never have been. I've also got other friends that are on the wrong side of the law." Oscar Moon came to mind. "But they ain't got nothin' to do with you and me, and I sure as hell ain't had nothin' to do with any woman but you. The sooner you accept that, the sooner you'll keep thoughts like that outta your pretty head."

She continued to look him hard in the eye, until she had to smile. It was the first time he had shown any side of himself other than an innocent confusion in her presence. "All right," she said, "I accept it." She took his hand then and led him to the sofa. "I just hope you're going to be home for a while this time."

"I hope so, too," he said. "I reckon I'll find out when I report in to Dan in the mornin'." She raised an eyebrow at the remark, but gave him a big smile. The rest of his evening was spent listening to the plans she had for their wedding. When they finally said good night, he was finding it hard to believe it was going to happen to him. He could only imagine the look on Miss Jean Hightower's face when she heard the news. Will could imagine it would seem to her like her son was taking a wife. As for Shorty and the boys at the J-Bar-J in Texas, they wouldn't believe it until he showed up with Sophie on a lead rope.

Chapter 3

After breakfast the next morning, when Will walked into Dan Stone's office, he was greeted with the words he often heard from his boss. "Will Tanner, just the man I wanna see. How soon can you be ready to ride?"

"Well, my horse is rested up, so I reckon whenever you say," Will answered. "Where am I goin'?"

"Cherokee Nation, and you need to get up there as fast as you can. I've been contacted by both the Kansas and Missouri Marshals Services. They're trying to track down a gang of outlaws that robbed the Missouri State Bank in Joplin and shot the bank guard down. They're not sure, but they think the gang is led by a fellow named Ansel Beaudry and he's leading five or six men. They're not sure on the number, either. The gang crossed over the line into Kansas and two Kansas deputies picked up their trail, figured the outlaws would head down into Indian Territory, but they didn't. Instead, they continued west on the Kansas side of the line, like they were headed to Coffeyville.

Two days later, another Kansas deputy marshal found the bodies of the first two deputies following Beaudry. They'd been ambushed in a blind gulch. The deputy that found 'em said he lost their tracks right after that, so he returned to take the bodies home. A day after that, the First Bank of Coffeyville was robbed. There were a couple of people killed when they tried to stop the outlaws, but they got away clean. Folks on the street said they rode north outta town on the road toward Independence."

"I didn't know Coffeyville had a bank," Will said. "There wasn't one there when I was up there about a year ago." He remembered the two banks in Independence, however, all too well, for he had thwarted a bank robbery there and received a dressing down for his part, since he was not authorized to work in Kansas.

Stone paused to gauge Will's reaction to all this. Satisfied that he was listening carefully, Stone continued. "I've got a feeling that gang is planning to drop down below the line and disappear in Indian Territory."

"I'm thinkin' the same thing," Will said. "It looks like they planned to hit a couple of banks close to the Oklahoma line, so if the law got onto their trail, they could head for Osage territory in the Nations."

"Exactly," Stone responded, thinking he and his deputy were of the same mind. "That's why I need somebody up in that territory to find 'em. I know you just got back from Atoka, but everybody else is out on assignment. You're the only man here right now and we need to get an eye on this gang right away. They're a mean bunch and nobody to take on by yourself, so all I'm charging you with is to find 'em and keep an eye on 'em till I can get more men up there to help you. We might have to get some help from the army at Fort Gibson."

"What do you know about this fellow, Ansel Beaudry?" Will asked.

"Like I said, they *think* it's Beaudry, but nobody has definitely identified him yet. It just looks like his work—hits a bank with enough men to take over the town, doesn't hesitate to shoot anybody who gets in his way. He and two other prisoners broke outta prison up in Missouri about a year ago and they hadn't seen hide nor hair of them since." Stone paused for effect. "Till now, so it looks like he's had time to get up another gang of trigger-happy outlaws. I know, if it is Beaudry, we sure as hell don't need him down here."

"I'll head out in the mornin'," Will said, and got up to leave.

"Good man," Stone said. "Remember what I said: find 'em, don't take any chances on trying to arrest 'em." He got up from his chair. "Wait a minute and I'll walk out with you." Will waited while Stone locked his desk and paused again while he locked his office door. Downstairs on the street, they said so long and parted, Stone to the hotel for a late breakfast, and Will to check back at the stable to make sure his horses were going to be taken care of. He was almost out of all supplies, but he figured he'd best count on taking care of that somewhere on his way. He could have told Dan he could start out that afternoon, but he figured he had put enough strain on Sophie's wedding plans as it was.

* * *

He hesitated, reluctant to inform her, but knowing it couldn't be helped. "I have to leave first thing in the mornin'," he said.

"What?" she demanded before he could say more. "Why?"

"There's a real bad situation up on the Kansas border," he said, "and I've gotta get up there as quick as I can." He went on to explain that it was a joint effort with marshals in Kansas and Missouri to run a gang of dangerous outlaws to ground.

"You just got back from Indian Territory," Sophie complained. "Why can't Dan Stone send one of the other deputies for a change? It seems to me like he sends you out more than anybody else, and Kansas is a long way from here."

"He is gonna send some other deputies to help, but right now, I'm the only one in town, except Ed Pine. And Dan can't send him up there, so he doesn't have much choice."

"Why can't he send Ed Pine?" When Will explained that Ed had never really recovered from some serious wounds he had received a while back, she was not sympathetic. "Damn it, Will, I need you here, especially right now." She seemed as mad as Will had ever seen her.

"I'm just as sorry as I can be," he said, "but I can't very well leave Dan high and dry."

"But you can leave me high and dry," she replied.

"Sophie," he replied, "we ain't plannin' to get married till Christmas. We've got plenty of time to get ready for the weddin'. There's gonna be folks up in the Cherokee and Osage Nations that could be in some real danger if that gang is allowed to ride free in that territory." He saw readily enough that his argument was falling on deaf ears, but he didn't know what else he could say. When he glanced at her mother, there appeared to be a contented expression of *I told you so* on her face, and he realized that he was helping prove Ruth's opposition to their marriage. "Sophie, I'm real sorry about this. I'll be gone for a spell, but when I get back, we'll take a trip down to Texas, so I can show you the J-Bar-J."

"*If* you get back," she spat, her anger growing by the moment. "I don't believe you've even got a ranch in Texas." She turned toward the hallway door. "I hope you have a good trip," she slurred, and left him standing there bewildered.

Will started to go after her, but hesitated, deciding he would only make matters worse. He looked at Ruth, standing there with a smile approaching benevolence that he was sure could be more rightly defined as satisfaction. "She'll probably be a little more understanding after she calms down," she said in a rather halfhearted effort to placate him. "Anyway, we're glad to see you safely home. You'll be here for breakfast in the morning?" she asked.

"I don't know," he replied at once, then hesitated. "I reckon I will." He was thinking that she would get over her little snit by the afternoon and he would surely be talking to her that night. He was to find that she busied herself in the kitchen with Margaret for most of the afternoon. When suppertime came, she continued to keep him at a distance and afterward complained of a headache, so she retired to her room. Ruth said good night then, even though it was early still, and left him to ponder the trouble he had caused simply by returning home. At that moment, he wished that he had set out immediately for the Cherokee Nation, when he left Dan Stone's office, instead of coming back to Bennett House.

He made himself available for a while in the parlor, then on the porch after Ron and Leonard had retired to their rooms. He felt certain Sophie would seek him out after she had a chance to cool down, but she never came to look for him. Finally, when he decided that she was not going to, he went upstairs and tapped lightly on her door. He was surprised when the door opened to find Ruth there to answer his knock. She informed him that she was sorry, but Sophie had gone to bed with a bad headache. "Oh," he responded. "Well, tell her I was lookin' for her, and I'm real sorry she's got a headache." *It'll most likely be gone before breakfast in the morning, since I reckon I'm the headache,* he thought as he turned and went to his room at the end of the hall. He had seen a side of Sophie that night he had never seen before, and he wondered how much of it was caused by her mother.

Sleep proved to be an off-and-on affair that night, due to an inability to turn his mind off. Sometime during the wee hours of the morning, he decided that he had no experience in playing a lovers' game, and wanted none now. He had important things to concentrate on and he would deal with Sophie's problems when he got back. So, when it was five-thirty, according to his watch, he got dressed and left the house, knowing that Vern would be arriving at the stable about this time. Margaret Thatcher, preparing breakfast, looked out the kitchen window in time to see him going out the back door. She shook her head slowly, unable to prevent a feeling of compassion for the earnest young man and knowing the competitor he was facing in Sophie's mother.

As he had assumed, Vern Tuttle was at the stable when he arrived. "Mornin', Will," Vern greeted him. "You gettin' ready to ride early, I see. I fed your horses like you said. I'll help you saddle up and you'll be ready to go."

"I 'preciate it, Vern. I need to get an early start if I'm gonna get up to the Kansas border in three and a half days, especially since I'm gonna have to stop to get some supplies on the way."

"You're right about that," Vern said as he helped tighten a strap on Will's packsaddle. "You ain't got much in these packs. How far you figure it is to the Kansas border?"

"Where I plan to strike it, it's about a hundred and seventy or eighty miles," Will replied, "and I'm gonna have to push ol' Buster here to go a little farther than he's used to every day."

When he was packed up and ready to ride, he led the big buckskin out to the street to discover Dan Stone hurrying down to the stable. "When you said you were leaving first thing this morning, you meant it," Stone said.

Genuinely surprised to see his boss at the stable, or for that matter, anywhere this early, Will asked, "Something wrong?"

"No," Stone answered. "I just wanted to remind you to find that bunch and not try to arrest them until you get more help. Right now, this operation is in the hands of the Missouri and Kansas services, but it'll be our responsibility if that gang decides to get lost in Indian Territory. So the sooner we can find them, the better off we'll be."

"Right," Will said, "I'll see what I can do to help."

"And, damn it, Will," Dan continued, "you be careful. This gang has left a trail of dead folks everywhere they've been. They're as mean a bunch of rattlesnakes as have ever straddled a horse."

"I plan to be," Will said, and stepped up into the saddle. He nodded to Vern before saluting Stone with his forefinger to his hat brim. "I'll keep in touch when I can get to a telegraph," he said, and nudged Buster with his heels. His boss had never shown this much concern for his safety before. *This Ansel Beaudry must be the devil himself,* he thought.

"Check at the telegraph office when you get to Tahlequah," Stone called after him. "I might have more information for you. I'll be in touch with Kansas and Missouri."

"Right," Will answered, and turned Buster toward the river.

"How long you thinkin' about stayin' here, Ansel?" Luther Curry asked.

"I was wonderin' that, myself," Whip Dawson said. They had been camped there in a horseshoe-shaped bend of the Verdigris River, a good ten miles south of the Kansas border, for two days, and Whip wasn't the only one ready to move on. They had enjoyed a fairly good payday from the Joplin bank and the small bank in Coffeyville above the border, but there was no place to spend their loot in this wild country.

"What's the matter, boys?" Ansel Beaudry answered. "You gettin' a little itchy with a little money in your pockets?" He was riding with a rough collection of gunmen, but there was no question who was the boss. "We'll be ready to ride in the mornin', after the good folks up in Kansas tell the lawmen we rode straight north. They ain't smart enough to think we doubled back and headed down here. Even if they were smart enough, they ain't likely gonna want to head down here after us."

"I reckon not," Cecil Cox spoke up. "After seein' what happened to them other two deputies that came after us, they'd just figure we was Oklahoma's problem now." He grinned at Ansel, much like a dog looks at his master for approval. He, along with Whip Dawson and Tom Daly, had joined up with the three escaped convicts at an oft-used hideout near Springfield, Missouri. With Ansel calling the shots, the newly formed gang's first robbery was the bank in Joplin, and it had gone as smoothly as Ansel had said it would.

A man of average height, Ansel Beaudry nevertheless stood out among other men. Heavyset, with wide shoulders, Beaudry was a solidly built man. His dark hair and full black beard reminded some of President Ulysses S. Grant. Recognizing him as a natural-born leader, Bo Hagen and Luther Curry were drawn to him while in prison and never hesitated to follow him when he told them he planned to escape. Ansel had realized early on that his tastes were much too rich to ever be accommodated by honest work. It was obvious to him that the quickest way for him to attain the wealth he desired was to take it from those who earned it. And he found that the easiest way to do that was with overpowering force in the form of himself and five ruthless gunmen.

"Rider comin'," Whip warned, and drew his rifle in case there was a need for it. He relaxed after a moment and announced, "Look who's comin' here." They all relaxed their guard after they saw Tom Daly approaching the camp, leading a cow.

"Hot damn!" Bo Hagen exclaimed. "Where'd you find that cow? When you said you was goin' huntin', I figured you thought you might find a deer or somethin'."

"There's a ranch grazin' cattle about two miles down the river," Tom said. "Wasn't much of a herd, but this one followed me home. I reckon he wants to join up with us."

"Well, he's damn sure welcome," Bo declared. "I'm gettin' damn sick of nothin' but bacon to eat."

Equally sick of bacon, but concerned with more important things, Ansel got up from his seat near the fire. "Damn it, Tom," he stressed, "anybody see you take that cow?"

"Ain't nothin' to worry about, Boss," Tom answered. "There weren't nobody anywhere around those cows. This 'un was in a little bunch of strays, only a dozen or so, musta wandered off from the main herd. If somebody rides out lookin' for those strays, they won't even know they're one short."

"If you're wrong," Ansel replied, "you're gonna cause us some trouble we hadn't counted on."

"I swear, Boss, there ain't nothin' to worry about. I was extra careful to make sure there weren't nobody ridin' herd on those cows, and I knew some fresh beef would taste pretty good right now."

"I reckon you're right about that," Ansel conceded. He was aware of the look of expectation in the eyes of the other men, so he decided not to come down too hard on Tom. It was not good news to hear there was a ranch downriver somewhere. In view of that, he decided it was lucky Tom hadn't run up on a deer. His rifle might have alerted somebody of their presence there. "Well, don't just stand there lookin' dumb," he said. "Get to work butcherin' it. I ain't plannin' on stayin' here more'n another day or two. Then we'll head farther on down in Injun Territory where those Kansas marshals ain't got any jurisdiction." His announcement was met with a chorus of gleeful grunts, eager for the slaughter. "No gunshots," Ansel warned, "since we found out we got neighbors."

"Ain't no need to shoot the damn cow," Whip Dawson snorted. He drew his skinning knife, walked up to take the cow's head, and twisted it around. Then while the cow was trying to keep its neck from breaking, Whip slashed its throat. When the cow finally quit its feeble kicking, Whip released its neck, jumped out of the way, and let it drop. "Now you can skin it and butcher it," he crowed as he scooped up a handful of sand to clean the blood from his hands.

"I swear, Whip," Bo remarked, "damned if you

ain't a regular savage. You sure your daddy weren't an Injun?"

"I reckon if he was, he'da been a Comanche," Whip replied proudly.

Ansel listened to the banter between the members of his gang, always interested in judging the usefulness of the men riding with him. He was sure of Bo Hagen and Luther Curry. They had proven themselves to be loyal and willing when they served with him in prison. He also had no doubts about Whip Dawson. Big and powerful, Whip had a lust for killing, but needed someone to tell him which way to go. Ansel was confident that Cecil Cox was in awe of him and would be useful if the need to sacrifice someone ever arose. Tom Daly had ridden with more than one band of cattle and horse thieves. More important, he knew the territory in Oklahoma and that's where Ansel planned to hole up for a while. Unlike Whip, Tom had nothing to prove. Ansel felt sure he could be counted on to do his job. He was confident that he had assembled an outlaw gang that could operate like an army patrol, striking suddenly and viciously, then escaping before the law or the military could react. The thought of it brought a faint smile to his face when he thought about his next strike. It would be at a fledgling little settlement called Bartles Town, where he planned to restock his dwindling supplies.

It was close to sunset when Will reached the Illinois River and followed it into the town of Tahlequah. On the chance of finding Raymond Two Trees at the tiny room he used for his office, he turned Buster toward the back of the two-story brick building that served as the capitol of the Cherokee Nation. He didn't bother to go inside to look for Raymond because the little corral behind the building was empty. Raymond had already gone home, if in fact he was even in town. No matter what, Will was going to have to camp for the night and his horses were tired, so he could stop by the Cherokee policeman's house later. Right now, however, he would check the telegraph office to see if there were any wires from his boss, so he turned Buster toward the railroad depot.

"Howdy, Will," Billy Higgins greeted him when he walked into the telegraph office. "I figured you'd be showin' up pretty soon."

"That so?" Will replied. "Why'd you figure that?" He hadn't been in Tahlequah for some time. It would not have surprised him if Billy didn't remember him at all.

"'Cause I've got a couple of telegrams here for you, and I ain't seen you in a coon's age," Billy said. He reached down, pulled the two messages from a cabinet under the counter, and handed them to Will. Then he recited the messages at the same time Will read them, "'Confirmed, two Kansas deputies killed—STOP—Be extra careful—STOP.' The second one came in right after I got the first one yesterday." He went on to recite the second one. "'Beaudry robbed bank in Coffeyville—STOP—Two men killed—STOP—Headed north toward Independence—STOP—No sign of them since—STOP—Do not follow into Kansas—STOP.'" He stood there waiting for Will to read what he had just recited. When Will looked up from the messages,

Billy said, "Looks like you'd best get ready for a rough time, if you run into those boys."

"Does look that way, doesn't it?" Will replied. His thoughts were on the town of Independence and the friends he had made there. He had been there on another occasion when there was an attempted holdup at both banks. He was not happy to hear those decent folks might be getting hit again. The image of a young woman came to mind, Marcy Taylor was her name. She was the doctor's daughter and she had been very nice to Will. He wondered if she was still working in the bank. Maybe she was married now. When he realized he had let his mind wander, he reprimanded himself and returned his thoughts to the present. "Have you seen Raymond Two Trees?" he asked then.

"Not since yesterday," Billy answered. "He said he was headin' down to Muskogee—figured he'd be gone for a couple of days." He paused, waiting for Will's reaction. When Will said nothing, his mind still on Independence, Billy continued. "You caught me just as I was fixin' to go to supper. I eat over at the boardin'-house. That woman over there fixes a right fine supper for twenty-five cents. You wanna go with me?"

"I reckon not," Will said. "I've gotta buy some supplies over at Todd's and I'd best not wait too long, or he'll be closin' up." He was tempted to go to the boardinghouse with Billy, but if he failed to catch Kirby Todd before he closed, he'd have to wait until morning. He planned to be long gone from Tahlequah by the time Kirby opened up in the morning. He said good-bye to Billy and led his horses across the street to the General Merchandise Store.

He caught Todd just in the process of closing up for the day, as he was moving a display of kitchen brooms from the boardwalk to be locked up inside for the night. "Am I too late to buy a few things before you close?" Will called out.

"Well, hello there, Deputy," Todd responded. "Long time, no see. No, sir, it's not too late to serve an officer of the law. What can I sell you?"

"I'll be needin' some flour, some coffee, some bacon, a little salt, and some .44 cartridges," Will said. "I could use a little grain for my horses, if you've got any."

"Sounds like you're running short of about everything," Kirby said. "Come on inside and I'll fix you up." Will followed him inside, where Kirby's wife, Eunice, was busy counting the money in the cash drawer. "You can hold up a minute on that, honey," Kirby said. "We've got one more customer."

Eunice paused to give Will a smile. "Good, we can sure use the business." She gathered the items from the shelves when Will called them out, while her husband cut a slab of side meat and weighed it. When the bill was totaled, Will paid it and, with Kirby's help, loaded everything on his packhorse.

"'Preciate the business," Kirby said when Will stepped up into the saddle. "I'd say I hope you'll come to visit us more often, but that would likely mean we'd be having some outlaw trouble."

"Reckon so," Will said, "but not this time. I'm just passin' through." He gave Buster a light nudge with his heels. His horses had already done a day's work, so he rode up the river only far enough to be well away from the town before he picked a spot to camp. It was only after he had taken care of his horses and built a fire to fry some supper that he allowed himself to think again about the conditions under which he had left Bennett House. Sitting there by his fire, eating a supper of nothing more than fried bacon and coffee, he had to question his recent decisions. Before the day he asked Sophie to marry him, he didn't seem to have so many worrisome thoughts running around in his head. He had assured her that he was ready to settle down on his ranch in Texas, but was he really? He couldn't say that he enjoyed the life of a U.S. Deputy Marshal, no one in their right mind could. It was a hell of a rough life and one with a decidedly short life expectancy. It wasn't much of a guarantee to offer Sophie. He could understand her insistence that he should turn in his badge, but marshaling was a calling that just happened to some men, often when they didn't expect it. It happened that way for him. A lawman was the last thing he wanted to be when Fletcher Pride made the decision for him. He thought of Pride now and again, and found it ironic that he had been killed on the first job they had worked together. At the time, it should have warned him of the hazards of dealing with the most vicious of outlaws. Instead, it created a calling for him to stop those who preyed upon honest people and murdered good people like Fletcher Pride. He thought then of Sophie's mother and her relationship with Fletcher and realized that he really couldn't blame her for her attitude about her daughter marrying a deputy marshal.

Returning his thoughts to Sophie, he had to admit that he was sure that he loved her and wanted to spend the rest of his life with her. But for right now at least, he had a responsibility to do the job he had signed on for. He expected her to understand that. "And right now, I've gotta shut my mind down and go to sleep," he suddenly announced to Buster, "else I ain't gonna be good for anything."

Chapter 4

He awoke to a light rain that created a low mist to hang over the river under heavy dark clouds. It did little to help his mood as he saddled his horses and started out along the riverbank, looking for a good place to cross. He might have considered crossing the river the night before, but he liked the grassy bank on this side. It offered better grazing for his horses. He had expected the rain to start sometime in the early hours of the morning, so he figured he'd be wet in the morning, anyway. Crossing the river wouldn't make much difference then, and he could at least go to sleep that night while he was dry.

Once across the river, he left the Illinois and headed in what he figured to be a more northwest direction, hoping to strike the Neosho River after about twenty-five miles or so. If he did, he'd know he was heading in the right direction. The rain let up after a couple of hours and by the time he reached the Neosho, the sun began to peek through the scattered clouds. With the sun to go by, he was able to confirm that he was generally on the right course. He stopped by the river to give his horses a good rest and eat his breakfast, with still two full days' ride to reach the Kansas border.

With horses rested and ready to go, Ansel Beaudry led his gang of ruthless gunmen into the thriving new settlement of Bartles Town on the Caney River. It was early yet and the town was still rubbing the sleep from its eyes. The gang casually rode past the rooming house and the post office, heading directly toward the two-story building that housed the general store, with a residence on the second floor. "The owner lives upstairs over the store," Tom Daly said when he rode up beside Ansel. "Feller by the name of Jacob Bartles built it," Tom continued. "Started out with nothin' but a tradin' post on Turkey Creek. Now he's got a nice little town growin' up here."

"Looks that way, all right," Ansel said. "Has he got a sheriff?"

"Nope," Tom answered. "Least there wasn't one last time I rode through here, but that was almost a year ago."

"Well, it looks like there ain't much happenin' here this mornin'," Ansel commented, then looked up and down the street for a diner. "I'm partial to havin' a good breakfast before we load up on supplies, but I don't see anyplace to get one."

"Roomin' house yonder," Tom said, and pointed to the two-story house they had just passed. "We can get us some breakfast there. I've et there. It's more like a diner with rooms to rent than a regular boardin' house, and the food's good. Least it was when I et there."

"That sounds to my likin'," Ansel said, and turned

his horse in that direction. When they pulled up to a hitching rail beside the house, he cautioned his men. "You boys mind your manners. We're just lookin' for some breakfast. This ain't no saloon and I don't want to get the folks all riled up before we're ready to take care of our business."

"Lord a-mercy, Kitty, look who's comin' here," Bertha Ballard exclaimed to her thirteen-year-old daughter when she glanced out the window and saw the group of riders and packhorses pulling up to the hitching rail. "You'd best put on a fresh pot of coffee. If they're all lookin' to eat breakfast, you might have to run to the smokehouse and slice off some more of that ham. They might want more'n bacon." Caught in the process of cleaning up the long table, she turned around hurriedly then to finish collecting the remaining dirty plates. Luckily, it was late enough, so most of her boarders had already had their breakfast and were gone. By the time she had carried the dirty dishes to the kitchen and stuck a few more pieces of firewood in her stove, she heard them come in the door. "Grab that rag," she blurted to Kitty while she picked up another, and they hurried out to meet their customers.

"For goodness' sake," Bertha greeted the impressive-looking figure that Ansel Beaudry presented, with only a fleeting glance at the entourage behind him. "We wasn't expectin' a party of customers this mornin', were we, Kitty?"

"Good mornin', madam," Ansel responded. "I must apologize for not bein' able to give you advance warning, but we weren't sure we'd be passin' this way. My men and I are hungry, but if we're too late, we can certainly move on." He favored her with a warm smile. "I have to say, though, if I'd known such a charmin' lady was in charge of this dinin' room, we would have made it a point to get here earlier." In spite of herself, Bertha felt a blush threatening, forgetting the damp rag she held in her hand. Bo Hagen looked at Luther Curry and winked.

"Why, no such a thing," Bertha was quick to respond. "We'll be happy to fix you and your friends some breakfast. My daughter's already put on a fresh pot of coffee for you, we've got plenty of eggs, and either ham or bacon; whichever you want." She glanced at Kitty, who was busy wiping off the table. "And if you've got time, I can put some more biscuits in the oven. You gentlemen set yourselves down." She paused a moment when she took a longer look at Tom Daly. "I believe you've been in here before."

"Yes, ma'am, I have," Tom replied. "'Bout a year ago."

"Well, we're glad to have you back," she said cheerfully. "We must have pleased you."

They filed in then and took a seat around the table, Ansel at the head, as befitted his importance. Kitty disappeared into the kitchen to return shortly with a stack of clean dishes. Not as charmed as her mother, she eyed the group of men as she dealt the plates, and decided they were a pretty rough-looking lot. *What*, she wondered, *is their business in BartlesTown?* When she became aware that they were eyeing her as well, she was prompted to ask, "What are you men doin' in Bartles Town? Are you just passin' through?"

"That's a fact, sweetheart," Whip Dawson answered her with a wide grin while he blatantly looked her up and down. "Just passin' through."

Concerned that the men might become too bold with the young girl, Ansel quickly interrupted. "That's right, young lady, we're on our way to Oklahoma City.

I'm a federal judge and these rugged men are an escort for my protection." He was not at all opposed to his gang raising a little hell, but he preferred they wait until after they had acquired all the supplies they needed.

When Bertha heard his reply to Kitty's question, she could not help being impressed. "Well, we're proud to have you stop here for breakfast, Your Honor. We'll sure try to fix you a good meal."

"I would have bet on it," Ansel responded. "And I know my escort will appreciate it. They're a mangy-lookin' lot, but they have to be. There are some dangerous outlaws ridin' these parts."

"I know that's the gospel truth," Bertha said. "We'll have you some breakfast in a jiffy. I'll get a new batch of biscuits in the oven and Kitty'll start fryin' up some eggs and bacon." She left them to wait for coffee and went into the kitchen to mix up the biscuits. "We'll bring you some coffee as soon as it's done," she called back over her shoulder.

When she returned to the kitchen, she found her daughter waiting to comment. "They're about as mean-lookin' a bunch of men as I've ever seen."

"I wouldn't worry none," her mother assured. "The judge looks like he doesn't have any trouble handlin' them. Besides, one of 'em has already eaten with us, and he didn't cause any trouble."

"Yes, sir, Judge Beaudry," Luther Curry quipped, "we'll have Your Honor some coffee right away." His comment caused the others to chuckle.

"I hope you ain't a hangin' judge like that feller over in Fort Smith," Whip japed, causing a second round of laughter.

Ansel laughed with them, but cautioned again,

"Don't do nothin' to get these women upset. I wanna keep everything nice and peaceful till we've got what we came for."

They did as he instructed and after a substantial breakfast, they prepared to leave. Ansel told them to go on outside and mount up, while he remained to settle up with Bertha. "I hope your breakfast was satisfactory," she said when he turned his attention back to her.

"I would say it certainly was, madam, more than that, and I'd like to compliment you on fixin' such a magnificent meal on such short notice. I apologize again for poppin' in on you so unexpectedly. I do believe those were the best biscuits I've ever eaten. I'll bet you have a secret recipe." When he saw her blush, he continued, "What would be the chance of getting you to bake up another batch of those biscuits to take with us?" Her wide smile and eyes glowing with pride told him she was more than willing. "I'll tell you what, why don't you mix up another batch, then figure up what I owe you for everything? I've got to get some supplies at the general store. Maybe by the time I'm done, you'll have the biscuits baked, and I'll come back and settle up with you."

"I'll try to have 'em done by the time you're ready to go," Bertha replied, still basking in the light of his compliments.

"Don't hurry your recipe," he said as he went to the door. "If we get back too soon, I'll gladly wait for your biscuits." Outside, he climbed up into his saddle and turned his horse toward the general store. "Come on, boys. We've wasted enough time here already. We've got to take care of business now."

* * *

Ned Carter had his back toward the door while he straightened up some items on the shelves behind the counter. When he heard them come in the door, he turned to greet them, alarmed at once by the look of them. Moments later, however, he was somewhat relieved when Ansel pushed past the others and strode forth, businesslike and friendly. "Good day, my good man," Ansel said. "We're gonna need a fair amount of supplies. Are you here by yourself?"

"Right now, I am," Ned answered. "My wife and my son help in the store. They're upstairs. I can call my boy down to help you carry your goods out." Judging by the looks of the men with him, Ned couldn't help wondering why they couldn't do the loading.

"No need to do that," Ansel quickly responded. "My men will take care of it. Now, let's see if you've got everything we need." He proceeded to call out items as they came to mind while his eyes roamed the shelves. Ned, in a panic to keep up with the list, found himself racing from the shelves to the counter, hustling in between to jot down the items on a piece of paper. Led by Bo Hagen, the outlaws immediately started to carry the supplies out and load them on the packhorses. In a short time, half of Ned's shelves were emptied. Ansel summed it up by asking, "Do you have any more .44 cartridges than those that were on the shelf?"

"No, sir, You've cleaned me out," Ned answered while he frantically raced to sum up his bill. "Does that about do it?"

"Now, let's see," Ansel mused. "Let me have that sack there." He pointed to a canvas sack on the end of the counter. "I'm gonna need one more thing." He pushed his coat aside and drew the Colt .44 he carried. "I'm gonna need the cash outta that drawer yonder."

"Oh my Lord," Ned uttered. The fear that had steadily increased during the unusual transaction suddenly became a fact. It was a holdup, and a massive one. "You low-down dirty . . ." he started, then thought better of it. "For God's sake, mister, you've done cleaned me out. Don't take what little bit of money I've got in the cash drawer."

At that moment, they heard a door close upstairs. In a hurry now, Ansel ordered, "Get that damn drawer open and dump it in that sack, or you're a dead man." He cocked his pistol and leveled it at Ned's head. Fearing for his life, Ned did as he was told. Ansel took the sack and started to back away toward the door when he was suddenly distracted by Ned's son, who came down the stairs at that moment. The boy stopped halfway down, and seeing what was happening, turned to run back upstairs, only to fall forward on the steps when a bullet from Whip Dawson's .44 slammed him in the back.

"Tommy!" Ned screamed and ran to his son.

"Let's get the hell outta here!" Ansel yelled, and they all ran to the horses. Spurring their horses to a gallop, the outlaws charged out the end of the street, their guns blazing at any innocent soul who happened to step out of a door to see what was going on. In a matter of seconds, they were out of range of anyone who had run for their weapons. Since the horses were rested and fresh, they held them to a fast lope for a couple of miles before easing up on them, confident there would be no posse after them. They would rest the horses at Bird Creek, about twenty miles away, according to Tom Daly.

* * *

After holding his horses to a steady pace for two full days, Will reached the Verdigris River at a point he figured had to be about twenty-five or thirty miles south of Coffeyville, Kansas. It was his intention to follow the river to that town, hoping he could get some information regarding the actions of the Kansas deputies. Dan Stone's telegram had instructed him not to cross over into Kansas. How, he wondered, could he possibly be useful to the Kansas deputies if he didn't go to Kansas to find them? It wouldn't be the first time he had crossed out of his jurisdiction, and likely not the last. Hopefully, he could connect with the Kansas lawmen and determine what he could do to help out. As he rode farther along, the trail following the river became wider and obviously more traveled, with signs of wagon tracks as well as horses. He figured he couldn't be more than ten miles south of the Kansas line when he saw two riders descending from a low ridge and riding to intercept him.

Until he knew their intent, he decided to take precautions, so he drew the Winchester from his saddle sling and let it rest across his thighs. When they were within about forty yards, he pulled up and waited for them to approach. When they closed to about fifteen yards, he held his rifle in one hand with the butt resting on his leg and the barrel straight up. They had the look of farmers or ranchers, but he could never be sure. "Howdy," he said. "What can I do for you boys?"

"This here is our rangeland," one of them spoke. "We was wonderin' where you might be goin'. Don't see many strangers travelin' this road." A rail-thin man with red hair and a mustache to match, he pulled his horse up almost nose to nose with Buster.

Will looked at him, then his companion, who was

also a redhead, maybe a little younger than the other one. There was such a definite resemblance that Will was sure they were brothers. He pulled his vest aside to show his star. "I'm U.S. Deputy Marshal Will Tanner," he said. "Who might you two boys be?"

"Well, I'll be go to hell, Johnny . . ." one of them exclaimed, obviously the younger of the two. "I didn't think they could send somebody that quick."

"Hush, Dave," his brother admonished. "He ain't here 'cause of us. We didn't send the telegram till yesterday." To Will, he said, "I'm Johnny Whitsel. This is my brother Dave."

"Did you wire Fort Smith for some help?" Will asked. "What kinda help are you lookin' for?"

"I'm sorry, Deputy," Johnny apologized, then backed up his horse a few paces. "We thought you mighta been with them fellers who killed one of our cows."

"Somebody's been killin' your cattle?" Will asked, thinking that he didn't want to get delayed with a job to find some poor Indian family who needed some food.

"Well, they didn't kill but one," Johnny said. "They didn't even butcher the whole cow. Looked like they just cut off enough for supper and left the rest for the buzzards. Me and Dave found their camp, but there was six of 'em, so we rode into Coffeyville to send a telegram for help. We didn't know how long they was gonna stay there, eatin' our cows."

"They're gone now," his brother volunteered. "They weren't there yesterday."

Will's interest was raised considerably now. "You say there were six of 'em?" Both brothers nodded. "And they weren't Indians?" They nodded again.

"They were a pretty rough-lookin' bunch," Johnny said. "Looked like a gang of outlaws to me."

"Can you show me where they camped?" Will asked. "I'd like to take a look around." He told them why he happened to be riding by their ranch, and that there was a good chance the men they saw were a gang of bank robbers that lawmen in Kansas, Missouri, and Oklahoma were trying to catch up with. "It's probably good you didn't try to confront them about killin' your cow. They've left a trail of dead men behind, killed two deputies up in Kansas just a few days ago."

"We can show you where they camped," Johnny said. "I hope to hell they don't come back."

"Yeah," Dave added. "We thought you mighta been one of 'em when we saw you come ridin' up the river trail."

"Let's go take a look at that camp and maybe we can see which way they went when they left your range," Will said. Eager to show him, they wheeled their horses and led him on up the river. They rode for no more than a couple of miles before they pulled up where the river took a horseshoe-shaped bend and pointed to a grassy area near the water's edge.

It didn't take much looking around to get a picture of the camp, for there was plenty of sign that didn't require an Indian to read. The gang was obviously there for a couple of days before they decided to move again. Scouting the perimeter of the camp, it was easy to see where they had come and gone. Tracks of all of the horses had clearly come from the north, and other than a few random prints from single riders, it was apparent that what the Whitsel brothers had told him was true. The gang stayed put for a day or two. When they left, they crossed over the river and their tracks on the other side showed that they set out to the west. It was obvious to Will that they had come down from Coffeyville, planning all along to move down into Indian Territory. The reports that had the gang heading north toward Independence were dead wrong. When he had seen all he needed to see, he told the Whitsel brothers that he appreciated their help. He might have ridden past the outlaws' camp and never seen it. "I doubt you'll ever see that gang again. If my guess is right, they were just layin' low to give the law time to look for 'em in Independence, since witnesses reported that they had escaped north on the Independence road. I expect they were hoping that posse would keep ridin' north till they had to give up lookin' for 'em."

"Glad we was able to help you out," Johnny said. "Our house is just about half a mile on the other side of that ridge yonder. If you're hungry, my wife will be fixin' somethin' to eat about now. You'd be welcome to share it with us."

"That's mighty kind of you," Will replied, "but I need to get along after that bunch as quick as I can, so I'd best keep ridin'." He bid them farewell and crossed over the river, where he picked up the tracks of six riders and probably three packhorses where they came out of the water.

It proved to be a relatively easy task to follow the trail left by that many horses, especially since most of the horses were carrying riders. At first starting directly west, they had not ridden far when they turned more toward a southwesterly direction. From having ridden in this part of the country on prior occasions, he wondered if the outlaws were heading to a little town on the Caney River, called Bartles Town. If they continued on the same line they were now on, they would most likely strike the Caney in about twenty-five miles. He wondered if they knew where they were going or were just riding to find a place to hide. He was not really sure how far behind them he now was. At least two days, he figured, judging by how much the tall grass had recovered from their passage.

Holding Buster to a pace the buckskin could maintain for a long distance, Will continued across a land of open and rolling prairie with only a lone tree here or there. *A long way between shade spots,* he thought. It was as if the Maker had planted one every once in a while, just so you wouldn't forget what they looked like. After a ride that he estimated to be close to twenty miles, he saw a creek ahead, easily identified by the trees and bushes that lined its banks. *Just about the right time to water my horses,* he thought, and figured the men he was trailing probably thought the same thing. Their tracks led straight to the creek, and as he had guessed, he found the remains of a campfire and obvious signs of a temporary stop. That caused him to think they had not known about the little town less than five miles farther, or they might have pushed on to rest their horses there. Then it struck him that they might possibly be planning to raid the small settlement. If that was the case, they would likely stop here to rest their horses, so they would strike the town riding fresh mounts. In light of the reputation these men had already established, he was at once concerned for the good folk of Bartles Town. It was enough to convince him to push on to the town, instead of resting Buster and the bay there at the creek.

* * *

He noticed a couple of new buildings in the little town since the last time he had traveled this part of the territory. There was little activity on the street this close to suppertime, but he saw lights still on in the general store. Knowing they would most likely be out pretty soon, he decided to go there first, so he pulled Buster up at the rail and walked inside. As he had figured, Ned Carter and his wife were covering the counter with a dustcloth, preparing to close the store. They both turned when they heard the door open and stood watching the stranger. There was no welcome greeting from either. "I reckon I got here when you were about to close up," he said. "I won't be but a minute or two."

"What can we help you with?" Ned finally asked. There was still no hint of welcome in his tone.

"My name's Will Tanner. I'm a deputy marshal outta Fort Smith." He saw eyes blink with surprise. "I'm on the trail of a gang of outlaws that rode down this way." That was as far as he got before Marjorie Carter interrupted.

"Well, you're late," she charged. "My son is lying upstairs with a bullet in his back and we've been robbed of almost everything we own." She made a sweeping gesture with her arm. "We ain't got half the merchandise we usually stock on these shelves."

"Easy, Marge," Ned said. "It ain't the deputy's fault they shot Tommy." Turning back to Will, he offered an apology for the chilly greeting. "I reckon we're just suspicious of any stranger that hits town after the other day."

"I can understand that," Will said. "I was afraid

those men were going to cause trouble here. How bad is your son's wound?"

"Well, like she just said, he's got a bullet in his back," Ned replied. "He's bled a lot, but he ain't dead. There ain't no doctor nowhere near here, but he's a right strong boy. I reckon he'll make it all right."

"I'm sure sorry your boy got hurt," Will said. He could see by Marjorie's frown that she felt that he was somehow responsible. "I'm sorry I couldn't have gotten here sooner to help you, but we just got the word about this fellow, Ansel Beaudry, and his gang a few days ago. I left Fort Smith the next mornin'."

"I don't know if you coulda done much against that gang of outlaws by yourself," Ned commented. "They were a pretty rough-lookin' bunch. You shoulda brought a posse with you."

"You're right about that," Will agreed, "but I couldn't wait for some more deputies to get here. I'm hopin' I can at least stay on their trail, so we'll know where they end up."

"In the meantime," Marjorie couldn't resist saying, "they'll just keep stealing and killing all across the territory."

"Well, I hope not," Will responded, "but you might be right. I'd appreciate anything you can tell me about Beaudry and his men. There were six of 'em altogether, right?"

"That's right," Ned answered. "That Beaudry fellow and five of the meanest-lookin' men I've ever seen. The only reason we weren't scared to death when they walked in the store was because Beaudry didn't look as evil as his friends. He looked like somebody important, and he talked like a real gentleman, until he stuck a gun in my face." He glanced at his wife before continuing. "When he said he was on his way to Oklahoma City, why, hell, I believed him—said those five were escortin' him to protect him."

"Ned wasn't the only one that got fooled by that man," Marjorie was quick to point out, lest the deputy might think her husband was an easy mark. "Bertha Ballard fed the six of them in her dining room and believed him when he told her he was coming back to pay her after they came here."

"That's right," Ned commented. "He even talked Bertha into makin' up a whole new batch of biscuits he said he wanted to take with him." He shook his head slowly, still picturing Bertha's angry face when she told them about it. "She was fit to be tied, but I told her she was lucky. At least nobody got shot at her place."

"I reckon that's true," Will said, and expressed his sympathies again for their son's wounding. "Can you give me some idea of what they looked like?" he asked. "Especially Beaudry, I don't have any description of any of them."

Ned did his best to describe the outlaws. He summed it up by saying four of the gang looked little different from trail-hardened cowboys, the other two were easiest to describe. "Like I've been saying, their boss did most of the talking, and he could pass for a lawyer, a judge, a preacher, or whatever else he said he was. The other one was as wild-looking as a coyote. A big fellow, he's the one who shot Tommy. I'll never forget that face."

"What about their horses?" Will asked. "Any of 'em

ridin' unusual-lookin' horses, or fancy saddles?" He needed anything that would identify them.

Ned scratched his head while he gave it some thought. "I'm sorry, Deputy, they kept me so busy takin' stuff off the shelves till I didn't take time to look at their horses. Then when they left, me and my wife were more worried about takin' care of our son. It wasn't safe to go out in the street, anyway, what with them shootin' the town up when they charged outta here."

"Bertha said the judge rode a gray horse," Marjorie volunteered, referring to Ansel Beaudry. "I didn't pay any attention to what the rest of the scum were riding."

"Thank you, ma'am," Will said. "That'll help." He apologized again for their loss and bid them good evening after they told him which way the outlaws had left town.

"You've been mighty patient, boy," he said to Buster as he climbed up into the saddle, "but we're gonna make camp just as soon as we get outta town and find us a good place." He rode south along Bird Creek until he found a spot that suited him, then unloaded his horses and let them drink while he gathered wood for a fire.

Chapter 5

After a peaceful night on Bird Creek, he set out at first light, easily picking up the trail left by the gang of six outlaws. Seeing no sign of wavering from their original line of travel, it was now Will's impression that Beaudry had a definite destination in mind. After a short mile, he came to a common wagon trail that led to the Arkansas River. The tracks did not cross it. Instead, they followed it, and if they continued on this course, they would be heading straight for Wilbur Paul's ferry. Will figured that to be a distance of about twenty-five miles, so he settled Buster into a comfortable gait, planning to eat his breakfast on the banks of the Arkansas.

The sun was high in a cloudless sky when he caught sight of the river. It had been a while since he had last used Wilbur Paul's services, and at that time he was trailing a wanted man, much like today. Seeing the ferry on this side of the river, he guided Buster toward it and the little shack on the bank. "Will Tanner!" Wilbur exclaimed in greeting when he saw the rangy deputy marshal rein Buster to a halt beside the shack.

"I ain't seen you in I don't know when." He dropped the ax he had been in the process of sharpening and got up from his stool. "I thought some of them outlaws you've been chasin' mighta shot you."

"Howdy, Wilbur—last time I saw you, you were ridin' that stool. I'll bet you ain't got off it since then." Will climbed down from his saddle. "Reckon I'll give you a little ferryin' business, if you ain't too busy to take me across."

"Hah!" Wilbur snorted. "I ain't had much time to do nothin' but operate my ferry since the river's been so high this month. And I sure wouldn't wanna delay one of our brave deputy marshals from goin' about his official business." He responded in the same sarcastic vein as Will had. He and Will were accustomed to japing each other on the few occasions they crossed paths. "Where you headed?"

"Across the river right now," Will answered. "After that, I ain't sure where I'm goin'. I'm guessin' you mighta got some ferryin' business from some men I'm tryin' to catch up with."

"Six of 'em, I expect," Wilbur spoke up at once. "I ain't surprised you showed up. I figured some lawman would be after that gang of coyotes. What did they do?"

"Bank robbery and murder," Will replied, then went on to tell Wilbur the story behind their appearance in Indian Territory. "I don't reckon they said anything about where they were headin'."

"No, they didn't do a lot of talkin' anytime I was nearby, and that wasn't any more times than I could help. Tell you the truth, I just pulled 'em across as fast as I could. I was surprised when we got across and they paid the fare. I was gettin' ready to have a gun stuck in my face when I asked for it, but the feller that looks like a banker or somethin' paid me before I even asked. There ain't no doubt he's the boss."

"That'd be Ansel Beaudry," Will said. "The folks back in Bartles Town general store thought he was a judge before he robbed 'em and one of his gang shot their son. How long ago were they here?"

"Day before yesterday," Wilbur replied.

"They stay on the road when they left?"

"Yep, rode on down the road toward the Pawnee Agency, at least until they was out of sight." He paused a moment, studying Will's reaction. "Will, I ain't so sure you'd wanna catch up with that bunch. You'd be better off waitin' till you can get some help."

"You might be right," Will said, "but I'd like to find out where they're headin', so I can keep an eye on 'em till I get some help. If I'm real lucky, maybe they'll keep on the same line they're ridin' and pass right on into Texas. Then they'd be the Rangers' problem." Even as he said it, he knew it was unlikely, because the western border between Oklahoma and the Texas panhandle was a good distance away.

Will led Buster and his packhorse onto Wilbur's flat, bargelike ferry while Wilbur untied it and pre- pared to pull it across. When they reached the other side, Will told him that he planned to rest his horses before starting out again. When told this, Wilbur decided to continue his visit, offering to contribute some smoked antelope for Will's breakfast. While they ate, Wilbur tried to describe all the gang of outlaws. "I'd seen one of 'em before," he said. "Drifter, don't know his name, but he's been by here two or three times in the last year or two. The feller you need to watch out for is the big one. I think I heard one of the others call him Whip, or somethin' like that."

"Why is that?" Will wondered, since Wilbur said he had heard very little of their conversation.

"I don't know, he's just got a look about him, the way he stares at you, like a big cat thinkin' about havin' you for supper."

From Wilbur's description, Whip, or whatever his name was, sounded like the one Ned Carter described as the man who shot his son. Everyone had warned him that this gang was going to be a problem he was not going to be able to handle by himself. The more Wilbur talked about them, the more Will was convinced of it. When his horses were ready to go again, he said so long and started out again on the common road toward the Pawnee Agency on Black Bear Creek, a short ride of maybe a dozen miles. He had limited experience with the Indian agent at Pawnee, for he had never been sent there for any trouble. Since the government had relocated the population in the Osage reserve, the Indian police seemed to handle their troubles without the help of the deputy marshals. For this reason, he felt no obligation to contact them, but since it was beginning to look like the men he followed were going to ride right through the agency, he would check in with the agent. The man assigned to the post was a conscientious man who lived in a frame house with his wife and three small boys. His office was housed in an addition built onto the back of his house.

It was close to the noon hour when Will rode up to the agency headquarters. Seeing no one in the office or the broad clearing that held the house, the barn, a small warehouse, and a few outbuildings, he figured that he might have arrived just when Franklin Tatum was having his noontime meal. That proved to be the case when Tatum, alerted by one of his sons, stepped out the kitchen door to signal him. "Deputy Tanner," he called out, and waited until Will walked over.

"Mr. Tatum," Will replied, mildly surprised that Tatum remembered him. "Looks like I mighta caught you at a bad time."

"No trouble at all," Tatum responded. "We were just sitting down at the table. You're welcome to come in and join us—nothing fancy, but we've got plenty."

"No," Will said. "Thank you just the same. I didn't wanna pass through without stoppin' to say howdy. I just had something to eat back at the river."

"I wouldn't be far off if I said I'm betting you're following a group of six men that rode through here day before yesterday, would I?"

"No, sir, you wouldn't. Did they cause you any trouble?"

"No, they didn't even stop," Tatum replied, "and from the looks of them, I'm happy they didn't. They just rode straight on through and took the trail toward Stillwater Creek. You sure you don't want to eat something?" When Will declined again, Tatum insisted, "How about a cup of coffee? I know you're probably in a hurry to catch that bunch, but you can spare time for a cup of coffee, can't you?"

"Ain't many times I can remember turnin' down a cup of coffee," Will relented. "I hate to drop in on your wife like this, though." He was thinking that, if Beaudry passed through here day before yesterday, he might be gaining on him, maybe half a day.

"Nonsense. No trouble." Tatum turned to yell back inside. "Lucille, it's Deputy Will Tanner. Set a cup out

for him, will you?" He held the door wide for Will to
enter. "I won't keep you long. Tell me about those
men you're following." It was obvious that Tatum
seldom had any opportunities to pass the time of day
with a white man.

After Will told him who the men were that he was
chasing and what they had recently done, Tatum
was even more relieved the gang had found no reason
to stop there. "I guess that's one good thing about
being an Indian agent," he joked. "You don't have
anything worth stealing." When Will finished the cup
of coffee Lucille Tatum had poured for him, he
thanked them both and took his leave. Since the
common road ended at the agency, Will scouted
the clearing to make sure the outlaws had left the
agency on the trail to Stillwater Creek, as Tatum had
said. When he was sure of the tracks, he headed in the
same general direction Beaudry and his men had
held to since leaving their camp on the Verdigris. He
figured he was a half-day's ride from Stillwater Creek,
so that was where he planned to camp for the night.

As he continued on throughout the afternoon, following a trail easily determined, he unintentionally let
his mind wander back to Fort Smith, and more specif-
ically, to Sophie Bennett. He had not left there on a
particularly good note. There were issues that Sophie
wanted to discuss and she wasn't too happy when he
left so soon after he had just returned from the field.
The situation troubled him and he told himself to put
it out of his mind as he guided Buster through the
cottonwoods guarding Stillwater Creek. The big buckskin gelding whinnied as they neared the creek and
Will leaned forward to stroke his neck, just as he
heard the sudden snap of a bullet as it passed directly

over his head. When he heard the report of the rifle that fired it, he was already galloping down the creek bank, seeking cover and cursing himself for his carelessness. It was the second time he had barely missed being shot out of the saddle in the last couple of weeks. The last time, the shooter had been Lyla Birdsong. A couple more shots rang out to rustle the tree leaves above his head before he found a washed-out section of the creek that offered protection for him and his horses. He came off Buster in a hurry, grabbing his Winchester in the process. Not knowing for sure who, or how many, he scanned the creek bank frantically, trying to pinpoint the source of the shooting.

Still angry at himself for being so carelessly surprised, he had to assume it was the gang he had been trailing, but he couldn't believe that he had caught up to them this quickly. At any rate, he had had no intention of letting them know he was tracking them. *So much for that now,* he told himself, and realized that Buster had tried to tell him he was approaching strange horses and not that he sensed water. If he hadn't leaned over to pet him, he would most likely have taken that bullet that passed over his head. Now that he had blindly ridden into an ambush, he had to figure out where his assailants were hiding, and that might not be so easy.

After those first three shots, all was quiet along the creek, as he strained to see some indication of movement upstream from his position. If he had, indeed, caught up with Ansel Beaudry, he was going up against six hardened outlaws, and he didn't particularly like those odds. He couldn't help looking over his shoulder when the possibility occurred that they might be circling around behind him. Those thoughts prompted him to find out where they were, and since the shooting had stopped, he could only guess. As he scanned the banks upstream, he tried to pick a spot where there was plenty of cover. His gaze settled on a group of hackberry trees with thick bushes around their feet. *As good a place as any*, he thought. Next, he picked out a gully on the other side of the creek from where he now knelt. Ready then, he rose up and fired two quick shots into the hackberry trees, then ran, splashing across the creek to dive into the gully, just as a couple of shots plowed into the bank he had just left. They were followed by a couple more impacting in the dirt of the gully he now occupied.

His move had been successful in drawing their fire, although it had not come from the hackberry trees. In his frantic dash through the creek, he happened to have caught sight of a muzzle flash about a dozen yards upstream from the spot he had picked to fire upon. He was thinking now that there were no more than one or two in ambush. Had there been six, he would have been running through a hail of bullets. Was it just bad luck that he had run into a couple of dry-gulchers and not Ansel Beaudry's gang after all? That made more sense than thinking he had caught up with the six. No matter, he couldn't stay there and try to exchange shots. He had to smoke them out and he couldn't do it hunkered down in that gully, so he popped up and fired a shot at the spot where he had seen the muzzle flash. Then he quickly crawled up the gully to the top where it started in the cottonwoods, hearing the pounding of their bullets in the dirt of the gully behind him. He was counting on his assailants thinking he was pinned down in the gully, and he wanted to get around behind them before they came up with the same idea and circled around behind him.

With enough cover from almost-head-high bushes to shield him, he got to his feet and ran upstream until well past the spot from which their shots had come before he crossed back over the creek. Confident that he was behind his attackers, he started working his way back downstream, moving as carefully as he could. A few dozen yards farther and he stopped, for he could hear them talking, even though he still could not see them. Very cautiously, he parted the branches of a thick laurel bush before him—slowly, lest he might encounter a rifle muzzle looking at him. What he saw, however, told him he had guessed right. There were only two men, both intently watching the gully he had crawled out of. He had to decide what to do about them. He was not sure what their motive was for bush-whacking him. It would be easy enough to shoot them both from his position behind them. But if he did, he would still not know why they tried to kill him. He was honor-bound as a deputy marshal to attempt to arrest them, but being frank with himself, he had to admit that he was a little busy at present to take two prisoners back to Fort Smith. *Maybe*, he thought, *I can arrest them and take them back to the Indian agency I just left.* Franklin Tatum surely must have a room in his ware-house where he could hold them until he returned for them, or got word to Fort Smith to send someone to get them. It would delay him again in his pursuit of Ansel Beaudry, but he decided he had little choice.

In an effort to get a little closer before announcing his presence, he pushed through the bushes, his rifle

ready to fire. He was close enough then to see both
men straining to look for any movement in the gully
they had fired at, both oblivious to his presence
behind them. About to surprise them, he paused a
moment when he recognized one of them, Tom Daly.
He had arrested him some time back for horse and
cattle rustling. Evidently, he had served his time, because there had been no notice from Little Rock of
his escape. He was not surprised that Tom hated him,
but he would not have suspected him to be the kind
of man to seek vengeance by bushwhacking him. Daly
seemed more the type to just run away. As for the man
with him, Will had never seen him before. He was a
big man, half again as big as Tom.

"Tom Daly!" Will suddenly shouted. "Drop those
rifles! You're under arrest!" He did not expect their
reaction. Befitting his nature, Tom immediately
bolted like a rabbit into the bushes behind him, while
the big man beside him whirled around, his rifle blazing away as fast as he could fire and cock it. Will dived
to the ground for cover, saved from being hit because
the man had not had time to take aim. Before he
could, Will placed a well-aimed round in the center of
his chest that caused him to stagger backward. Still,
he brought his rifle up to shoot again, forcing Will to
place another round in his gut. The huge man's knees
buckled and he dropped like a gunnysack full of
horseshoes. One last shot from his rifle whistled
harmlessly through the branches of the trees over
Will's head. Only then was he aware of the sound of a
horse galloping away through the trees. He thought
to give chase, but discarded the notion when he realized how far away he had left his horses. *Better check on*

this one first, anyway, he thought, and went to see if he was still alive. He wasn't. Looking at the placement of the shot in the man's chest, Will figured he was already dead before his second shot hit him.

Will pushed through the bushes where Tom Daly had fled and discovered the dead man's horse tied to the branch of a tree. He found it highly unlikely that Tom was riding with the gang from Missouri. A small-time cattle rustler, Tom spent most of his time popping back and forth across the Red River, trying to avoid getting caught by the Texas Rangers. The man he had just shot was no one Will recognized, but maybe he was a relative of someone he had arrested, or killed. He would have assumed he was a member of the gang he had been following, had it not been that he was riding with Tom Daly. On the other hand, any lawman was a target for assassination west of the MKT Railroad in Indian Territory. It was a constant risk of the job.

In his haste to run, Tom had not wasted the time to take the other horse with him. A big black horse, befitting the big man's size, stood calmly watching Will as he approached. Will took hold of the horse's bridle and gave him a few reassuring pats on his neck, then took a look at the double-rigged saddle with the fancy design on the skirt. He started to search the saddlebags when he realized that the etching was so fancy that he hadn't at first noticed the word spelled out in the center of it. He took a closer look. The word was *Whip.* It immediately struck a chord in his mind. Wilbur Paul had told him he thought one of the men with Beaudry was called Whip—and Wilbur said he was a big man. Then he recalled that Wilbur had said that one of the men with the gang was a familiar face, even though he didn't know his name. *So Tom has moved up to the business of robbing banks,* he thought, and that thought caused Will to stop and speculate on the situation as it now stood. Had Ansel Beaudry somehow discovered that he was being followed, so he sent these two back to ambush him? Or was he just taking precautions to make sure he wasn't followed, and they were sent back to find out? *It doesn't matter,* he thought, *they damn sure know it now.* "I'm gonna have to be a helluva lot more careful from now on," he said aloud.

He led the horse back to Whip's body and tied it to a bush while he relieved the body of everything useful, including a hefty roll of paper money. A good rifle and handgun were packed on his horse, along with an even more substantial amount of money in his saddlebags, no doubt his share of that stolen from the banks in Coffeyville and Joplin. It was wrapped securely in a canvas bag, so he didn't take the time to count it, but stuffed it under a sack of flour in one of his packs. As an official U.S. Deputy Marshal, it was his responsibility to dispose of the body, usually by burial. For Whip, however, he chose to leave the body where it lay to feed the wildlife. Now it appeared that he was tracking five men, instead of six, or would they be tracking him? He was going to have to be doubly careful from this point forward. With that in mind, he climbed up on Whip's horse and rode it back down the creek to the place where he had left Buster and his packhorse. After rigging a lead rope from his packhorse, he climbed on Buster and went back to pick up Tom Daly's trail, trailing the packhorse and Whip's horse behind him.

* * *

"Somebody's comin'!" Cecil Cox called out from the bluff above the camp.

"How many?" Ansel Beaudry responded from the campfire close to the edge of the Cimarron River.

It was rapidly getting dark, so Cecil waited a moment to be sure before calling back. "Looks like one rider."

That served to prick Ansel's curiosity, since he had sent two men to backtrack their trail just to be sure there had been no posse assembled after he had raided the store in Bartles Town. "Let him come," he called. "Might be Tom or Whip."

After a couple of minutes, Cecil sang out again. "It's Tom Daly."

Fearing something had gone wrong, Ansel walked up the bank to meet him. He didn't get a chance to ask before Tom pulled his lathered horse up before him and slid out of the saddle. "He got Whip!" Tom yelled. "Shot him down!"

"Who shot him?" Ansel demanded as the rest of the men gathered around Tom.

"Will Tanner!" Tom responded, still in a state of panic.

"Who the hell's Will Tanner?" Ansel demanded.

"U.S. Deputy Marshal Will Tanner," Tom replied, as if the name alone should mean something to them all. When it was obvious that it did not, he went on, "He's the son of a bitch that hauled me off to prison for cattle rustlin', and one man you don't want on your trail."

"How many men's he got with him?" Ansel asked.

He and the rest of the gang were already straining to see into the darkness Tom had just emerged from. "How far back is he?" Ansel pulled his handgun from his holster, getting ready to welcome a posse. The others did the same, immediately on the alert to defend themselves. When Tom said the deputy was alone and he wasn't sure how far behind him he was, Ansel holstered his weapon in disgust. "One deputy? And you come ridin' in here like the whole army was chasin' you?"

"He shot Whip," Tom reminded him.

"And you ran off and left him," Ansel accused him.

"There weren't nothin' I could do for Whip. He was dead with the first shot, and there weren't no chance for me to get a shot at Tanner," Tom lied. "Whip tried to draw down on him, but Tanner cut him down before he could get off a shot. Like I said, I didn't have a good chance for a shot, and I knew I had to get back here to warn you, if I didn't do nothin' else."

"Damn it!" Ansel cursed. If he didn't need Tom as a guide, he would have been tempted to shoot him down right then, but Tom was the only one who knew where Grassy Creek was. Whip Dawson was a good man, one he didn't think he could afford to lose. In addition to losing one of his men, now he had a deputy marshal on his tail, and that had to be taken care of. In spite of what Tom said about this Will Tanner, he was only one man, and one man was not a problem. Kill him and get on with the ride to Grassy Creek.

Grassy Creek was the name of the place where he planned to make his permanent hideout. It was a place so remote that he would be free to ride out on strikes against towns in Kansas, Texas, and Colorado, then disappear before a posse could be raised to come after him. He had heard about this wild part of Oklahoma from a man he met in prison, and he knew it was the place to build his hideout. It was in the western part of Indian Territory, close to the Texas border and he couldn't afford to lead a U.S. Deputy Marshal there. He had been fortunate to meet one of the few men who knew the place he wanted to find. It was disappointing to discover that Tom Daly was more rabbit than cougar, however.

Impatient for Ansel's decision, Bo Hagen declared, "Well, we can't stand around here talkin' about it. Whaddaya say, Ansel? Whaddaya wanna do?" It was already dark and this deputy marshal in all likelihood had followed Tom to their camp. Like Luther Curry, Bo had accepted Ansel as their leader, even before their escape from prison, but he was now questioning some of Ansel's decisions. They shouldn't have stopped to camp on this river for an extra day, just so they could check on anybody trailing them. If they hadn't, they'd be a whole day ahead of this lawman and Whip Dawson wouldn't be dead.

"What are we gonna do?" Ansel echoed. "We're gonna wait for Tanner to show up. That's what we're gonna do."

"You think maybe we oughta saddle up and get outta here?" Tom Daly asked.

Ansel favored him with a look of disgust. "Hell no," he said. "You think the five of us are gonna let one single lawman chase us all across Indian Territory? Let him come. I plan to kill him." He looked back at Bo. "Since we don't know how far behind Tom this deputy is, we'd best get our camp ready for him right now. I wanna see just how crazy this fellow is." Moving quickly then, he had his men arrange their blankets like sleeping bodies around their campfire. Then he positioned each one of them around the camp so that it was surrounded, cautioning them to be sure of their target. "So we won't end up shootin' each other," he cautioned.

"If he's chasin' Tom all the way from that creek," Bo questioned, "ain't he gonna think it's mighty funny that we all rolled up in our blankets and went to sleep?"

"Maybe," Ansel allowed. "If he's got a lick of sense, he ain't gonna come ridin' right into the middle of our camp and get himself shot outta the saddle. Most likely, he'll wait till he thinks we're all asleep. That's when he'll make his move." He looked back at Tom then, not without doubts himself. "Are you sure there ain't but one man trailin' us?"

"He's the only one showed up at that creek," Tom assured him.

"Then he's a damn fool to think he can ride in here and arrest all five of us," Ansel said. Then he hesitated while he thought back on Tom's accounting of the confrontation at Stillwater Creek. "You say he tried to arrest you and Whip. How'd he get the jump on you? You were supposed to be watchin' the trail from that Indian agency."

"We were," Tom said. "We saw him followin' our trail and Whip took a shot at him, but he missed. Then he got around behind us somehow."

"You left that part out," Ansel said, "that part about Whip shootin' at him. He wasn't plannin' on arrestin' us. He was just plannin' on trailin' us." He looked at Bo and nodded. "Now he knows that we know he's onto us, so he's gonna have to decide what he's gonna do. And it ain't likely gonna be to ride into the middle of our camp and say *You're all under arrest,* is it? I think we've got him where we want him. He might think about sneaking up here while we're asleep and try to shoot as many of us as he can before we can wake up. I hope he does. He'll just be shootin' holes in our blankets. Then, if one of us doesn't get a shot at him, we'll chase him till we catch up with him and settle his hash."

Chapter 6

As Ansel Beaudry had surmised, Will knew that the outlaws were onto him, and it was now a question of what they would choose to do about it. Tom Daly was on his way to warn the others that a lawman was tracking them. To chase after Daly was not an option for Will at this moment for several reasons. His horses were tired, too tired to go after Daly at a full gallop, and it was already getting dark, so to follow his trail might be difficult, as well. And if he did find their camp, he was sure to be met with a ready welcoming party. Their camp could not be far up ahead. If he had to, he would guess that it was probably at the Cimarron River. There was also the possibility that they might decide to come back, looking for him. He had to rest his horses, so to play it safe, he decided to ride on down the creek to find a better spot to camp, then wait until morning to pick up the chase.

He rode about two miles downstream before he found a spot that he thought offered him the best place to camp. Not sure that he might now be the hunted, he considered making a cold camp to make sure a fire didn't expose his campsite. A rude gnawing sound from his stomach reminded him that he hadn't eaten much all day. It was enough to persuade him that there was probably enough cover from the trees to hide the smoke, especially in the dark.

The night passed peacefully with no visit from the five outlaws, so he stirred up the few remaining sparks of his fire enough to start a flame for a cup of coffee before he saddled his horses. This was a change in his usual routine, but he figured he might need a little boost to get this day off to a good start, not knowing how busy the day might get for him. When he was ready, he climbed aboard Buster and backtracked to the place where he had confronted the two outlaws. "I coulda camped right here," he told Buster when he found Whip Dawson's body lying just as he had left it. *Good*, he thought. *They didn't come after me. Maybe they'll just keep going.* Even as he thought it, he figured there was very little possibility of that. Tom had departed without taking time to think about it, but surely he had seen that Will was alone, and that made it more than likely they would come after him. Until he found out for sure, he had little choice but to keep tracking them.

It was easy to see where Tom Daly had crashed through the bushes when he made his departure the night before. Will followed his trail across the creek and out to the open prairie beyond. He paused briefly to see if he could find any tracks to tell him the gang had returned to look for him, but there were none. In a mile or so, Daly's tracks led him back to the common trail and the gang's general line of travel that had changed very little over the past few days.

* * *

Up ahead, on the banks of the Cimarron River, the band of outlaws were saddled up and ready to leave their campsite. Ansel Beaudry and Bo Hagen stood at the edge of the trees, looking back over the way they had come a couple of days before, as if they might see a horseman on the distant horizon. After a moment, Ansel turned and looked back at the campsite they were preparing to leave. He was disappointed that the deputy had not chosen to visit the camp during the night. They had been ready for him with five decoys around the fire and everyone hidden to receive their visitor. He had hoped it would be a simple solution to the problem. When he turned back again, Hagen asked, "We goin' back after him?"

"I was thinkin' about it last night," Ansel replied, staring out again across the way they had come. "I had an idea he would try to come sneakin' in here last night and start shootin' while we were asleep, but he didn't. Maybe he's smarter than I gave him credit for. Might be, he's smart enough to know he'll most likely get himself shot. Whaddaya think, Luther?" he asked when Luther Curry came to join them. "You think that deputy got some common sense and decided to let us be?"

"Maybe," Curry replied. "If he's got half a brain in his head, he oughta be able to figure out five-to-one odds in our favor ain't too healthy for him. We goin' after him?" He repeated Hagen's question.

"I'm tempted to," Ansel answered. He had been thinking the situation over during the night just past. If one deputy marshal was trying to follow them, it was for the purpose of telling a posse where to find them. Ansel was in a hurry to get to the hideout before they could assemble that posse, then they could lie low until the law gave up looking for them. And that would depend a lot on whether this hideout on Grassy Creek was as difficult to find as Tom Daly claimed. He had cooled off considerably since he found out the lawman had killed Whip. Ansel hated to lose Whip, but he had no burning desire to avenge his death. Now, in the light of day, he deemed the most important thing for him and his men was to get to this hideout that he had been told was unknown to the law. "I think not," he finally answered Luther. "I think this lawman, this Will Tanner; is that what Tom called him? I think he's most likely on his way back for help. Let's get mounted and get goin'. Maybe we'll drop one of us back after a while, just to make sure, but he's gonna have to stay a helluva ways back to keep us from seein' him."

"This time we'd best make sure it's one of us, so's we don't make a mess of it like Tom and Whip did," Bo said.

More than five miles behind them, Will was faced with a situation that favored the men he was chasing. The farther west he rode, the more open the prairie became. With no mountains or mesas, and a scarcity of trees, except along the banks of rivers and creeks, he could not risk closing the gap between himself and the outlaws. He kept his eyes on the distant horizon, lest he'd suddenly see them and fear that they had spotted him as well. Over the rolling grassland, he could have easily followed their trail at night, but the next morning when the sun came up, he would have to stay hidden until they lengthened the distance again. His only objective was to stay on their trail until

they finally got to where they were going to stay put.
Those were the orders Dan Stone had given him and
he was happy to obey them. As one day led to the next,
with nothing to change the routine, he began to hope
they would keep going until they passed into Texas.
Then he could turn around and head for home, and
as soon as he reached a telegraph line, wire Dan that
the outlaws were now a problem for the Texas Rangers.

When the outlaws left the Cimarron, they continued
in the same southwest direction for about twenty-five
miles before they struck the winding river once again.
Will reached the spot where they had rested their
horses and decided to use the same place to rest his.
With that in mind, he made a very careful approach
to the tree-lined banks to avoid a surprise like the one
he had endured back on Stillwater Creek. It was then
that a cloudy sky that had been threatening all morning decided to release its burden. He spread his rain
slicker over some low bushes to make a rain shelter
for himself and sat there drinking his coffee while
he watched his horses down near the water's edge.
The rain held steady for quite a while, long enough to
cause Will some concern about the trail he had been
following. It might cause that trail to become less obvious, as the tall grass began to come back from being
trampled by the gang's horses.

In the saddle again, he found that the sudden rain-
storm, now reduced to a light drizzle, had not been
enough to restore the grass completely, but had caused
him to be a little more careful when the trail led over
patches of bare ground and sand. Riding across one
such patch, which also had a gravel area, he found no
sign of tracks on the other side. He reined Buster back
and guided him in a circle around the perimeter of

the barren plot until he came to a place where the outlaws had left it. "Now, why the hell did they decide to quit on the general line they've been riding for days?" he asked the buckskin gelding as he peered out to the southwest in the direction the tracks were leading. After all this time, were they just now thinking about losing him?

Half a day's ride found him at a shallow crossing of the North Canadian River, and he could plainly see tracks where the outlaws had started across. Planning to stop there for the night, he crossed to the other side, but found no sign of the outlaws leaving the river. He realized that the men he pursued were in the same state of uncertainty as he was. The difference was he knew he was following them. They weren't sure if he was or wasn't, so they had evidently decided to start covering their trail just in case. He would have to wait until morning to find out if they were successful, since it was rapidly becoming darker, so he proceeded to make his camp.

When morning came, he saddled his horses and followed the river north. He figured Beaudry would not likely follow the river's course south toward its confluence with the Canadian, since that would take him in a direction opposite the one he had followed for days. Will continued along the North Canadian for almost two miles before he reached a shady bend with a grassy apron spreading down to the water. *The best place, so far*, he thought, and paid particular attention to the thin strip of sand between the water's edge and the grass. *Figured*, he said to himself when he spotted the hoofprints left by the horses leaving the water. They set out on a line that would take them toward the Canadian, a distance of twelve or fifteen miles from the north fork.

When he reached the Canadian, he was faced with the same puzzle to solve as he had been on the north fork. He followed the tracks into the river, only to find none on the other side. This time, however, he was not so fortunate. He spent the rest of the day searching the banks of the river, but found no sign of horses leaving it. By the time he was forced to stop to rest his horses, his frustration was nearing a peak. How, he wondered, could a herd of horses leave the river without leaving a clue? He was almost ready to believe they swam up the river to Texas. *It would be hard to convince Dan Stone of that one*, he thought. Thinking realistically then, he had to assume that they must have headed in the opposite direction, possibly leaving the water on the same side they had entered it. It was hard to convince himself that they had reversed their line of travel, however. He was still inclined to keep following the river north, even though he had to admit that he had lost them. "I reckon I ain't the tracker I thought I was," he confessed to Buster. "We might as well make our camp right here. I'm about to starve and I s'pose you and the other horses are ready to rest. Maybe tomorrow will bring us some better luck." It was most likely that the outlaws had come out of the river at some point behind him, and he had simply missed it. Still, he was reluctant to turn back, fearing the possibility that he might be just short of the sign he searched for. "I'll ride a little farther up the river in the mornin'," he declared. "If I don't see sign pretty soon, I'll turn around and go back." With that decision, he went about the business of making camp.

* * *

At first light, he continued up the river for almost two miles before being stopped by the sound of a rifle shot. Moments later, he was startled by a couple of deer that would have collided headlong into Buster, had they not split to flee on either side of him. With no time to think, he pulled his rifle from his saddle sling and wheeled Buster toward a group of cottonwoods, the closest cover he could see. Out of the saddle then, he scanned the riverbank upstream. It figured he had run up on a hunter, but was the hunter with the gang he was searching for? *They must feel pretty confident that they have lost me,* he thought, *else they would hardly risk shooting at a deer.* His concern now was the likelihood the hunter, in trying to follow the deer, might spot him and his horses in the trees and think them deer. With that a possibility, he decided to try to head the hunter off before he got that far, so he left the horses there and proceeded upstream on foot, still hoping he wasn't mistaken for a deer.

He had not advanced far when he had to duck behind another tree to keep from being seen by a lone hunter bending over the carcass of a deer, his knife in hand. He wore a buckskin shirt and his hair was long, braided Indian style in two braids. With only the descriptions of Ansel Beaudry and his men, given to him by Ned Carter and Wilbur Paul, he could not be certain if he was looking at one of the gang or not. He didn't remember anyone describing one of them with long braided hair and a buckskin shirt, however. Since the hunter's back was turned toward him, he cautiously moved closer to a couple of cottonwoods no more than ten yards from the man. Suddenly, he was struck with a feeling of familiarity. "Moon?" he called out, not really questioning as much as reacting in astonishment.

"Jesus!" Oscar Moon blurted, and stumbled over the carcass in his panic to defend himself. Landing on his behind, he frantically fumbled to find his rifle before he was able to recognize his surprise visitor. "Will," he gasped, "you scared the hell outta me!"

"Sorry," Will replied, "you kinda surprised me, too." He walked over and extended his hand to help Moon up from the sitting position he had landed in. "I didn't expect to run into you up here."

"Well, I don't know why not," Moon said as he got to his feet. "I told you last time I saw you I was movin' my camp up here on the Canadian. What are you doin' up this way?"

"I was trailin' a gang of five outlaws up until I struck this river," Will said, "but I lost 'em somewhere downstream from here. I don't suppose you saw 'em come up this way, did you?"

"Nope, I ain't seen a soul but you in the last few days. Who is it you're chasin'?" Will told him about the joint efforts of the three territorial Marshals Services to run the vicious gang to ground. "Where were they headin'?" Moon asked.

"If I knew that, I'da just rode on up there and waited for 'em," Will replied.

"If these five jaspers are as bad as you say they are," Moon asked, ignoring the sarcasm, "how come they sent you up here by yourself? Sounds to me like your boss is tryin' to get rid of you."

"I expect he might at that, especially if he finds out I lost the trail of five men leadin' three packhorses across a prairie without a place a rabbit could hide in," Will said. "They went in the river downstream from here, maybe five or six miles back. If they didn't come by you this far upstream, then they came out somewhere between here and there, and I missed it."

"You figure they're just passin' through?" Moon asked, and Will said it was his guess that they were looking to hole up somewhere until the law got tired of searching for them. "So you figure they're headin' someplace that the law don't know nothin' about?"

"I expect so," Will answered. "At least that's what I think makes the most sense. They've already got marshals stirred up in Missouri, Kansas, and now the Nations. I would think they're lookin' to lay low for a while." He paused to take another look at his friend. Moon had changed somehow since he had last seen him. For one thing, he was wearing a buckskin shirt that looked almost new, with fancy needlework and tasseled sleeves. It was a sharp contrast to the plain old shirt he'd worn that was stained with dirt and smoke. And while he still wore a beard, it looked as if it had been trimmed. Will couldn't resist commenting. "What's got into you? You look like you're dressed up to go to a weddin' or a funeral. Did you come into some money?"

The question obviously made Moon nervous. His face flushed a little and he sputtered in his reply. "Nah," he answered, hesitating, knowing that Will was well aware that he crossed back and forth across the line of the law with regularity. "I ain't come into no money. My old shirt wore out, that's all." Quickly changing the subject then, he said, "I reckon I know where those fellers you're lookin' for mighta gone."

"Is that so?" Will responded. He was not surprised, because Oscar Moon knew Kansas and Oklahoma better than any man he had ever met, and he seemed to know the comings and goings of every outlaw in the territory. He had helped Will on a number of occasions. He was the man who led him to Sartain's on Muskrat Creek, a favorite hideout for outlaws on the run. For that reason, he didn't press him on the matter of his apparent recent prosperity. He wasn't sure he wanted to know, anyway, because it was bound to be from an illegal source.

"The place I'd look is Grassy Creek," Moon continued. "West of here about two days' ride, near the Washita River. That's where they're headin'. I guarantee it."

"Grassy Creek?" Will replied. "I never heard of it." He was somewhat familiar with the area of Oklahoma where the Washita flowed, but he had never crossed a creek with that name. He had to allow for the fact that he had not spent a great deal of time in this area where General Custer had fought Black Kettle's Cheyenne. There were no white settlers in this part of the grasslands since it was a Cheyenne and Arapaho reservation now. "I never heard of Grassy Creek," he repeated.

"That's why them fellers are headed there," Moon said. "Ain't nobody else heard of it, neither."

"How do you know about it?" Will asked, and wondered why he bothered to ask as soon as the words left his lips. Moon knew about everything in the Nations and the prairie west of them.

"Used to be Sartain's was the place where all the outlaws ran to hide," Moon answered, "but too many folks got to knowin' about Sartain's—even lawmen." He paused to grin. "And Elmira's business sorta petered out, so when Tyler Brinker offered to go partners with her if she'd move closer to his business, she decided to take him up on it."

"Who's Tyler Brinker?" Will asked.

"Feller runs a tradin' post on the Canadian River, across the line over in Texas," Moon replied. "I reckon he'd heard about the money Elmira was makin' hidin' outlaws and figured he'd get in on it, too. So Elmira decided to pull up stakes and move her business to Grassy Creek. Darlene went with her, and of course, Elmira's son, Eddie. I helped her move her stuff over there and stayed long enough to help her and Tom Daly build a right sizable cabin. Tom's the one who knew where Grassy Creek was."

With the mention of Tom Daly, all the pieces were beginning to come together. This place, Grassy Creek, surely had to be Ansel Beaudry's destination. Will told Moon about his encounter with Daly and the shooting of the outlaw called Whip. Moon nodded confidently, then went on with his story. "Brinker's plannin' to build another cabin for Darlene, just like she had on Muskrat Creek," he said, "and another one for a bunkhouse for their customers. Slim didn't go with 'em. He stayed there at Sartain's. I stop by to see him every once in a while."

Will paused to consider all Moon had just said, astonished that it had been done in the year not yet passed. And it was all news to him. Elmira Tate was evidently still going strong, and Darlene Futch, too. Elmira had taken over the business of hiding outlaws when Elmer Sartain died, and she was strong enough to deal with the kind of customers who fled there. Equally tough, but several years younger, Darlene provided for the lonely needs of those so inclined to seek her particular services. Will wondered if they still knew him as Mr. Walker, the name he had given them when he had been there before. The only way they might know he was actually a deputy marshal is if Moon had told them. And Moon wouldn't do that. At any rate, his decision was made. He could continue his search for the tracks of Beaudry's gang, in case Moon was wrong, but Grassy Creek was where Beaudry was headed. He was sure of it. He had taken Moon's advice before and it had never proven wrong. To strengthen it, he knew that Tom Daly was riding with Beaudry, and Moon had just said that it was Daly who guided Elmira to Grassy Creek. That was enough to persuade him to rely on Oscar Moon once again. "Will you take me to Grassy Creek?"

"If you'll wait till I take care of this deer," Moon replied. It didn't bother him that he was operating on both sides of the issue, as long as his customers on the lawless side never found out about his friendship with Will Tanner. Will was a special friend of his and the only lawman who was.

"I'll help you butcher it," Will said, "but first, I'd best go get my horses.

When he returned with his horses, Moon was especially interested to hear about the black gelding with the fancy saddle. "Like I said," Will reminded him, "I shot the fellow that was waitin' for me at Stillwater Creek with Tom Daly. That's his horse."

Moon gave the horse a good looking-over, then commented, "He sat a fancy saddle, didn't he?"

The rest of that day was spent smoking the meat, so Moon could carry it on his packhorse. They dined on fresh venison that evening for supper with Will no longer worried about falling too far behind Ansel Beaudry. He decided that Moon was right, Beaudry was heading for Grassy Creek. It still stuck in his craw that the outlaws had managed to lose him, however. Marshal Dan Stone was probably wondering what was going on. It had been over a week since he had left Fort Smith, but there were no telegraph wires in this part of the Nations, so there was no opportunity to check in with Stone to keep him abreast of his progress. He was at least two hundred miles from the telegraph on the MKT Railroad, but he could start back as soon as Moon took him to Grassy Creek. He was 99 percent sure the outlaws would be holed up on Grassy Creek. He had to be one hundred percent sure, however, and that meant he had to see the men he trailed settled in at Grassy Creek. He never was one to act on assumptions.

The more he thought about the job he was charged with, the more he wondered if he wasn't on a fool's errand. Moon's questions and comments didn't help matters. "After you see these jaspers with your own eyes, whaddaya aim to do about it?" Moon had asked. Will told him that it was his duty to report the location of the outlaws, then a posse would be sent to take the outlaws in custody. More than likely, the Marshals Service would call upon the military for help. Oscar interrupted his chewing on a large piece of venison while he gave that some consideration. "That's gonna take a heap of time for you to get somewhere that you can tell 'em where they're holed up. It's gonna take longer'n that for them to throw a posse together and longer again to get 'em out here. Seems to me like a helluva waste of everybody's time. Those boys up at Grassy Creek might likely be long gone by then." Will shrugged helplessly. He realized he had no argument.

"You still gotta see 'em with your own eyes, though. Right?" Moon concluded.

"Right," Will answered, and pulled another slice of roasted venison from the fire. As he blew on it to keep it from burning his lips, a random thought came to him. Dan Stone was not the only one wondering about him. *Sophie's most likely fit to be tied*, he thought. As soon as it occurred to him, he hastened to discard it. *I'll think about that some other time.*

Chapter 7

It was only after they had traveled a full day and were resting their horses with a half-day's ride left to reach the hideout, that Moon confessed. "Well, I'll be . . ." Will started when he heard. "Why didn't you tell me you were headin' to Grassy Creek all along?"

Moon shrugged. "I figured you'd find out when we got there. That's where I'm takin' this meat—for Elmira," he quickly stressed. "I ain't gonna tell nobody where Grassy Creek is, but I can't help it, if some lawman follows me to it." He shrugged again as if blameless.

"I reckon not," Will agreed. He understood and respected Moon's position and his simpleminded idea of right and wrong.

After resting the horses, they continued on until reaching the Washita River, where Moon pulled up and waited for Will to ride up beside him. "I expect this is about as far as you oughta be ridin' with me. I'm goin' on up Grassy Creek, so you'll have to follow me from here if you wanna see the creek. It's easy to miss it if you don't know what to look for. Just keep a sharp eye out for a rock 'bout the size of a wash-tub, shaped like an arrowhead 'cause that's where Grassy Creek empties into the river." He paused to make sure Will understood before continuing. "The creek comes down through the trees from a little slope that runs parallel to the river. It gets pretty narrow by the time you get to the cabin, and anybody up there can see you comin'." He paused again. "You ain't plannin' on chargin' up there, blazin' away, are you?" Will assured him that he was not. "Good, 'cause I wouldn't want 'em to think I led anybody up there, especially a lawman. No offense."

"None taken," Will replied.

"Even if you tried that, they'd most likely shoot you down before you got to the clearin'." He gave his horse a nudge with his heels and started off along the river. "Take care of yourself, Will," he called back over his shoulder. "I won't likely come back down till after breakfast in the mornin'."

"I will," Will answered. "You do the same." He gave him seventy-five yards, then started out after him.

The path along the river was narrow and well hidden by weeds and tall grass. The trees were so dense along this stretch of the river that Moon was soon out of his sight, causing him to be more careful to search for the rock. He almost rode past it, but reined Buster back when the horse's hooves splashed through some water. Then he saw the rock, almost hidden by the grass growing around it, and realized that the narrow grassy bed was actually a creek bed, the grass growing on the bottom was obviously the reason for its name. The creek was squeezed in on both sides by the thick growth of trees on its banks. Moon had not lied when he had said that the only path up to the cabin was the creek, itself.

Although only late afternoon, the trees were so thick that their branches formed a ceiling overhead, making the creek seem like a dark tunnel as it gradually climbed upward. He continued on up the middle of the creek, that being the only path possible, until he thought he heard the sound of voices ahead, possibly challenging Moon. He stopped at once, alerted to the fact that he would certainly be challenged as well, should he ride a few yards more. Leading two horses, one of them saddled with the property of a late member of their gang, he would most likely have little time to explain. He had to admit they had found a hard place to attack, and he carefully turned Buster around and squeezed past the two horses he was leading.

Once he had returned to the river again, he decided the next thing he wanted to do was to scout above the site of the camp to see if he could get a look at the layout from behind to determine if the creek was the only way into it. Moon had said he wasn't coming back until morning, so he was going to have to make camp where he could keep out of sight and wait for Moon to return. Moon could tell him for sure whether Ansel Beaudry and his gang were actually there. Eager to scout the woods behind the camp while the light was still good, Will went downstream until beyond the line of trees that hugged Grassy Creek. Then he rode along beside them for a distance he estimated to be beyond the outlaw hideout. He pulled his horses inside the tree line and tied them there while he continued on foot, working his way back to the creek. He could see at once that it would be hard to ride a posse or a platoon of soldiers into the backside of the camp. With some difficulty, he finally managed to push through the bushes to a stone ledge where he could see the log cabin sitting beside the creek in a small clearing. He could not see any back way into the hideout, at least not on horseback. Maybe a man on foot could climb over the ledge, and even that might be somewhat difficult.

At first glance, he wondered where they were going to put the other cabins Moon said were planned. The clearing looked only large enough now to support the one large cabin, a small barn, a smokehouse, and an outhouse for the two women, all located in a small pasture, already crowded with horses. Will counted a dozen horses, two of them he recognized as Moon's. *It is not going to be easy to attack this camp, even with a large posse,* he thought, as he surveyed the log cabin wedged up against the creek. He shrugged then. *My job is done,* he thought, *I found them. At least I'll know for sure when Moon comes back down in the morning.* Even though that was true, it didn't feel right to ride away and leave it up to a posse, whether it be marshals or soldiers, to come and attempt to arrest Beaudry and his men. He shook his head and backed slowly away to return to his horses.

Ansel Beaudry sat at the big table in the center of the front room, a coffee cup half-empty before him. "Who the hell is this Oscar Moon jasper?" he asked Tom Daly. He glanced toward the kitchen door where he could see Moon inside talking to Elmira. "I thought you said nobody knew about this place."

"Oscar ain't nobody," Tom replied. "He brought Elmira over here from Buzzard Creek. He helped build this place. You don't have to worry about Moon. He ain't gonna cause you no problems, and he's right handy in bringin' Elmira fresh meat, like that deer he brought with him. And it ain't always deer meat, most of the time it's prime beef. No, sir, Moon's all right."

Ansel glanced at Bo Hagen. "He damn sure better be, ain't that right, Bo?"

"That's a fact," Bo replied.

"We're gonna be spendin' a lotta money in this damn squirrel's nest 'cause I plan to be here for a while," Ansel said. "So I'm gonna want me and my men to be taken care of like we were in a fancy hotel."

Elmira walked in from the kitchen in time to hear Ansel's last statement. "And that's what I'm plannin' to do," she said. "We ain't been set up here but a few months, but I ain't heard no complaints from nobody. You boys were lucky you got here right after Tyler's son brought in a heap of supplies, so we ain't been short of nothin'."

"He sure as hell didn't bring enough whiskey, if them three bottles is all there is," Luther Curry replied. "We'll drink that up in two nights."

"As long as you wanna spend your money on it," Elmira responded, "that ain't no problem. Tyler's place ain't but half a day's ride from here. It's over the border in Texas, so he gets all the whiskey he can sell." She stood in the middle of the doorway, hands on hips, and grinned confidently. "Now, you boys ready to eat? 'Cause it's on the table." As they filed by her, she nodded toward Moon, already at the table, and said, "Don't let Moon get a head start on you, he'll be hard to catch."

Moon didn't look up to acknowledge her remark. His plate full, he was already working hard to empty it. Having spent a good many years dealing with folks who operate on the wrong side of the law, he was a pretty good judge of people, and it didn't take long to determine he was in the midst of evil without conscience. While he didn't want Elmira to be deprived of the money they would spend while they were there, it would suit him just fine if Will Tanner was able to bring a cavalry patrol down upon them. Consequently, he was making an effort to learn their names, so he could report them to Will. There was little doubt who the leader was, so it was Ansel Beaudry's name he learned first.

Moon's obvious concentration did not go unnoticed by Beaudry, who fancied himself a judge of people, too. "You don't talk much, do you, Mr. Moon?" Ansel asked.

Moon looked up from his plate then, aware that all conversation at the table had stopped and all eyes seemed to be upon him, awaiting his answer. He was smart enough to realize that Beaudry's tone was evidently a signal to his men that he was not convinced that Moon was to be trusted. He looked at Beaudry and grinned. "Not when I get a chance to set down at Elmira's table," he said, and took a big bite out of the biscuit he was using to load his fork. "Besides, I found out that too much talkin' always seemed to let folks see how little I knew about everythin'."

"'Bout the only way to shut him up is to set the

table for supper," Elmira stated, coming to his rescue. Beaudry hesitated a fraction of a second, then chuckled, causing the other men to laugh.

Their attention was drawn away from Moon then, when Darlene walked into the kitchen. "Looks like I'd best get me a plate before it's all gone," she commented.

"I expect you'd better," Bo Hagen remarked. "You might have a hard night's work ahead of you." That brought another round of laughter.

"Only a jackass brays before he does any work," Darlene shot back, turning the laughter back on him.

The mood seemed to be light and cheerful around the supper table, even though Elmira was concerned about pleasing Beaudry. He seemed to fancy himself as someone who expected to be catered to, and he had already complained about the crowded conditions. Even with two rooms available to house the five men, he thought he should have a private room, since he was paying a lot to stay there. She tried to explain that they were still in the building stage and Tyler Brinker was planning to build one or maybe two more cabins. "That doesn't do me a helluva lotta good right now, does it?" Beaudry had responded, prompting her to offer her own room to him and make herself a bed in the pantry. She didn't expect him to accept her offer, but he did, and she was forced to move most of her belongings out of her room. She first offered to let him share her room with her, but he replied that he wasn't that desperate. She told Darlene that she wanted to tell him to haul his royal ass somewhere else, but she couldn't. They needed the money, and these boys were carrying plenty. In their present situation, she didn't even have a room for her son, Eddie. He was sleeping in the barn with Moon. She wasn't surprised that Moon said he was leaving right after breakfast.

After supper, Bo grabbed one of the bottles of whiskey sitting on the sideboard and retired to the front room. He was joined at the big table by Cecil Cox and Tom Daly. Beaudry and Luther Curry remained at the kitchen table, finishing off the rest of the coffee while they speculated on the best towns to target after they had lain low long enough. In a little while, Darlene joined the three in the front room. "How 'bout it, honey?" She sidled up beside Bo's chair. "You still brayin', or are you plannin' to put your money where your mouth is?"

He tossed a drink of whiskey back, then smirked at her. "I ain't drunk enough yet. When you start to look halfway decent, I'll let you know."

"You do that," she came back. "The drunker you get, the higher the price goes up." She turned at once to Cecil. "How 'bout you, honey, you wanna play house? I'll give you a gettin'-acquainted price." He got to his feet right away and followed her back to her room.

Bo and Tom Daly were joined by Moon, who sat down for a drink before retiring to the barn for the night. Bo poured him a drink, and before long, they put quite a sizable dent in the bottle. The conversation naturally centered on the camp there on Grassy Creek and the plans that Tyler Brinker and Elmira had for it. "That's a far piece from where it is right now," Bo commented. "I ain't been here but one night and I'm already gettin' cabin fever." He nodded toward the hallway door Darlene and Cecil had just gone through. "And ol' Darlene looks like she's about ready to be turned out to pasture."

"Darlene can be right comfortin' on a cold winter night," Tom said in her defense.

"Maybe so," Bo allowed, "but it ain't winter for a spell yet." He picked up the half-empty whiskey bottle and inspected it. "We're gonna be outta whiskey before you know it. How far is it to get some more—that feller's store—Brinker, was it? How far is that from here?"

"Half a day's ride," Tom answered.

"What else is over there?" Bo persisted. "Any women that ain't old enough to be your mama?"

Tom and Moon both laughed. "Yep," Moon answered. "There was two the last time I was over there. Brinker's got a store and a saloon in the same big room. He's in Texas. He don't have to worry about the law comin' down on him."

"Now, that sounds more like it," Bo declared. "I might take me a little ride over there tomorrow. We're gonna need more whiskey, anyway. So we might as well go ahead and get it."

"Whaddaya reckon Ansel might say about that?" Moon asked. "I thought you boys wanted to stay hid."

"I ain't in the habit of askin' Ansel if I can do somethin' or not," Bo immediately flared. "If I take a notion to do somethin', I don't reckon I gotta ask anybody." He paused to consider that. "You said there wasn't no law anywhere around that store, right?" When Tom said that was so, Bo went on. "Then there ain't no reason not to go, as long as I don't lead anybody back here. You wanna go with me to show me the way?"

"Sure," Tom said. "I'll take you to Brinker's. When you wanna go?"

"Hell, tomorrow's as good a day as any, after breakfast, but not too soon after breakfast. I got a feelin' I'm gonna wanna sleep a little of this whiskey off in the mornin'." He looked over at Moon then. "How 'bout you, Moon, you wanna go with us?"

"Sounds temptin'," Moon replied, "but I reckon not. I've gotta get back to my camp and make sure ain't nothin' been nosin' around in it."

Will was up with the first rays of light that crept through the branches of the cottonwoods along the Washita River and he wasted little time in packing up his camp and saddling his horses. Moon had told him he would not return until after breakfast, and he guessed that wouldn't be very early, but he didn't want to take a chance on missing him. He toyed with the idea of bringing his campfire back to life just long enough to boil a cup of coffee, but decided against it. When his horses were ready, he climbed up into the saddle and rode back down the river to a spot he had picked out the night before. About fifty yards downstream from the rock that marked the mouth of Grassy Creek on the opposite bank, he dismounted and led the horses back into the trees before returning close to the bank. He sat down with his back against a cottonwood, where he could see anyone coming down the creek to the river. A low mist hovered over the river, giving it a peaceful feeling. He might have enjoyed it had it not been for knowing what lay a hundred yards or so up that creek. Suddenly, the form of a horse and rider appeared in the mist. In a matter of moments, it took on the solid form familiar to him. It was Oscar, riding along the river now, leading his packhorse behind him. Will got to his feet and waited a few seconds to make sure Moon was alone, and when no one came out of the creek after him, Will returned to his horses. He guided Buster out along the riverbank, where Moon could see them. When he did, he signaled with a wave of his arm, directing Will to ride farther downstream. After riding about two hundred yards, Moon drove his horses across to join him.

"We was right," Moon said upon dismounting. "Them's your bank robbers up there, all right. Ansel Beaudry's the big dog and he's got a couple of dangerous-lookin' gunmen with him, name of Bo Hagen and Luther Curry. Listenin' to 'em talkin', I think they was in prison with him. The other two— well, you know Tom Daly—and a little feller name of Cecil Cox."

Will couldn't help laughing. "Well, Moon, you did a helluva job. I'd best write those names down, else I'll forget 'em before I get back in the saddle." He got a piece of a paper sack and a stubby pencil from his saddlebags and asked Moon to repeat the names.

After Will wrote the names down and put them away in his saddlebag, Oscar scratched his chin whiskers thoughtfully. "That ain't all," he said. "There's somethin' else that might catch your interest." Then he reported the conversation he had heard the night before between two of the outlaws. "So that's what they decided they was gonna do," Moon summed up.

"Tom Daly is gonna take this Bo Hagen feller over in Texas to Tyler Brinker's tradin' post." He paused to give Will an impish grin. "Course, you ain't got no authority in Texas, but I s'pose that don't make no difference to you, does it?"

"Not a whole lot, for a fact," Will answered. His mind was galloping. His job was to find Ansel Beaudry's hideout and lead a posse to arrest him and his gang, but this surprising piece of news offered an opportunity to make an arrest right away of two of the gang. As he and Moon had speculated, with all the time and distance hampering the arrest, by the time a posse was formed, it might be too late to capture any of the gang. He didn't have to deliberate long. "When are they goin'?" he asked, and Moon said after breakfast. He also told him that it was possible that Bo would change his mind about leaving Grassy Creek when Beaudry found out what he was planning.

"Ain't no doubt, Beaudry's the boss," Moon repeated, "but Bo Hagen ain't the kind of man that lets people tell him what he can and can't do."

"This might be the only chance to arrest any of that gang," Will said, "so I reckon that's what I'll try to do."

"That's what I figured you'd say," Moon said, "so that's the reason I had you ride down the river a piece. When Tom and that Hagen feller come outta Grassy Creek, they're gonna ride down this way about fifty yards. Then they're gonna take a little game trail up over the rise to the west." He pointed to a spot upstream by a dead tree, even though the trail was not easily seen due to the overgrowth of bushes. Will nodded and Moon continued. "That game trail will cross an old Injun trail to the Canadian River, and that trail will lead you to Brinker's place if you stay on it. I figure you're gonna have to trail 'em a pretty good ways before you make a move on 'em, so if there's some shootin', you'll be far enough away that they won't hear it back at Grassy Creek."

"You figure right," Will said. "That's just exactly what I'm aimin' to do." There was nothing to do now but wait to see if Bo Hagen was going to show up. Judging by Moon's impression of Ansel Beaudry and his obvious position as the boss, Bo Hagen's boastful claims that no man told him what to do might just be the whiskey talking. "What are you figurin' on doin' now?" Will asked. "You gonna take off for home?"

Moon hesitated for a moment before answering, not sure if Will was going to ask for his help in capturing Hagen and Daly. "Well . . ." he drew out, "I expect I at least oughta wait till we see if they show up to take the trail to Brinker's. I was figurin' on headin' back to my camp up on the Canadian today. I don't really have no business here right now with Elmira, and I've got some things that need took care of at my camp."

Will couldn't help being amused by Moon's predicament, and he understood it. Moon considered Will a friend, but he couldn't afford to have the people he routinely dealt with know that. If word got out that he helped a deputy marshal capture a couple of outlaws, it would be too dangerous for him to show his face in this part of the territory. He decided to relieve Moon's anxiety. "I think it's best if you're not seen with me. You've been a helluva lotta help to me on more than one occasion and I'd hate to mess that up. This ain't the first time I've had to arrest two or more outlaws at the same time. And after I arrest 'em, they might get word back to their friends that you helped me, so it's best you don't lend a hand."

"I see what you're sayin'," Moon responded eagerly. "It might keep me from helpin' you down the road sometime. I'll do what you say. I'll keep outta the way." Sometimes his friendship with the young lawman bothered Moon. Although he didn't like to think of himself as being a double-crosser, he had no trouble picking sides when it involved men like Ansel Beaudry. In Moon's way of thinking, there was nothing wrong with operating on the shady side of the law, but Beaudry and his gang were downright evil. He reached in his saddlebag, pulled out a piece of smoked venison, and handed it to Will. "Here, I brought you some breakfast."

Will took it gratefully. "Thanks. I ain't had any breakfast."

"That's what I figured," Moon replied. "Maybe that'll hold you for a little while." He was about to apologize for not having any coffee for him, but he was interrupted at that moment by the appearance of two horses at the mouth of the creek. "Uh-oh, there they are!"

Will watched the two riders as they turned downstream and followed the river until they reached the dead tree Moon had pointed to. Then they pushed through the bushes and were soon out of sight. "I recognized Tom Daly. Was that the one you called Bo Hagen with him?"

"Yep," Moon replied, "that was Hagen, and Will, you'd best be real careful with that feller. He's just naturally rattlesnake mean." They both climbed aboard their horses. "That little game trail will lead you to the trail to Brinker's," he reminded him. He started to leave, but paused to say one more thing. "I ain't got no idea how in the world Tom Daly wound up ridin' with that bunch. He ain't nowhere near as mean as they are. He's a cattle rustler, he ain't no killer."

"That's pretty much the way I see it, too," Will said, "and thanks again, Moon. Be seein' ya."

"Be seein' ya," Moon replied, then he turned his horse downstream while Will crossed over to the other side, heading toward the dead tree and the game trail beside it.

Chapter 8

Will guided Buster through a patch of berry bushes beside the dead cottonwood tree on a game trail he never would have discovered had Moon not pointed it out to him. He was careful to take his time, lest he catch up with the two men he followed too soon. While trying to keep his mind on the trail he followed, he could not help wondering if what he was doing was foolish. Instead of riding as fast as he could to the closest telegraph wire to report Beaudry's location, he was on the trail of two of the gang with the intention of arresting them. He was planning to do this even though he would be crossing into Texas, where he had no authority to arrest anyone. And after he arrested them, what was he to do with them? He couldn't afford the time it would take to transport them all the way across Oklahoma Territory to Fort Smith. There was another possibility, however, and that's what he ultimately decided to do. Camp Supply was located on the Beaver River where Wolf Creek emptied into it. The camp was only about twenty-five miles east of the Texas line. According to what he had learned from Moon, Brinker's trading post was probably about sixty miles southwest of Camp Supply, a day and a half's ride. He felt sure the army would hold the two outlaws in their guardhouse for him and maybe send a message to Fort Smith. That would leave him free to return to keep a watch on Grassy Creek. That was his plan. The only thing left to do was to put it into action. With that settled in his mind, he turned all his attention to the job of arresting Hagen and Daly.

He set a comfortable pace when he turned onto the old Indian trail when the game trail reached it. He was in no hurry to catch the two outlaws until he was well away from the camp at Grassy Creek. Ideally, he would like to make his move before they reached the trading post, but he doubted they would stop to rest their horses before reaching Brinker's. It was hard to say what the situation might be at the store. According to what Moon had told him, Brinker was a partner with Elmira, so he might feel obligated to help the outlaws. Maybe it would be best to wait Hagen and Daly out and strike them on their way back. "I reckon we'll just have to wait and see," he informed Buster, and nudged him with his heels.

The sun was high overhead when he saw the trees that marked the course of the Canadian River, so he slowed Buster once again while he tried to see if he could spot the trading post. Knowing Tom Daly would recognize him at once, he wanted to be careful not to ride blindly into their midst. When within fifty yards of the log building that faced away from the river, he stopped to look over the situation. The path he had followed led right past the front entrance to the store and continued on in a northern direction. Outbuildings and a barn were on the other side of the main building. There was a hitching rail in front of the porch, but there were no horses tied there, causing him to wonder until his gaze was attracted by some movements down at the river's edge. Nudging Buster forward a few more yards gave him a better view of the river, and he spotted a couple of horses down near the water. In a moment, a young boy came into his view. Will guessed that the boy had been given the job of watering the outlaws' horses, because both horses were saddled. Thinking to gain some information that he could use later, he turned Buster toward him.

Young Thomas Brinker turned when the horses he was watching nickered and he heard Buster answer from the bluffs behind him. He stared at the man riding a big buckskin with two horses following behind him. He knew right away that the man was no one he had ever seen before, and outlaw or honest man, it made little difference to him. Both kinds came to trade at his father's store, so he felt no need to sing out to announce the stranger. Instead, he stood by the water's edge and continued to stare at him as he approached.

"Howdy," Will said when he pulled Buster to a halt beside the boy and stepped down from the saddle.

"Howdy," Thomas returned.

"These your horses?" Will asked, knowing they were not. He just wanted to see if the youngster was prone to conversation with a stranger.

"Nope," Thomas replied. "They ain't my horses. I'm just waterin' 'em for two fellers in the store."

"Is that so?" Will responded. "Those fellows pay you

to watch their horses? That's a big job for a young fellow like you."

"They ain't payin' me to watch 'em, they just told me to. Anyway, it ain't no big job for me, I've took care of horses before. I ain't so young, either. I'm nine years old and I take care of my daddy's horses all the time."

"Sounds to me like you know what you're doin'," Will went on. "You reckon you could handle three more horses? My horses need waterin', too. It's worth a nickel a piece to me to have somebody watch my horses. Whaddaya say?"

"Yes, sir," Thomas responded at once. "I'll watch 'em for you. I'll see that they get a good drink. Those two fellers in the store said to bring 'em up to the porch and tie 'em at the rail. You want me to bring yours up there, too?"

"Yep," Will answered. "Bring mine, too. Keep 'em all together. I'll walk on up to the store. There's a couple of things I wanna pick up." He reached in his saddlebag, pulled out a small purse that he kept coins in, and took out three nickels. When he handed them to Thomas, he commented, "You must do a man's job around here. Ain't your daddy got anybody else to help him?"

"He don't need nobody else to help him," Thomas answered. "Me and him do all the work and Mama does the cookin'."

"I declare," Will said, "you're a hardworkin' man, all right. I'll go on up to the store now." He drew his rifle from the saddle scabbard and turned toward the store, then paused to ask, "If I stay on that trail I rode in on, where am I gonna wind up?" The boy told him he'd wind up in Kansas, so he asked another question, confident that the youngster would tell him the truth. "What if I was goin' to Camp Supply, back in Oklahoma? Do you know where that is?"

"Sure, I know where Camp Supply is," Thomas answered. "We get soldiers comin' by here from time to time." He shrugged. "Only it won't be Camp Supply for long. The soldiers told Daddy they're changin' the name of it to Fort Supply in December."

"Is that a fact?" Will replied truthfully. "I did not know that." He nodded thoughtfully. "So what trail did the soldiers come in on?"

"Same one you came in on," Thomas said. "Only you have to take that trail that forks off to the right when you get about five miles past our store, if you wanna go to Camp Supply."

"What's your name, son?"

"Thomas."

"Well, Thomas, I'm mighty pleased to meet you. I appreciate all the help you've been."

"Yes, sir," Thomas replied, then asked, "What's your name?"

"Will Tanner . . . I'll see you later." He walked around to the other side of his packhorse, pulled two sets of hand irons out of one of the packs, and hooked one end of each on the back of his belt, so his hands would be free. Then he left Thomas to watch the horses, confident that he had gotten more information from him than he ever would have from Thomas's father. He didn't really need anyone to watch his horses. Buster wasn't going to wander off without him and the other two horses had to follow Buster, since they were tied to him by a lead line.

He took a good look around him as he walked up
to the front porch, in case there might be someone in
the barn or the outhouse, but it appeared everyone
was inside the store. He noticed that the back part
of the building was two stories high, no doubt to
accommodate the two prostitutes Moon had mentioned, or anyone else who wanted to take a room for
the night. There were two steps up to a wide front
porch with four large rocking chairs. He couldn't
help thinking it looked mighty fancy for a trading
post. It more nearly resembled a resort. There were
two doors off the porch, one opened directly to the
general store, the other to the half of the room that
served as a saloon. Thinking it to be less noticeable,
Will chose the door to the store.

Effie Brinker looked up from behind the counter
when he walked in. "Well, howdy, stranger," she greeted
him. "I didn't hear you come up. I thought that was
Thomas coming in the door."

"I left my horses with Thomas down by the river,"
Will said. "He'll probably be up in a little while. He's
got a couple other horses he's watchin', too."

"Yeah, they belong to the two fellows in the saloon,
talkin' to Myrtle and Gracie." She studied him for a
moment, thinking he didn't look as if he wanted to
buy anything. "If you're lookin' for my husband, he's
in the saloon, too." Her attention was drawn to the
Winchester rifle he held casually in his right hand,
and the two short chains hanging behind him. She
wondered if she had made a mistake when she told
him where Tyler was. "Was there something I could
help you with? He's tendin' bar for those two men at
the table. They're friends of his." She thought it might

be a good idea to let him know that her husband was not alone.

He realized then that he had obviously caused her some concern by his solemn manner, so he smiled and said, "I'll go over and maybe we'll have a drink. I've never been in your store before. I'll go take a look at the saloon."

"Everybody's friendly to strangers here," she felt compelled to say. "You won't need that rifle. You can leave it here by the door if you want to."

He looked at the rifle as if just then remembering it. "I declare, I forgot I was carryin' it. I reckon I'm so used to carryin' it, I walk off balance when I ain't got it." He gave her another smile, then continued walking toward the saloon section of the store.

With his eye on the table, he took the one step up to the saloon floor. Tom Daly was seated with his back to him, and while Bo Hagen glanced at him, he showed no interest. He was more interested in visiting with Gracie Johnson at the moment. Tyler Brinker, leaning on the front side of the short bar, noticed him and spoke. "Howdy, mister, whaddle it be?"

Will didn't answer. Instead, he walked toward the table, his rifle now in both hands and leveled at the table. Myrtle Mayfield was the first of the four seated around the table to see the rifle aimed at them. She was suddenly struck dumb, her eyes seeming to bulge, her mouth open to scream, but no sound came out. Confused, Tom Daly turned his head to see what had caused her to freeze. His reaction upon seeing the relentless lawman was decidedly more violent than Myrtle's. "Will Tanner!" he exclaimed, and went over backward in his chair when he tried to push it back while reaching for his pistol, crashing to the floor in the process.

Gracie screamed and Bo made a move for his .44, but stopped when Will brought his rifle to bear on him. "It would be a mistake," Will calmly warned him. His tone convinced Hagen, so he immediately lifted his hands up over the table. "Miss"—Will nodded toward Myrtle—"with your left hand, draw that pistol out of his holster and throw it over here on the floor." She nodded nervously and reached for his pistol. "With your left hand," Will repeated sternly when she naturally started to reach for the weapon with her right. She obeyed, using only her thumb and forefinger to withdraw the pistol. "You stay right where you are," Will warned Brinker when he started to slide toward the end of the bar, "and you won't get hurt. I'm arresting these men for bank robbery and murder." It was enough to convince Brinker to do as instructed. He was further convinced when Tom Daly, still on his back, straddling the seat of his chair, made the mistake of thinking Will was distracted by all that was happening at the same time. He reached again to pull his pistol, but succeeded only in getting it halfway out of the holster before the bullet from Will's rifle ripped into the floor beside him, barely grazing his wrist. Daly screamed in pain, echoed by screams from both women at the table as well as one from Effie Brinker when she heard the shot. Will quickly cranked another cartridge in the chamber and told Brinker to tell his wife that everything was all right, they wouldn't be hurt as long as they didn't interfere with the arrest. Brinker did so and told her to stay in the store.

Shifting back to Bo Hagen again, he ordered, "Get

on your feet." Hagen pushed his chair back and slowly rose to his feet. "You stay right where you are!" Will warned Tom when he started to get up from the floor.

"Who the hell are you?" Hagen demanded, even though Tom had blurted out his name. He could not believe the deputy had found them again.

"I'm a U.S. Deputy Marshal," Will answered. "Turn around." When he did, Will quickly laid his rifle on the table and grabbed Hagen's wrists. He clamped one set of hand irons around them and ordered, "Get on your knees." When Hagen was on his knees, his hands behind his back, Will turned again to Tom Daly. "All right, Daly, it's your turn now. Get up from there."

Seeing as how he had little choice, and having experienced an arrest by Will before, he struggled to free himself from the overturned chair and submitted himself to the procedure of handcuffing. It was only after Will clamped the hand irons closed that it occurred to him. "Hey, you can't do this. We're in Texas!" He looked frantically at Bo Hagen. "He's a deputy marshal in Oklahoma! He ain't got no authority in Texas!"

A ray of hope flashed in Bo Hagen's eyes. "He's right, we're in Texas now, there ain't nothin' you can do with us. You ain't got no authority here. Tell him, Brinker," he yelled at him.

With no idea what he should do, Brinker could only respond, "He's right, Deputy, this is Texas."

"Not today, it ain't," Will replied. "These two men, and three of their partners, are wanted in Missouri, Kansas, and Oklahoma for robbin' banks and murderin' five men that I know of, so I have the authority to arrest them anywhere I find 'em." It was not true, but he thought it might give Brinker something to think about if he was considering coming to their aid. "Now, tell your wife to come in here." When Brinker looked apprehensive, Will said, "No harm's gonna come to her if she doesn't interfere with my arrest." Still reluctant to call to her to join them, he hesitated before calling for her. She came almost immediately, having been peeking at the activity in the saloon ever since hearing the shot. When Will had them all gathered in the saloon, he told them what they were to do. "We're all gonna go out on the porch. I ain't got any argument with any of you but these two outlaws, but I wanna know where everybody is till we ride outta here. When we get on the porch, I want you to call your son to bring all the horses," he said to Effie. "Can you do that?"

"I reckon I can," she replied after getting a nod from her husband, and when they were all gathered on the porch, she called to Thomas and told him to bring the horses.

In the few minutes they waited for Thomas to gather the five horses, Bo Hagen attempted to bluff his way out of his predicament. "Tanner, damned if you ain't a regular bloodhound. I'll give you that." Will made no response, but Bo went on, "You're makin' a terrible mistake, but you can get out of it, if you're smart enough. It's a helluva long way from here to Fort Smith. Ain't that where you ride out of?" Again, Will did not respond. "Ansel and the rest of the boys will be coming after us, doggin' you all the way across Oklahoma. You ain't gonna be able to close your eyes the whole time, and sooner or later you're gonna make a mistake, and it's gonna cost you your life. You think about that." He paused to let his words sink in. "But if you let us go and ride on outta here, we won't hold no hard feelin's against you—let you go without nobody comin' after you. Whaddaya say, Tanner?"

"I say, the horses are here, time to get in the saddle." Will went down the steps to meet Thomas, who was wondering why everybody was waiting for him and who fired the shot he had heard.

Hagen recognized Whip Dawson's horse, and as soon as Will stepped off the porch, Hagen whispered to Brinker, "Send your boy back to Grassy Creek to tell Ansel what happened." Brinker nodded vigorously in response.

"Much obliged," Will said to the astonished young boy and took the reins from him. Then he proceeded to secure a lead line to trail the outlaws' horses behind his horses. As a precaution, he took another coil of rope and fashioned a loop on the end. He hung the rope on Buster's saddle horn and motioned to Tom Daly. "Step up in the saddle." When Tom replied that he couldn't do it with his hands behind his back, Will said, "Yes, you can. I'll boost you up." Having ridden as a captive of Will's, Daly knew there was no use in balking, so he went dutifully to stand beside his horse and waited for Will to give him a boost. While he was in the process, Hagen saw it as an opportunity to make a run for it, in spite of any odds for escape. Daly was already high enough in the air to throw his leg over, so Will gave him one final shove as Hagen stepped off the porch and started to run. Will grabbed the rope from his saddle horn, shook out the loop, and roped Hagen before he had gotten more than thirty feet away. With his hands anchored behind his back, Bo could not fight the rope when Will drew the loop tight and reeled him in. The silent crew of spectators watched in astonishment.

"I coulda told you there ain't no use to run," Tom said. "He worked cattle for a livin' before he was a lawman."

"Is that so?" Hagen spat, angry enough to defy the seemingly unperturbable lawman. He was encouraged to balk when Will ordered him to step up on his horse, since the deputy had not simply shot him down when he had tried to run. That told him that Will was intent upon taking his prisoners in alive, and he told himself that he'd be damned if he was going to go willingly. "Well, I reckon I ain't gonna get on that damn horse," he informed Will. "Whaddaya gonna do, shoot me?"

"Get on your horse," Will ordered.

"Nope," Hagen replied, more confident than ever that Will would not shoot him.

Will shrugged. "Suit yourself," he said, and tightened the loop even more, then wrapped the rope around Hagen's body half a dozen times before tying a knot. He reeled out the rest of the rope and tied it to his saddle horn. Ready to ride, he climbed aboard Buster. This was not the first time he'd had a prisoner who refused to go, so it didn't surprise him when Bo sat down in defiance. Will gave Buster a firm nudge and the buckskin responded, spinning Hagen around to land on his back, tumbling and bouncing as he was dragged over the rough ground toward the trail along the bluff. It didn't take long before Bo was yelling for Will to stop. Will gave him a little more of the treatment, then stopped and asked him if he was ready to ride.

Still defiant, although bruised somewhat in body and mind, he did not want to submit to the lawman's orders. "Let me get on my feet, you son of a bitch, and I'll walk to Fort Smith."

"Fine by me," Will replied, and waited for Hagen to struggle to his feet. Then he started out again at a pace that would not push Hagen too much. He figured it not a bad idea to tire Hagen out, so he planned to walk him awhile at a casual walk for the horses, a pace that would require Hagen to walk fairly briskly. After a few miles, he would increase the pace to a gentle lope that would require the walking man to trot to keep up. He was hoping that if he tired him out, he might be less inclined to protest his every order. To his credit, Bo Hagen held up pretty well in his protest. He was still on his feet when they reached the trail that branched off toward the east, which Thomas had told him was five miles from the trading post. They had gone only a couple hundred yards on that trail when Hagen stumbled and fell. When he made no effort to get on his feet again, Will stopped the horses, dismounted, and helped Hagen up on his horse.

When they were under way again, Tom Daly looked over at Hagen and said, "I'm still tryin' to figure out what the hell you were tryin' to prove."

"You go to hell," Hagen grunted. At this point, he had no patience for Tom, for it was Tom who had led them to Grassy Creek, a hideout that was supposedly unknown to lawmen, and very few outlaws. Yet, here was a U.S. Deputy Marshal waiting for them, no more than a half-day's ride from Grassy Creek. He was worn out, but still determined not to return to prison. It was a long way from where they now were to Fort Smith, Arkansas, and he was convinced that the deputy would slip up somewhere along the trail. They might not get far at all before Ansel and the others would be riding after them. Then he would personally deal with this smart-ass deputy.

Will kept them in the saddle for a distance he figured to be about twenty miles past the fork that led toward Camp Supply when he came to a creek. Since it was the first sign of water they had seen in that time, he decided to make his camp there. The horses were ready for a rest and he was ready for some coffee and something to eat, since a piece of smoked venison was the only breakfast he'd had that morning. He had enough food to feed his prisoners and himself, with still some extra smoked deer meat he had gotten from Oscar Moon, and he could restock his supplies at Camp Supply. After a quick glance upstream and down, he decided to cross over and ride upstream toward a group of cottonwood trees. Grass was no problem, for there was plenty all along the creek, and the cottonwoods offered cover and firewood, as well as other requirements, which Tom was familiar with. "Reckon it's time for some tree huggin'," he commented to Hagen when Will reined Buster to a stop.

"What the hell are you talkin' about?" Hagen barked. It was the first words he had spoken since he had ended his walking protest.

"You'll see," Tom answered.

"Since you know what to do, I'll get you settled first," Will said. He waited then, his rifle in hand, and watched while Tom threw one leg over and slid from the saddle. When he hit the ground, Will pointed to a young cottonwood and said, "That one." Tom walked over to the tree and stood beside it, waiting for Will to unlock his handcuffs. When one hand was free, he dutifully put his arms around the tree trunk and stood patiently waiting while Will locked the cuffs together again. Will walked back to the horses and motioned with his .44 for Hagen to dismount. When he did, Will pointed to a tree about five yards from the one Tom was chained to. "That one looks like it's about the right size."

When both prisoners were occupied with getting acquainted with their trees, Will unloaded the horses and turned them loose to drink and graze. As a precaution, he hobbled all of them except Buster, then he built a fire and filled his coffeepot with the cool creek water. When he had fried up a supper of bacon and hardtack, he released one prisoner at a time to eat, while he watched them with his rifle ready to fire if necessary. He fed Tom first, and when he had finished, Will locked his hands around the tree again before unlocking a scowling, complaining Bo Hagen. "Why can't you let both of us eat at the same time?" Bo griped. "Hell, you got your rifle on us. There ain't much we can do without gettin' shot."

"I'll let you go first in the mornin'," Will said. "I ain't got but one extra plate and cup, anyway, so you'll have to eat one at a time."

"How come we're followin' this trail?" Tom decided to ask. He knew the territory as well as anybody, and he was beginning to wonder about Will's familiarity with it. "We keep goin' this way, we'll end up in Kansas somewhere. Fort Smith's far enough already without addin' extra miles. I'm thinkin' you might be lost."

"The longer, the better," Bo growled. "We'll get to spend more time gettin' to know Deputy Tanner." Although sarcastic, his remark was sincere in that he figured the longer the journey took, the more time Ansel, Cecil, and Luther had to overtake them. And the more nights Tanner tried to sleep with one eye open, the more likely a chance to jump him would occur.

Will didn't bother to respond to either of the grumbling prisoners, which prompted Tom to complain further. "I hope to hell you've got more grub in those packs than bacon and hardtack. We'll be starved to death by the time we get to Fort Smith— won't be nothin' left of us to hang." He paused to think again about the direction they had held to ever since leaving Brinker's, and it suddenly occurred to him. "Unless . . ." he started, then sure of it, he declared, "You're goin' to Camp Supply! You ain't goin' to Fort Smith a-tall."

Again, Will didn't bother to respond. He was not surprised that Tom figured it out. He was surprised, however, that it had taken him this long. Still, he had hoped his destination would not be discovered until well along the way the next day. It would have been better if they thought they had more time for him to become careless. Hit hardest by Tom's sudden declaration, Bo Hagen strained at the shackles trapping him against the tree. "Where's Camp Supply?" he demanded.

"About a day's ride from where we are right now," Tom said, unable to keep from grinning at the sight of fury in Hagen's eyes. He knew his partner would risk everything in an attempt to attack the deputy and he hoped he might slip away in the process. What he hoped for was that Tanner would make a mistake between now and tomorrow this time, because once they were locked inside that stockade at Camp Supply, they were lost.

Will was in the process of rinsing his coffeepot in the creek when he heard Hagen call out, "Hey, Tanner, I need to go to the bushes. My bowels are crampin' up. That slop you gave us for supper ain't settin' too good in my gut."

Here it is, Will thought. *He didn't wait long to make his first try.* "All right," he answered him. "Soon as I pick up these plates." He never denied a prisoner's right to answer a call from nature, even though he was highly suspicious of Hagen's urgency.

He could feel Hagen's eyes on him while he put the plates and the coffeepot back in one of the packs. When he approached the tree where Hagen was shackled, he was further alerted by the seemingly cooperative tone of his voice. "I 'preciate it," Hagen said respectfully. "I reckon it hit me kinda sudden-like."

Will decided he might as well play along, since Hagen was set on making a break for it, and they might as well get it over with. He sensed the tension in Hagen's forearms as he unlocked the cuff on his left wrist. When it was unlocked, he stepped quickly back a couple of steps to await his move. Not surprising, there was none. Hagen let his arm drop by his side, the chain and open cuff dangling almost to his knee. His first intention, to brain Will with the open cuff, had been anticipated and rendered impossible when Will stepped out of range, with his Colt .44 aimed squarely at him. "Step lively, Hagen," Will ordered. "You can do your business right up there by that big elm tree."

Hagen was struggling to hold his temper after missing his first plan of attack, but he was not ready to give up. "I need to go to them berry bushes down by the creek," he complained. "I can't do no business settin' up there with you two lookin' at me."

Pretending to have empathy for his predicament, Will said, "Probably something you got used to in prison. I mean, with all those private toilets they have in there." He shrugged. "But I reckon if that's the only way you can go, you can go do it in the bushes, and there won't be anybody watchin' you but me and this .44."

"To hell with it," Hagen snapped. "Might as well be out in the open, if you go in the bushes to watch me. We done talked about it too much, I ain't gotta go no more."

"Let's get your hands back around your tree," Will said. "Maybe it'll let loose while you're sleepin'. You got any clean britches in your saddlebags?"

Hagen didn't answer, his face a mask of uncontrolled rage. He raised his uncuffed hand to be shackled, but when Will reached for the open handcuff, Hagen suddenly jerked it away and swung it like a mace at Will's head. It all seemed to have happened within the span of a second. Will was able to deflect the swinging weight on the end of the short chain, catching the blow on his shoulder, at the same time pulling the trigger of his .44 to put a bullet into Hagen's leg. The impact of the slug in Hagen's thigh caused him to drop to the ground, screaming in pain. Before he could recover, Will dropped down and grabbed Hagen's wrists, locking them securely around the tree again. "You son of a bitch!" Hagen blurted. "Turn me loose, so I can tend to it. I'm bleedin' bad."

"Stay still and I'll take care of it," Will said, "but I can't do anything if you don't hold still. I reckon I oughta tell you what my rules are. You just took your first try to escape—you've got two more tries. The second time you try, you'll get a bullet in the other leg, the third time, you get one in the chest. So you'd best be thinkin' about how much trouble you wanna give me on the rest of this little ride." With Hagen groaning in pain, Will had to turn him sideways behind the tree, so he could unbuckle his belt and pull his trousers down to his knees. He took one look at the bullet hole in Hagen's underwear and the rapidly expanding bloodstain before he went to his packs to get some bandaging. His source was an old worn-out bedsheet he had gotten from Ruth Bennett for this purpose. He tore off a couple of strips and tied them tightly around Hagen's leg. "Maybe that'll stop the bleedin' and hold you till we get to Camp Supply tomorrow. Then I expect we'd best have the surgeon take a look at it." When he was finished, he went back to the creek to rinse the blood from his hands, and now that he had time, he pulled his shirt off to take a look at the already sizable bruise on his shoulder. Luckily, his shirt had prevented an open cut.

"You reckon them two are comin' back here for supper?" Elmira Tate asked Ansel Beaudry. "I'm ready to set food on the table."

"Go ahead and put it on the table," Ansel said. "It's their own damn fault if they ain't back by suppertime."

"They're most likely spendin' all their money on those young whores at that tradin' post," Luther snorted, and glanced in Darlene's direction to see if she was insulted.

If she was, she didn't show it, seeming to be more interested in a pan of biscuits she was carrying to the table. When she had placed it in the center of the table, she commented on Luther's remark. "Bein' young ain't as good as bein' experienced," she declared. "Too bad some men spend all their money before they find that out."

"Maybe they ain't thinkin' they need no mother's love," Luther japed, remembering the remark Bo had made the night before.

There was little concern for the absence of Tom and Bo, even when bedtime came with still no sign of them. It was easy to imagine their two partners had found themselves with a real opportunity to catch up on the high times they had missed while running from the law. They figured the two would come dragging into camp sometime around noon the next day. Only Darlene was a little perturbed over their preference to have their party at Brinker's instead of with her, even with Cecil's attempts to soothe her pride. It was not until after breakfast the next morning, with still no sign of Bo and Tom, that Ansel began to be concerned. "If they don't show up by this evenin', we'd better ride over to Brinker's to see what's goin' on," he said to Luther. "That damn deputy might still be doggin' our trail. I shoulda gone back and killed Tanner after he shot Whip. I didn't figure he'd stay on our trail after that, figured we'd lost him for good at the Canadian."

"Mighta been him," Luther said, "but you know how crazy Bo is. They're likely just to still be shackin' up over at Brinker's. They've got plenty of money to do it."

"You might be right," Ansel allowed, "but we'd best ride over there, if they ain't back by tonight." He had no sooner said it when Cecil sang out a warning that someone was coming up the creek.

Ansel and Luther went immediately to the front porch, where Cecil was standing, peering at a rider approaching. "That ain't Bo and Tom," Cecil said.

"Who the hell is it?" Ansel demanded as the rider drew closer. "Looks like a kid."

"It's Thomas, Tyler Brinker's boy," Darlene said, coming out behind them when she heard them say someone was coming. "Wonder what he wants?"

Ansel had a feeling that something was wrong. He walked out in front of the hitching rail to meet Thomas. "What is it, boy?" he asked before Thomas climbed down from the saddle.

"He got 'em!" Thomas exclaimed. "Both of 'em! Walked right in the store and arrested 'em."

"Arrested them?" Ansel demanded. "Who arrested them?" he asked, even though he suspected he already knew the answer.

"Will Tanner, he said his name was," Thomas answered as he slid out of the saddle. "My pa told me to ride over here and tell you they was caught."

Will Tanner! The name burned in Ansel's brain like a glowing, hot branding iron. An insignificant Oklahoma lawman he'd never heard of, this Will Tanner seemed to have been sent here by the devil, himself, just to torment him. And now he had wiped out half of the gang he had built to carry out his plan to thrive off the toil of honest businessmen. One thing was clear in his mind now, Will Tanner had to be stopped. He turned back to the boy. "Where are they? Are they still at the store? Where did he take them?"

Thomas tried to answer the questions, but they came too fast. When he finally got the chance, he said, "I don't know where he took 'em, but they ain't at the store no more."

"Was there just one man?" Luther asked. "Did he have anybody with him?" His first concern was that Tanner might have led a posse to the store.

"No, sir," Thomas replied. "He was just by hisself."

"Just walked right in and arrested 'em?" Luther asked, finding it hard to believe that one lone lawman could take Bo Hagen by himself, and impossible to take him and Tom without help. "Was anybody else in the store? How 'bout Oscar Moon, was he there?" He was still not sure of Moon, even though Tom Daly and Elmira were certain he could be trusted.

"No, sir, Moon weren't there," Thomas assured him. "There weren't nobody else there."

Luther looked at Ansel, who still appeared to be battling his anger. "Whaddaya reckon we oughta do about it? Looks like that was a big mistake, Bo and Tom ridin' over to Brinker's yesterday." Ansel didn't reply right away, so Luther continued, "It sounds to me like Tanner don't know where we are. If they'da stayed here, he wouldn't have ever had a chance to jump 'em. I bet Tanner is holed up somewhere where he can watch Brinker's and he saw them ride in."

"We need to find Tanner and kill him," Ansel muttered, as if talking to himself.

"That'd be good if we knew where he was," Luther said. "Where do we go to look for him? Right now, he's most likely on his way to lock Bo and Tom up somewhere—if he ain't shot 'em by now. Our best bet is to stay right where we are. He don't know where this place is. Even if he finds out, then he's got to come up this creek to get us, and that would be his last mistake."

Chapter 9

The night passed without further incident for Will and his prisoners, although Tom complained about Hagen's almost constant mumbling and groaning. He joined Hagen in complaining when Will made no preparation to feed them breakfast before starting out again. "We'll eat when the horses need rest," he told them. He was as good as his promise, stopping after about twenty miles when they came to a healthy-looking stream. Although Hagen didn't look to be in any shape to give him trouble, Will was still cautious when he pulled him off his horse and made him limp over beside a tree. He dutifully held his wrists out to be cuffed around the tree. "Since you're wounded, I'll let you eat first," Will said. His remark was met with only a scowl. "Cheer up," Will went on. "Tonight you'll have a cot to sleep on and a doctor to take care of that wound."

"Is that so?" Hagen came back. "You know, there's a bullet waitin' for you somewhere, and it ain't gonna be too long from now."

"Gives me something to look forward to, doesn't it?" Will answered.

The vertical log walls of Camp Supply came into view a little before four-thirty in the afternoon, according to Will's railroad pocket watch. As he approached the open gate of the fort, the sharp notes of a bugler pierced the air with the afternoon "Stable Call." He was not that familiar with the various bugle calls that sounded during the day. But he had learned from his brief experiences at Fort Gibson that this particular call at four-thirty was followed about half an hour later with "Mess Call." *Maybe,* he thought, *I might have supper with the soldiers.* He was counting on the same cooperation and hospitality he had received at Fort Gibson on an earlier occasion. Of course, it would depend on the character of the commanding officer—he might not feel inclined to accommodate the Marshals Service at all. First, he had to get through the gate. With no trouble with the Indians at the present time, the gates of the fort were open to civilian traffic until locked down for the night. The guard posted at the front gate seemed not to challenge anyone coming and going, but when a man rode up trailing four horses behind him—two carrying riders with their hands chained behind their backs, and one with an empty saddle—Will was not surprised when the young soldier stepped in front of Buster and held up his hand.

"Mister," Private Waters challenged, "what is your business in the fort?"

Will pulled his vest aside to reveal his badge. "I'm U.S. Deputy Marshal Will Tanner," he said. "I've got two prisoners that are wanted in Missouri, Kansas, and Oklahoma for murder and bank robbery. I'm lookin' to keep 'em in your guardhouse for a time, so I reckon I need to see your commanding officer first." The private had obviously never been confronted with any situation similar to this, so he had to pause to decide what to do. When he turned to look behind him as if searching for assistance from someone, Will tried to help him. "Most often when I go to other forts, they show me where the commandin' officer works, and I go to see him."

"Yes, sir," Waters replied, "that's what you should do." He turned and pointed toward a row of buildings along the stockade wall, all built of logs. "That one with the hitching rail in front of it is Major Scott's head-quarters." Then he stood aside to let Will pass.

"Much obliged," Will said as he rode past. He led his string of horses up to the rail Waters had pointed out and dismounted. As he was tying Buster's reins to the rail, a soldier with master sergeant's stripes on his sleeve stepped outside to question him.

"Something I can do for you?" Sergeant Patterson asked, looking Will up and down after taking a hard look at his two prisoners.

"I'm lookin' to talk to your commandin' officer. I'm a U.S. Deputy Marshal and I've got two prisoners that I need to put in your guardhouse, if I can."

"We don't usually keep civilian prisoners in our guardhouse," Sergeant Patterson replied. "You need to take 'em to a civilian jail."

"Fair enough," Will said. "Can you direct me to the nearest civilian jail?"

Patterson shrugged, then scratched his chin while

he thought. "Well, there ain't one anywhere near that I know of."

"Well, you see, that's my problem, and that kinda puts me in a bind. You see, these two gentlemen behind me are part of a six-man gang that have been robbin' banks and murderin' folks in Missouri and Kansas, and now they're down here in Oklahoma. Marshals in all three of those territories are lookin' for 'em. I've gotta go back to a little creek in Texas to keep an eye on the rest of the gang till help gets here." He paused and waited while the sergeant thought that over.

"Let me get the major," he finally decided. "You can tell him your story."

"Much obliged," Will said.

In a couple of minutes, the sergeant returned, an officer following him. "I'm Major Scott," the officer said. "What is it you want to do?" He listened patiently while Will identified himself and brought him up to date on everything involving Ansel Beaudry and his gang. When Will had finished, and said that Major Vancil at Fort Gibson had worked with the Marshals Service on a similar operation, Major Scott was willing to help. "We'll certainly help the U.S. Marshals Service in any way we can," he volunteered.

"The U.S. Marshals Service certainly appreciates that," Will responded. "I can guarantee that, and you won't have to keep 'em for very long." He nodded toward Bo Hagen, sitting sullen while listening to the negotiations. "That one's got a bullet in his leg that maybe your surgeon oughta take a look at, and I'd like to keep these three extra horses I'm leadin' with you till I come back for the prisoners."

Scott smiled. "No problem at all. Anything else?" When Will allowed that there was just one more thing, Scott asked, "What's that?"

"Well, I've got a little problem I'm hopin' you can help me with. Like I said, these two fellows are part of a gang that robbed a couple of banks in Missouri and Kansas. I don't know the total amount of money they stole, but it was enough that each one of 'em was totin' a sizable share. I've got their shares and another share of one of the gang I had to shoot." Major Scott and Sergeant Patterson exchanged puzzled looks, wondering where this was leading. "That money has to be returned to the banks," Will continued, "at least what they ain't spent. I'd sure like to put that money somewhere safe, till we can round up the rest of 'em. Maybe we can count it and write down how much there is."

Major Scott interrupted before he went any further. "I think we've got a safe that'll do the job for you. We'll make an official count of the money and sign it, so you won't have to worry about it comin' up short."

"I sure appreciate it," Will said. "That's a lot better'n me totin' it all over the territory." He nodded his thanks to the major and the sergeant. "If I ain't mistaken, I saw telegraph poles when I rode in, and I didn't think there was any telegraph at Camp Supply. Is there?"

"There sure is, all the work of army engineers. Starting the first of the year, the army has been working to connect all our forts by wire. I'm guessing you need to contact your home base."

"Yes, sir," Will replied, "and I was thinkin' I'd have to ride close to two hundred miles to get to the telegraph.

I need to wire my boss to let him know where I am and what's happenin'. Can I do that here?"

"Yes, you can," Scott answered. "We'll count your money first and lock it up, then I'll have Sergeant Patterson take you and your prisoners down to the guardhouse, and he'll tell Sergeant Davis what to do."

"Much obliged, Major," Will said. "I surely do appreciate your cooperation." He shook Scott's hand when it was extended to him.

After the money was counted, the major stood by the door for a few moments, watching Will walking beside the master sergeant and leading the two outlaws on their horses. He let himself imagine how dangerous life could be for a deputy marshal working alone in a land as untamed as Oklahoma Indian Territory. He smiled to himself when he thought about the money and wondered how many deputies would have fallen to the temptation of taking the money for themselves. He didn't know what the army's official stance was when it came to matters such as this, but he knew he was glad he could help.

Sergeant Patterson introduced Will to Sergeant Davis, who was the duty sergeant at the guardhouse, and the transfer of his two prisoners was handled in no time at all, with Davis taking responsibility for their welfare, including a visit to the surgeon to remove the bullet from Bo's leg. The bugle had already sounded for "Mess Call" while they were making arrangements for Will's extra horses, so Patterson invited Will to have supper with the troops afterward.

Things had worked out better than he had expected

at Camp Supply, so he thanked Patterson again after he finished his supper and said he hoped he'd be seeing him soon. Then he stepped up into the saddle and rode a short distance outside the fort to make his camp on Wolf Creek. As he watched Buster and his packhorse drink, he thought about the return message he had received from Dan Stone just before he left Sergeant Patterson. Dan instructed him to wait there at Camp Supply for a posse of Kansas deputy marshals to arrive from Wichita. Will considered that, but it would take a posse over a week to ride all the way from Wichita. Ansel Beaudry might not stay at Grassy Creek that long, especially since he'd lost two more of his men. He and the two remaining members of his gang might decide to disappear over in Colorado or farther away. *I need to be back at Grassy Creek to keep an eye on them,* Will thought, *since it'll be over a week before that posse gets here.* His decision made, he bedded down for the night, planning to head back to Grassy Creek at first light.

There seemed to be a cloud of tense uncertainty hanging over the cabin hidden halfway up the ravine formed by Grassy Creek. Elmira took a long look through the kitchen door at the imposing figure of Ansel Beaudry, still seated at the end of the table, drinking coffee. She turned to Darlene when she came in to help clean up the breakfast dishes. "I reckon he's gonna set there at the table all day," she whispered. "That deputy marshal has got him worried for sure, and it ain't makin' me feel too safe, either. I'm afraid we're gonna end up with a shoot-out right in our laps, and that ain't something I'm gonna enjoy. We need the money, but I'd just as soon see him and his two friends move on down the road."

"Where is Luther and Cecil?" Darlene asked. "I ain't seen either one of 'em since breakfast."

"Ansel sent 'em down toward the river to look around for any sign of that lawman's camp," Elmira said.

"I was wonderin' and I'm kinda glad he did—give me a chance to do something without bumpin' into Cecil every time I turn around. I swear, as old as that man must be, I don't think he knew anything about a woman till he came here."

Elmira chuckled at the thought. "I reckon it's a good thing for him that he found you, 'cause the way things are goin', he might not be around much longer with Will Tanner out there waitin' for 'em."

"You're runnin' low on whiskey." Both women were startled, surprised by the gruff voice. They turned to find Ansel standing in the doorway, glaring accusingly.

Not sure if he had heard all of their conversation, Elmira quickly replied with a question. "Did you fellers finish up all those three bottles I had in the cupboard?" She didn't wait for an answer before offering to send her son to Brinker's for more. "Eddie could ride over there and fetch a couple more bottles."

Beaudry gave that a moment's thought before replying. "I'll send Cecil over there to get it, so we don't get charged too much for it." Remembering then, he added, "Your son can go with him to show him the way."

"I'll call Eddie up from the barn," Elmira said, and went at once to the back door to do so.

When he came to the door, Ansel walked over to give him instructions "You need to ride down to the river and find Cecil and Luther. When you find 'em, tell Cecil you're gonna take him over to Brinker's. Tell him to buy three more bottles of whiskey. He can pay for it and we'll split it with him when he gets back. Tell him I said to keep an eye out for that lawman." Ansel could have sent either man to the store, but he preferred to keep Luther close by.

"If he's got a camp in these parts, it ain't nowhere close to Grassy Creek," Luther concluded. "It's like I said before, Tanner don't know where we're holed up. We might as well go on back to the cabin."

"Reckon you're right," Cecil agreed. They had ridden up and down the river for about a mile each way, finding no sign of even an overnight camp. Back at the mouth of Grassy Creek now, he started to say more, but was startled by the sound of a horse whinnying, causing him to jerk his pistol from his holster.

"Take it easy," Luther said. "That's somebody coming down the creek." They waited a few moments before Eddie appeared, riding a sorrel mare. "It's just Elmira's boy." When Eddie rode out on the riverbank, Luther asked, "Where you headin'?"

Eddie relayed the instructions Beaudry had given him. "Ansel said to show Cecil how to get to Brinker's store—said to tell you to buy some more whiskey, three bottles, he said, on account you've done drunk it all up—said to tell Cecil to keep an eye out for the lawman."

"You sure he said to take Cecil with you?" Luther

asked, thinking he and Ansel had decided they would all sit tight and wait Tanner out.

"Yes, sir," Eddie said. "And he said to tell Cecil to pay for it and you'd all split it when he got back."

Luther shrugged. He believed the boy had it straight, but he disagreed with the idea of sending Cecil to the store. It worried him to a degree that Ansel was letting this lawman get into his head a little, but Ansel was the boss. They had all agreed on that from the start. "All right, then," he said to Cecil, "but you be damned careful and make sure nobody follows you back here." Cecil assured him that he would, then nodded to Eddie, and the boy led him toward the game trail beside the dead tree.

"I expect we might be gettin' kinda hungry by the time we get to Brinker's," Cecil commented after they had struck the common trail to the trading post. "We'll see if they ain't got somethin' good to eat. That'd be all right, wouldn't it?"

"Yes, sir," Eddie replied enthusiastically, "it sure would." Of all the five gang members that had shown up at his mother's place, he liked Cecil best. He seemed a simple man, and he didn't have the menacing look about him that the others possessed. Besides, unlike the others, he didn't make mean remarks to, or about, Darlene.

When they reached Brinker's, Effie Brinker was just in the process of putting dinner on the table for Tyler and their son, Thomas. She was happy to set two more places for two paying customers. As far as Cecil was concerned, it was well worth the money, so they took their time and ate their fill. Much of the conversation between Cecil and Brinker had to do with the arrest of Bo Hagen and Tom Daly. "That feller, Will Tanner, walked right in, pretty as you please, and arrested them," Tyler said, then went on to tell how Tom had tried to draw on him and got tangled up in the chair. Cecil, of course, wanted to know if Tanner had been back since, but was not surprised that he had not, since the store was in Texas.

After dinner, Cecil went into the store with Tyler to buy the whiskey he had been sent after. While Tyler wrapped the bottles to keep them from breaking on the trip back, Cecil showed no interest in the two women sitting at one of the tables in the saloon section of the store. This in spite of the fact that one of them called out to him and invited him to join them for a drink. Instead, he showed more interest in a small bunch of blooms that Effie had fashioned into a nosegay for her own amusement. Cecil asked Eddie if he thought Darlene might be pleased by something like that. Eddie speculated that she might, and Effie was happy to sell it to the simple man for a quarter.

When the horses were rested and it was time to start back, Cecil packed the whiskey in his saddlebags and held the little paper bag with the nosegay in his hand, so the flowers wouldn't be crushed. They headed back down the old Indian trail halfway to the point where it met the game trail to the river, never noticing the lone man astride a buckskin horse standing in the shadows of the trees. Only when abreast of him and as he walked his horse slowly out of the shadows, his Winchester rifle aimed directly at Cecil, were they aware of him. "Make that move and you're a dead man," Will warned when Cecil started to react.

"Mr. Walker!" Eddie exclaimed. "It's me, Eddie Tate!"

"Howdy, Eddie," Will replied. "Who's your friend, here?" He kept his rifle aimed squarely at Cecil's chest.

"That's just Cecil Cox," Eddie said. "He's all right. He's stayin' at Mama's house with some other fellers."

That was all Will wanted to know. He could not have identified Cecil, since he had never seen him, but his name was one of those he had written down. "All right, Mr. Cox, I'm gonna ask you to take your left hand and draw that handgun real slow and drop it on the ground." Eddie watched, astonished, as Cecil, holding the nosegay in his right hand, dropped his reins from his left hand and did as he was instructed. He was smart enough to know he didn't stand a chance with the Winchester aimed right at him. "Now, climb down from there," Will ordered, and when he did, Will checked him for any other weapons. "I'm arrestin' you for your part in two bank robberies and five murders." He started to handcuff him then, but paused to ask, "What's in the sack?" When Cecil, fully aware that he had no hope of resisting, said that it was a nosegay, Will had to see for himself, since he didn't know what a nosegay was.

"It's for Darlene," Cecil said.

Will realized then that Cecil was evidently a simple soul and he guessed that explained why he had not shown the first sign of resisting. "All right, give it to

Eddie. He can take it to Darlene. Put your hands together." He handcuffed him, with his hands in front of him, and told him to climb back into the saddle, then he tied his reins to Buster's saddle. "I'll tell you what I tell every man I arrest. If you don't cause me any trouble, I'll not ride hard on you, but if you force me to, I won't hesitate to shoot you down." Cecil nodded his understanding, having already decided he was caught and there was nothing he could do about it. It was just bad luck, but he was used to it. He had always had bad luck.

Finally finding his voice again, after watching the effortless arrest of Cecil Cox, Eddie was still finding it difficult to believe that the Mr. Walker who had stayed with him and his mother when they were at Sartain's, was arresting Cecil. "Mr. Walker," he asked finally, "are you Will Tanner?"

"Reckon so," Will answered him. "Give my best to your mama and tell your other two guests I'll be seein' 'em." He climbed aboard his horse and wheeled him back in the direction they had just come from, leaving Eddie still confused over what had just taken place.

When they followed the trail back to Brinker's, but continued on past, Cecil spoke up. "Are you takin' me where you took Bo and Tom?"

"That's right," Will answered.

"I took part in those two bank robberies you talked about," Cecil volunteered. "But I never shot none of those people that was killed. I didn't have no part in shootin' that little boy at the store in Bartles Town, either. That was done by Whip Dawson. I never even shot *at* nobody."

"That's good to know, and you know what? I believe you, but that ain't for me to decide. That's up to the judge. Maybe he'll believe you, too." Based upon what he had seen so far of Cecil Cox, he wouldn't doubt but that he was telling the truth.

Chapter 10

"What?!" Ansel demanded. "He arrested him?" Almost beside himself with anger, this last piece of news was enough to send him into a rage. "How the hell could that happen? It sounds like every man I've got ridin' with me can't wait to run up and surrender to this son of a bitch. And now he knows where we are."

While Ansel continued to fume, Luther, somewhat calmer, asked Eddie, "Where were you when he arrested Cecil?"

"On the old Indian river trail, about halfway back to where the game trail cuts down to the Washita," Eddie replied. He turned to Elmira then. "It was Mr. Walker, Ma. He was the one who arrested Cecil. I asked him if he was Will Tanner and he said he was."

"Well, I never . . ." Elmira started, picturing the man in her mind whom they had come to know as *Mr. Walker*. "I ain't never been so wrong about a man in my life."

"Did Cecil tell that deputy where we are?" Luther asked.

"No, sir," Eddie answered. "He never asked Cecil where you were."

"That don't mean he ain't gonna," Ansel fumed.

Luther, still thinking about Eddie's answer to his question, tried to talk calmly to Ansel. "If he arrested Cecil where the boy says, then he still might not know where we are. He just knows that we're somewhere not too far from Brinker's. He don't know where this hideout is."

"This hideout!" Ansel exploded. "This is one helluva hideout—we're treed, that's what this is!"

"Well, what are we gonna do about it?" Luther pressed. "You're right, he's got us treed, whether he knows it or not. He can't find us, that's a fact, but we can't come outta this hideout, neither. He's cut us down to where there ain't nobody but you and me, two of us, and we were six when we started." He stopped to consider what he had just said, then changed his mind. "No, that ain't right. He knows where we're hidin'. That's why he didn't ask Cecil where we are, but he don't wanna risk his neck comin' up here after us."

Luther's calmness tended to temper Ansel's rage enough for him to try to think rationally about their situation and what action they should take. "You're right," he said after a moment. "He ain't gonna risk ridin' up this creek. We could just sit on the porch and wait for him to come up and pick him off without ever havin' to get up outta the rockin' chair." He thought about that a moment longer. "But I don't know if I wanna play a waitin' game with him. I'd sooner hunt him down and shoot him and be done with it." He paused again, his deep frown reflecting his concentration as he tried to work the problem out in his mind. "He ain't watchin' this camp right now," he suddenly announced, "'cause he's takin' Cecil to the same spot he took Bo and Tom." He looked at Luther for his reaction, but received no more than a puzzled look in return. "He arrested Bo and Tom, then it was three days later when he arrested Cecil. That sounds to me like he's takin 'em somewhere a day and a half's ride from here, and he ain't gonna show up around here again for three more days." He paused to swear. "Damn! We oughta get on his trail and catch him before he gets to wherever he's keepin' 'em. Maybe we can cut Bo and Tom loose in the bargain."

Luther listened patiently until Ansel was finished with his theory. He could not disagree with the speculation that Tanner was taking his prisoners somewhere maybe a day and a half away. But if he was taking them that far, it would seem that it would be to someplace where he could lock them up where he wouldn't have to worry about them. Otherwise, why bother to ride that far away? Maybe he just tied 'em up somewhere close by? Tom Daly was the only one of them who knew the territory, and he was gone, so Luther looked to Elmira for help. "Elmira, where's the nearest town around here? Maybe about a day and a half's ride from here," he continued.

"There ain't no town that close around here," she answered. "That's the whole idea behind buildin' this hideout in the first place—ain't near any town." She paused then to give his question more thought. "The only place about a day and a half from here is Camp Supply, if you count that as a town."

"Damn!" Ansel blurted, struck with the obvious answer to the question. "He's not got 'em tied up somewhere! He's takin' 'em to Camp Supply to lock 'em up."

"Well, I reckon I ain't plannin' to try to bust 'em outta a damn army fort," Luther declared without waiting for Ansel to comment. "I swear, though, that makes sense. He arrests 'em and takes 'em to the fort to hold 'em while he comes back here to wait for a chance to jump one of us."

"Maybe so, but that still means we've got three days to get ready for him," Ansel said, his mind back to his obsessive desire to kill this demon who was effectively destroying his master plan piece by piece. "He'll come back on the same trail as before, where he took Cecil, but we'll have plenty of time to set up an ambush for him. He won't be expecting that."

Luther didn't respond immediately—he had other thoughts. When he expressed them, it wasn't what Ansel wanted to hear. "If we've got this figured right, and he's gone for three days, I'm thinkin' that gives us a three-day head start on the son of a bitch. So we oughta pack up and get the hell outta here, head up Colorado way, or New Mexico Territory. If he knows about Grassy Creek, every other lawman in the territory's gonna know about it, too. I'm thinkin' we need to find us somewhere else to hole up, somewhere a helluva ways from here."

"I want him dead!" Ansel responded. "I want his guts on a fence post!"

Luther could see that he was not going to change Ansel's mind about killing the deputy, although running seemed to him the smartest thing to do. Grassy Creek was a good idea, but they were just unlucky that it was a spot that was known by a deputy marshal. It would be best to make use of the time they had to get a head start on the lawman and find a new hideout. Now that he was faced with a tough decision, maybe it would be best for him to go his separate way. He and Bo had joined with Ansel while in prison, and right from the start, Ansel was the one calling the shots. And from their initial success in robbing banks, Luther was satisfied to let Ansel make all the decisions. It wouldn't go well for him to go against Ansel at this point, however, when Ansel was already half-crazed with the passion to kill Tanner. *On the other hand, maybe he's right this time, too,* he told himself, still somewhat reluctant to quit him. Further discussion on the Will Tanner problem was interrupted at that moment by an alert from Eddie from the front door. "There's somebody comin' up the creek," he yelled.

With weapons drawn, Luther and Ansel ran out to the porch. As Ansel had commented earlier, they could see the rider approaching well before he got close enough to identify, and they could have picked him off sitting in a rocking chair. "Hello, the camp," a voice rang out from the dark tunnel created by the overhanging trees.

Recognizing the voice, Eddie announced, "It's Moon!" In another few seconds, they recognized the familiar figure of Oscar Moon, leading a packhorse behind him. Hammers were released and drawn weapons returned to their holsters.

Having overheard the discussion between Ansel and Luther, Elmira was not certain which of their plans she favored. She was beginning to think she had rather the two outlaws decided to run for it, in spite of the money she would surely earn if they stayed. She walked out on the porch to join them upon hearing Eddie say it was Moon approaching. It was she who answered his greeting. "Come on in, Moon." When he pulled up to the porch and dismounted, she said, "Didn't expect to see you back this soon. Whatcha got, some fresh meat?"

"Evenin', all," Moon replied. "That's a fact, I run up on some fresh deer meat that kinda has a beef flavor after I smoked it—thought maybe you folks might have a use for it."

Elmira chuckled in response. "I reckon we can always use more deer meat. Eddie can help you unload it."

He couldn't help noticing a feeling of tension in the air between Ansel and Luther, neither of whom had offered any greeting. "What's the matter with you boys, ain't Elmira treatin' you right?"

"That deputy arrested Cecil today when him and Eddie was ridin' back from Brinker's," Luther said. "I don't reckon you ran into him anywhere along that trail, did you?"

"I swear, that is a poor piece of news," Moon responded, and slowly shook his head to show his concern. "No, I ain't seen him, but I didn't come back that way."

Ansel had refrained from commenting to the crusty old cattle rustler, his mind still heavily occupied with his vengeful thoughts for Will Tanner. Another thought crossed his mind then, prompting him to ask, "You ever go to that soldier fort, that Camp Supply?"

Moon shrugged. "Well, I go by there from time to time." He glanced at Elmira and grinned. "They generally keep a small herd of cattle there to feed the soldiers, but the soldiers ain't what I'd call the best cowhands when it comes to watchin' the cows."

"How far is that place from here?" Ansel asked, still deadly serious, in spite of Moon's attempt at humor.

"'Bout a couple of days, or a little less," Moon replied. "You ain't thinkin' 'bout ridin' over there, are you? That ain't no town or nothin'. It's an army post."

"No, I ain't thinkin' about goin' there," Ansel answered, "but I expect you might go there more'n you let on. And maybe that's where you might be talkin' to that lawman that's arrestin' my men, and that's how the son of a bitch knows about this hideout."

There followed a stunned silence as everyone was shocked by Ansel's accusation. Elmira was the first to speak. "That don't make no sense! Moon wouldn't tell anybody where we are."

"Makes sense to me," Ansel replied, calmly satisfied with the possibility. "That lawman didn't just stumble over Grassy Creek, somebody had to tell him where it was. And ain't it funny how you showed up right after he got Bo and Tom?"

Moon took a step back, taken completely by surprise. "Now, hold on, Ansel, that's crazy talk. You've let Will Tanner get into your head so much you ain't thinkin' straight. I've been doin' business with Elmira for years, she'll tell you." He looked from Ansel to Luther. "Do you believe what he's sayin'?"

Luther, dumbfounded by Ansel's sudden attack on Moon, as were the other witnesses, gave his initial opinion. "No, I can't honestly say that I do."

Realizing he was facing an obviously crazy man, Moon attempted to dissuade him. "There, you see, Luther knows I wouldn't do nothin' like that."

"Sometimes Luther don't see the straight of things like I do," Ansel calmly replied. Then without a pause, he drew the .44 he wore and shot Moon in the chest, point-blank. The impact of the bullet caused Moon to stagger backward a couple of steps to keep from falling, the expression of complete shock frozen upon his face. He made one feeble attempt to draw his handgun before a second shot from Ansel's .44 dropped him to the ground.

The only sound heard after that moment was a little squeal from a horrified Darlene Futch, who was standing in the doorway. The others, including Luther, were shocked beyond belief at what they had just witnessed. Finally Elmira blurted, "You crazy fool! You've killed Moon!" She rushed to him, but too late to do anything to ease his dying. His eyelids opened wide as if trying to see through a thick fog and remained that way as he exhaled his last breath. Unable to understand how Ansel could have done such an evil act, she looked up at him and cried, "Why did you do that, you damn lunatic? Moon never did nothin' to hurt you."

Ansel cocked his pistol again and aimed it at her. "Maybe he ain't the only one needin' killin'," he said. "Maybe you'd best remember your place." He might have pulled the trigger, had not Luther stepped in.

"Easy, Ansel," Luther tried to calm him. "Hold on, partner, we need her. We don't wanna shoot Elmira." It appeared that he had gotten through to the crazed killer, even though there was a long moment of uncertainty before Ansel let the hammer back down. Although Ansel had remained calm throughout the entire incident, Luther was not sure that he did not have a maniac for a partner. For a fact, he didn't believe Moon had betrayed them, and he couldn't see why Moon would benefit from their arrest. So now he had to wonder who might be next to cause Ansel to go off half-cocked.

"We need to ride out on that trail tomorrow and find us a good place to set up an ambush for Tanner," Ansel said to Luther as he dropped his .44 back in his holster. There was no trace of agitation in his voice when he turned to Eddie and told him to drag the carcass away. "Drag him downwind somewhere, far enough so we won't have to smell him when he starts gettin' ripe."

"We need to bury him," Elmira said, finding her voice again. "That's the least we can do for him."

"Yessum," Eddie replied. "I reckon I can dig a grave." He took a rope from Moon's saddle and tied one end around Moon's ankles.

"Make sure to tie them good and tight," Ansel offered casually, "else you're liable to just pull his boots off when that horse starts up."

Darlene exchanged a look of total disbelief with Elmira, then said to Eddie, "Come on, we'll find him a good spot. I'll help you dig a grave."

Ansel turned to Luther and said, "I could use another cup of coffee. Let's go see if there's any left in that pot. If there ain't, we'll have Elmira make us another pot."

Luther didn't reply. He took another look at Oscar Moon's body as Eddie led his horse off toward the other side of the barn. Then he turned and followed Ansel inside. *Maybe I was wrong*, he thought, *and Ansel made the right call about Moon.* Maybe he had the right idea about ambushing Tanner. He decided he would back him one more time, partially because he was not sure he could risk arguing with him while he was in this fit of vengeance.

* * *

It was close to the noon meal at the mess hall when Will approached the gate at Camp Supply. His timing was not at all an accident, thinking he might take advantage of the army's hospitality again. This time, he told the private on guard duty that he was to report to Major Scott about turning over another prisoner. He made it sound routine enough that the private didn't question him at all and just waved him through. He rode over to the post headquarters and stepped down, leaving Cecil to remain in the saddle while he opened the door and stuck his head in. Seeing Master Sergeant Patterson at his desk, he said, "Howdy, Sergeant, I got another prisoner for your guardhouse."

Patterson was naturally surprised. "Another one? Whaddaya doin', pickin' them off one by one?"

"I reckon that's the safest way," Will answered. "If my luck holds out, maybe I can arrest the last two by the time that posse gets here from Wichita to pick 'em up. The last two might be a little bit harder, though."

"What's this one's name?" Patterson asked, since the major had him keep a record.

"This one is Cecil Cox and he's not as much of a threat as the other two. He didn't give me any trouble, just came along peaceful as you please. Matter of fact, I think he was just unlucky to join up with the others."

"I'll tell Sergeant Davis that when we lock him up," Patterson said. "It's about time to eat, so I'll go down to the guardhouse with you." He got up, about to stick his head in the office door to tell the major, when Major Scott walked out, having heard the conversation.

"Deputy Tanner," Scott greeted him. "I see you're

still working hard on the job, rounding up those bank robbers."

"Yes, sir," Will replied. "I'm doin' the best I can to earn my pay, and I surely do appreciate the army co-operatin' with us on this job. I've got some more money to put with that I brought last time."

"You keep making deposits and we're going to have enough to start our own bank," Scott said with a laugh. "First Bank of Wolf Creek, we'll call it." After he put the money away, the major wished him success with the capture of the two remaining outlaws and returned to his desk. Will couldn't help thinking how much quicker they could get the job done if Scott had offered to send a cavalry patrol back with him to arrest Beaudry and Curry.

As he had with Will's first two prisoners, Patterson walked down to the guardhouse with Will, while Cecil sat patiently in the saddle behind them, already hoping for a term in prison and not the hangman's noose. Sergeant Davis again took delivery of Will's prisoner and cheerfully japed him about the extra work he was causing his guards. "We might have to start charging you rent," he joked. "These birds you're bringin' in ain't the best guests we've had."

"The folks you need to see about the rent will be here pretty soon," Will joked. "They're the ones who pay all the bills." Then he asked if they had had any trouble with Hagen and Daly.

"None to speak of," Davis replied. "They ain't showin' any signs of likin' it here, though. You wanna visit 'em before you go back and round up their friends?"

Will's initial reaction was that he had no desire to see either of the two, then he changed his mind and followed Davis and one of the guards inside to the cell block with Cecil. "Well, I'll be damned . . ." Bo Hagen started when he saw Cecil being led in. A moment later, when he saw Will come in behind them, he got up from his cot and hobbled over to stand by the bars.

Lying on a cot against the back wall, Tom Daly raised up to get a look. When he saw who had caught Bo's attention, he sat up as well. Anxious to hear about the others at Grassy Creek, he asked, "Cecil, what about Ansel and Luther? Are they dead?"

"No, they ain't dead," Cecil replied, "but he knows where they're hidin'."

"He better hope he don't find 'em," Bo snorted. "He might not be able to sneak up on 'em like he did with me and Tom."

"How's your leg, Bo?" Will asked. "I see you're walkin' on it."

"Yeah, I'm walkin' on it," Bo shot back. "They told us they're sendin' a whole posse of marshals to take us back to Missouri. Is that so?" Will said that it was, and Bo continued, "I was kinda hopin' you'd be the one to take us back—things mighta turned out different."

"They might have at that," Will replied. "We mighta got to be big friends before it was done."

"Ha!" Hagen answered his sarcasm. "I'm more particular about who I call a friend."

Will said no more. He had satisfied his need to know that they were still behind bars and well guarded by the military. He turned about and walked back outside, where Sergeant Patterson was waiting for him. "Come on," Patterson said, "and we'll go get some grub." As he had done before, Will dropped his prisoner's horse and tack at the stable on their way to the mess hall, where he enjoyed another meal at the army's expense. He didn't waste any time after he finished eating before thanking the sergeant and taking his leave. He wasn't sure what effect this latest arrest would have upon Beaudry and Luther Curry, but if they decided to run, he needed to be back to Grassy Creek before their trail got too cold to follow. With that in mind, he figured to ride until after dark as soon as his horses were rested enough to go. He could not discount the possibility that they might decide to come after him, instead of holing up in their narrow fortress, however. That was going to be tough for them, because he could move his camp from day to day, but one way or another, he was going to have to lure them out of that stronghold. How to do that without getting himself shot was the problem he rolled over in his mind as he rode back toward Grassy Creek.

Chapter 11

It was late afternoon when he reached the fork where the trail from Camp Supply connected with the river trail five miles north of Brinker's trading post. Brinker's had figured in with all three of his prior arrests, but he didn't expect to find either of the remaining two outlaws there now. He was sure they were now too cautious to venture outside Grassy Creek, and that thought was verified by the empty hitching rail he saw when he approached. He was going to have to stop pretty soon to rest his horse after the extra hard day's ride. Ordinarily, the trading post would be the place to stop. However, Brinker was not likely to welcome him after he had started systematically thinning out his customers, and it might well be a good place to expect a bullet in the back. So he walked his horse past the saloon/store. "There's a nice little stream about four or five miles down this trail," he said to Buster. "We'll stop there and give you a nice long rest—might as well camp there for the night."

Buster isn't the only one who is tired, he thought, as

he continued along the trail. He had pushed on longer than usual the night before and that, added to the long day today, was enough to make him think about some coffee and something to eat. The setting sun threatening to settle on the western horizon seemed to signal it was quitting time as well. And sometimes, when he was feeling tired, his thoughts drifted back to Bennett House and the young woman waiting for him there. This was one of those times. A picture popped into his mind of the last time he had seen her. She was not too happy with him. *Maybe I should have sent her a telegram when I was at Camp Supply*, he thought, *at least to tell her I miss her and hope I'll be through with this mess before much longer.* Maybe in time she would be a little more understanding of a deputy marshal's job and the responsibility he had to go when and where he was needed. He knew that she was upset because he had promised to take her to see the J-Bar-J ranch in Texas where, hopefully, he would soon retire from law enforcement and return to his roots raising cattle. *I should have sent her a telegram*, he scolded himself as he approached the thick border of trees that traced the course of the stream up ahead. The thought was immediately swept away by the snap of the bullet that narrowly missed his head and the sound of the rifle that fired it a second afterward.

There was no need for thinking, instinct and automatic reaction took over. He wheeled Buster to his right toward the setting sun, at the same time lying low on the big buckskin's neck and yelled, "Go!" In that moment, when a second shot zipped over the horse's rump, he didn't know if he had kicked his heels sharply or not, but Buster didn't hesitate. Calling on all the reserve energy he had, the buckskin galloped full out. As more shots rang out, Will pointed the horse at an angle toward the trees that lined the stream, trying to put more distance between him and the shooters as he raced for the cover of the trees.

He knew he was gaining some distance because the shots were not as close around his body as before. The fact that the bushwhackers were forced to aim looking into the sun had to help some. He hoped they wouldn't start shooting at the horses, and as soon as he thought it, the bullets started kicking up dirt behind him. Moments before reaching the cover of the trees, he heard his packhorse scream just as its front legs buckled. He immediately dropped the lead rope to keep from being jerked out of the saddle when the packhorse collapsed. With another kick of encouragement when he started to stop, Buster bounded forward again and charged into the cover of the trees. Will came out of the saddle almost before Buster stopped. He quickly led the exhausted horse down beside the stream, then hurried back to the edge of the trees to see if he could pinpoint his attackers. Judging from the number of shots flying around him when he was in the open, he guessed that it was more than one man, and it was easy to speculate that the exact number was two. They had decided not to wait for him to make a try up Grassy Creek—they would hunt him down instead. While he strained to try to spot his assailants, he thought to count himself lucky. If they had waited only a couple of minutes longer, he would have probably been a target too easy to miss. He couldn't help thinking that it seemed that he was making it a habit to ride blindly into ambushes lately.

"Damn it! Damn it!" Luther complained to himself when Ansel fired before the deputy was close enough. They had decided Tanner wasn't coming back to Grassy Creek that day, after waiting for him to show since early afternoon. Then a figure on a horse, leading another, showed up in the distance, so they hurried to set up their ambush, with Luther on one side of the trail and Ansel on the other. If Ansel hadn't been so anxious to kill him, Tanner would have ridden right between them, but Ansel couldn't wait. Now they had the job of rooting Tanner out of the bushes around the banks of the stream, and that was not a job that Luther looked forward to. He got up from his kneeling position as Ansel ran across to join him.

"The lucky son of a bitch," Ansel exclaimed. "He ducked at the wrong time."

"You shot too soon," Luther said. "If you'da waited, he woulda rode right between us and he'd be dead right now. Now we're gonna have to find him."

"I had a good shot at him," Ansel insisted. "I can make that shot ten times outta ten. And the damn sun shined right in my eyes when I shot. He just ducked at the wrong time. We'll find him, but we need to get up this stream in a hurry before he has a chance to run."

"More likely he'll dig in up there and wait for us to try to come get him," Luther said. "So far, he ain't struck me as the runnin' kind."

"All right," Ansel said, becoming more impatient

by the moment. "Maybe he's diggin' in. We can see where he'll be." He pointed to Will's packhorse lying just outside the tree line. "He ain't gonna be far from there. We'd best leave the horses here and run up this stream on foot. He could see the horses comin' too easy." Luther agreed with that, so he went to his horse and pulled an extra handgun from his saddlebag and stuck it under his belt. Then they started up the stream at a trot to close as much distance as they could before having to become more cautious in their stalking.

A hundred and fifty yards or more up the stream, Will was hurriedly speculating on his best possible defense. There was plenty of protection beside the banks where he could take cover, but he didn't like the odds that he would be pinned down there for no telling how long. Then when darkness fell, it would be a dangerous game of hide-and-seek. He decided a better bet would be to close the distance between him and his ambushers and maybe catch them before they expected him, so he started running back toward them as fast as he could move through the trees and bushes. When he estimated that he was nearly halfway back to the trail, he came to a deep gully running down into the stream. Afraid to push on any farther, lest he run headlong into them, he jumped in the gully and waited.

In the gully for no longer than seconds, he heard the sounds of the two men running to surprise him, their breathing heavy as they pushed recklessly through the bushes. He crouched as low as he could in the gully, his rifle ready, when suddenly they appeared. Even in the fading light of the streambed, he recognized Ansel Beaudry by the description given him. Without a glance at the gully, they trotted by him, both men staring straight ahead into the sunlight shining through the leaves. Will raised up from the gully, his rifle aimed at the backs of the two outlaws and gave them warning. "Stop right there, or I'll shoot you down!" Startled, both men stopped, not sure where the voice had come from. "You're under arrest. Drop those rifles on the ground. Do it quick, my finger's gettin' itchy on this trigger."

There was a moment of hesitation on the part of both men, but Luther dropped his rifle, then Ansel reluctantly dropped his, his hands trembling with rage, and they stood there, their backs still toward him. "You gonna shoot us down, like you did with Whip Dawson?" Luther spat defiantly.

"He made a choice," Will answered. "It was the wrong choice. If you decide to make the wrong choice, I'll shoot you down. You don't give me any trouble and you won't get shot. Now, ease those pistols outta your holsters with your left hands and drop them on the ground, one at a time, you first, Beaudry." His arrest was hindered by the fact that he had no handcuffs with him and no rope, either. He was going to have to march them back to his packhorse to get them. "All right, start walkin', same direction you were walkin' in." They did as he ordered and when he came to their weapons on the ground, he started to reach down and gather them up. He decided against it, thinking it not wise to have his arms full of weapons, so he left them for later.

When they reached the spot where he had entered the trees, he directed them toward his fallen pack-horse. The horse was fatally wounded, though still alive when they got to it. Will did not want the horse to suffer any longer, so he pulled his Colt .44 and put a bullet in the suffering animal's head. Still facing away from him, both men jumped when the gun suddenly went off behind them, with Ansel releasing a little yelp of surprise. Will quickly covered him with his Colt. Luther, thinking Will at a disadvantage managing a gun in one hand and a rifle in the other saw it as his chance. He spun around, pulling the extra handgun he had shoved under his belt, the gun the deputy had been too careless to notice, and fired. His shot was wide of the mark, catching Will in the shoulder, and before he could cock it again, he doubled over when the .44 slug from Will's rifle ripped into his gut. Will turned to cover Ansel, who was already running in between the trees. He started to take a shot at him, but turned back quickly when he heard the sound of a hammer cocking. Seeing Luther struggling to raise his pistol, he fired. Luther dropped to the ground immediately, unable to get off another round before Will's fatal shot stopped him.

With no time to curse himself for failing to check both of them for weapons they might have hidden, he had no choice but to chase through the woods after Beaudry. He considered riding his horse after the fleeing outlaw, but decided he'd be too much a target on horseback, and Beaudry would reach the spot where he dropped his guns before he would. He took a brief look at the wound in his shoulder and decided it wasn't as bad as it was painful, so he started running after Beaudry.

Aware only of a stinging in his shoulder, he made his way through the laurel bushes that crowded the banks of the stream, moving as fast as he could while trying not to walk into an ambush. The light was quickly fading now and he was not certain he was back to the spot where he had left the weapons until he nearly tripped on one of the rifles. He paused to take a closer look on the bank and discovered the rifle, but nothing else. Beaudry must not have seen it in his haste. Will looked all around him before he continued along the creek, moving even more carefully now that he was sure Beaudry was armed. He was still about twenty-five yards from reaching the river trail when he heard the sounds of hooves on the hard dirt track. Beaudry was running! He had figured the outlaw would surely try to ambush him. Discarding all thoughts of caution at this point, he pushed through the bushes as fast as he could, but was only able to reach the trail in time to see Beaudry already galloping out of range. He fired a couple of shots after him in desperation, knowing it was wasted ammunition.

Feeling frustrated for having missed the chance to capture the last two of the six wanted men, he looked again at his shoulder and the large amount of blood that had soaked his shirtsleeve. Luther Curry was dead, but he should have captured him and Beaudry as well, if he had not been careless. He could have excused his carelessness, since he had not been prepared for the ambush, thinking it unlikely this far from Grassy Creek. "But, damn it, you shouldn't have been thinkin' about Sophie Bennett. You shoulda had your mind on your business," he scolded. At this point, he gave no thought of immediate chase, for his horse was about a hundred yards back upstream. And to make matters worse, Buster was already exhausted. He couldn't ask the horse to run itself to death. Catching Ansel Beaudry was important, but not as important as saving his horse. It was at that moment he heard the rustle of laurel branches behind him.

Acting on pure instinct, he spun around and dropped to one knee, his rifle ready to fire as a horse pushed through the bushes on the other side of the trail. Will released the hammer already cocked when he saw the empty saddle. It had to be Curry's horse wandering back after having strayed before. He was not surprised that Beaudry hadn't taken the time to try to find the horse. The thought occurred to him that this was a fresh horse and he could go after Beaudry right away. He only gave it a moment's consideration, however, for the same reason he wouldn't try to force Buster to chase Beaudry: he wasn't going to ride off and leave his horse. Besides this, he knew where Beaudry was going. He was going to hole up in that cabin and dare him to come get him—no easy accomplishment—and there was little chance of catching him before he reached Grassy Creek. There was no thought of leaving Grassy Creek without Ansel Beaudry. It would just have to wait until tomorrow. For now, his horse was tired, his packhorse was dead, his shoulder needed cleaning up, he was hungry, and he needed a cup of coffee. On the positive side, every member of the Ansel Beaudry gang was down but one, either captured or dead. And he had a replacement for his packhorse. "Come on, boy," he said calmly as he took the dark sorrel's reins, then stepped up into the saddle. *My orders from Dan Stone were to find 'em, but don't try to engage them, wait for the posse,* he thought as he turned the sorrel's head upstream. *Maybe I should learn to follow orders.*

Although Ansel Beaudry's horse was well rested when he jumped into the saddle and fled the site of the ambush, it was close to exhaustion by the time it climbed up the final rise of Grassy Creek. Elmira's son, Eddie, stood at the edge of the porch, squinting into the dark passage when he heard the splashing of hooves in the water. Eddie was always the first to spot anyone coming up the creek from the river below the cabin, and in a few minutes, he identified the rider. "It's Ansel comin' back," he yelled, then waited there, figuring Ansel would tell him to take care of his horse. "Howdy, Ansel," Eddie greeted him. "Where's Luther?"

Ansel stepped down and said, "Take care of him," ignoring Eddie's question. He pulled his saddlebags off the horse and hurried directly into the house, leaving the boy to wonder about the lathered-up horse.

Elmira and Darlene stared wide-eyed at the obviously agitated man when he stormed into the kitchen and went directly to the shelf where the last of their whiskey supply sat. "Damn," Darlene blurted, "you look like you saw a ghost." Both women looked toward the door, expecting Luther to follow him.

"Where's Luther?" Elmira asked.

Ansel didn't answer until after he poured himself a

stiff shot of whiskey, and then a second one. "Luther's dead," he finally told them.

"Uh-oh!" Elmira exclaimed. "Will Tanner?"

"Yeah, Will Tanner," Ansel responded, "and he damn near got me."

Immediately concerned, Elmira asked, "Is he chasin' after you? Is he comin' up here?" She was not sure how much hell Ansel had brought down upon them. From the first day he had arrived, she had regretted the fact that Tom Daly had led his gang to her cabin. Rough and demanding, he had forced her to give up her room, so he could have a private room. Then he cold-bloodedly shot down her friend Oscar Moon right in her front yard. She cursed the day when Ansel Beaudry entered her door. She feared she might lose everything she had gambled to build this place on Grassy Creek if Will Tanner led a posse of lawmen up here to clean her out.

"I don't know!" Ansel railed at her. "I don't know what he's gonna do." He snarled, "I hope he does try to come up here after me. I want that boy of yours to take his blanket out on the porch and sleep there tonight. Only, he'd damn sure better sleep with one eye open. I wanna know if anything comes up that creek tonight." He looked around him then as if just remembering where he was. "What the hell are you two standin' around gapin' at me for? I'm hungry. I pay you good money to cook supper and I need something to eat right now." The mention of money only served to infuriate him and he silently cursed Luther Curry for not tying his horse securely. When he got to his horse, Luther's horse had strayed. He didn't care about the horse, but Luther's share of the bank robberies was in his saddlebags. Now Tanner likely had it. Ansel was certain that explained Will Tanner's real reason for dogging them so hard—taking the bank money for himself. He got Whip Dawson's share and likely Tom's and Bo's—Cecil's, for sure, and now he had Luther's. He might be wearin' a deputy marshal's badge, but Ansel was sure he was as big an outlaw as he was, like a lot of lawmen. He stood there, scowling like an angry wolf before suddenly realizing the two women were glaring fearfully at him. "Get some supper on the table!" he roared.

"It woulda already been on the table if you hadn'ta come in here raising all that fuss," Elmira responded. "Go set down at the table and we'll bring it in. We can't do nothin' with you standin' in the way."

Ansel's eyes narrowed in a deep, angry frown as he focused his gaze upon her. "You keep up with that sharp tongue of yours and I'll rip it outta your mouth for you," he threatened. She was about to reply in kind, but decided not to push her luck. He had an insane look in his eyes, and she remembered the casual coolness he exercised when he shot Oscar Moon. He stood there, staring at her for a long moment as if hoping she'd say one more sassy word. When she didn't, he finally turned and walked out of the kitchen and sat down at the table.

"For Pete's sake," Elmira whispered to Darlene, "go take him some coffee. He's actin' like he's gone plum loco."

"I thought you were gonna get us both killed there for a minute," Darlene said, "talkin' back to him like that."

Elmira didn't answer right away, thinking about the insane way Ansel was talking. "He's scared," she finally declared, "scared outta his mind. Will Tanner's got him so buffaloed he don't know what to do."

Darlene paused, Ansel's coffee cup in hand. "Will Tanner's got me buffaloed, too. What's gonna happen to us if he comes up here after Ansel?"

"I don't know, honey. I don't know." She dipped out a plate of stew from the large pot on her stove, picked up a plate of biscuits, and followed Darlene into the dining room.

Ansel dived into the food as soon as it was placed before him. He had chosen a chair that faced the front door and nervously watched it while he ate. Elmira couldn't stop herself from commenting. "I made that stew with some of that beef Oscar Moon brought me. Reckon I'll have to find me a new source to get fresh beef." If Ansel heard her sarcastic remark, he showed no sign of it, his focus still on the door. Elmira looked at Darlene and shook her head, then walked to the door. "Supper's on!" she yelled out the open door. In a few minutes, Eddie appeared in the doorway and started to sit down.

"Fill your plate and take it out on the porch," Ansel said to him. "You can eat out there as good as you can sittin' at this table."

Puzzled, Eddie asked, "Why would I wanna set out there?"

"Because I'm payin' you twenty-five dollars to sit out there and keep watch tonight," Ansel replied. "I wanna know if anybody rides up that creek tonight, and I wanna know right away."

"Twenty-five dollars!" Eddie exclaimed. "Yes, sir, I'll

keep watch." He picked up a plate and piled stew on it. "What about Luther? Is he comin' behind you?" Elmira told him that Luther was dead, shot by Will Tanner. "Dang," Eddie huffed. "I reckon there's plenty of stew, then." He helped himself to another spoonful.

"You just make sure you keep your eyes open," Ansel said, "and I'll pay you in the mornin'."

Elmira got a quilt for Eddie to take out to the porch, since he was bound to get a little chilly during the night. Eddie took it, but insisted that he wasn't going to go to sleep, he was determined to earn that twenty-five dollars. When Ansel finished eating, he went straight to his room, instead of sitting by the fireplace in the dining room, as he had usually done. Darlene looked at Elmira and raised her eyebrows when they heard the door slam shut and the bolt being thrown.

Ansel stood in the middle of the bedroom surveying his situation as far as his self-protection was concerned. He was not completely satisfied that Elmira's young son could give him warning enough in the event Will Tanner showed up that night. Consequently, he decided to shove Elmira's bed over closer to the wall, away from the one small window. When that didn't seem to be protection enough, he decided to pull the quilts off onto the floor between the bed and the wall, using the bed for protection. All the while, he kept telling himself he was not afraid of the persistent lawman, he was just being smart. He could lay his rifle and pistol on the bed just above his head, so they would be readily at hand, should the need arise during the night. He could not say for sure that Tanner knew where this hideout was actually located. He and Luther had speculated that he might know, but was not willing to risk his neck coming up that creek. *I guess we'll see*, he told himself. *I hope to hell he does.*

The feeling he had experienced, when he was just able to escape after Tanner shot Luther, kept coming back to him as he sat in his bedroom fortress. He did not want to admit that it was fear, he had never felt fear of anyone, but it was a different feeling, and he was having trouble forgetting it. The recent talk between himself and Luther came back to him, when Luther had tried to persuade him that they should run while Tanner was evidently taking Cecil somewhere to be locked up. Maybe Luther had been right. Maybe it would have been smarter to leave the cursed lawman's territory and make a new start. Maybe the smart thing to do would be for him to do that now, instead of trying to hold out up here. *Treed*, the term came back to him, and he felt more treed by the moment, and never more alone than now with no one to back him.

He sat there between the bed and the wall long after there were no more sounds from the kitchen and the dining room. Then the sounds of the women's voices as they prepared for bed faded away until they, too, were gone, until there were no sounds at all. That was when it was the worst, for that was when he strained to listen for sounds that weren't there. As the night crawled slowly by, he nodded off in spite of his determination not to, only to awaken a few minutes later in near panic for having left himself vulnerable for that time. He decided that Luther had been right and he made up his mind to leave Grassy Creek in the morning as soon as it was light enough to see.

Chapter 12

With the first rays of light that shone through the small window, a stiff and bleary-eyed Ansel Beaudry eased himself up from his tiny fortress, creeped to the door, and listened for any sounds that might indicate anything out of the ordinary. When he decided there were none, he drew his pistol, then slowly slid the bolt back and opened the door. Relieved to find no one in the short hall, he started toward the front door, passing through the dining room, when he heard a sudden noise to his right. He spun around, his .44 cocked, and drew down on a startled Elmira in the kitchen doorway, holding the coffeepot. "Damn you!" he spat. "I almost shot you!" Frightened by the insane look in his eyes, she made no response and just stood there while he went to the front door. *Wake up, Eddie*, she pleaded silently as Ansel slowly opened the door. Seconds later, she heard the commotion on the front porch.

"You lazy little bastard!" Ansel roared when he found Eddie nodding off. "I told you to keep your eyes open! A whole posse of lawmen coulda rode up that creek while you were sleepin'."

"I wasn't sleepin'," Eddie pleaded. "I stayed awake all night, just like you said. I didn't close my eyes till just a few minutes ago when Ma came out and said she was makin' some coffee for me."

"That's your story," Ansel charged. "I ain't payin' you for sleepin'. Get up from there and go saddle my horse. Bring him and one of the packhorses up here to the porch." Eddie scrambled to his feet and ran to do Beaudry's bidding. Ansel stood watching him until he disappeared into the barn. Then he turned to go back inside, but stopped and turned back around, stepped off the porch, and went to the corner of the cabin to answer nature's call. When he was finished, he went back in the kitchen to get some coffee. When Elmira brought him a cup, he said, "I'm leavin' this rat's nest you call a hideout and I'm gonna need some things to take with me. Then he started calling off items of supplies as he could think of them.

"That's gonna put a helluva hole in my supplies," Elmira said when he had finished. "You ain't hardly paid me for that much stuff." Judging by his crazy actions during the last two days, she was a little cautious in her complaining to him, even now uncertain if he was really going to leave. At this point, however, she was happy to hear he planned to go, whether he paid her all he owed or not.

"I've already paid you more money than you deserve," he claimed. "You ain't gettin' no more. I'm leavin' two extra packhorses. That'll make up the difference."

"All right," she said, not willing to rile him up again,

"if you think that's fair." Ready for an argument from her, he paused for a moment, then went into the bedroom to get his things and bring them out by the front door. She couldn't resist asking then, "You expectin' him to come ridin' up here this mornin'?"

"Maybe," he said, calmer now. "But I ain't gonna be here when he does." He cocked a suspicious eye at her. "What are you worried about? He ain't after you."

"I'm just worried about you," she said. She couldn't help making the snide remark.

When Eddie brought the horses up to the porch, he helped Ansel pack the supplies in sacks on the packhorse. When they were finished, Ansel asked him a question. "I know there's a back way outta here, ain't there?" He was thinking about the chance of meeting Will Tanner on his way up.

"Yes, sir," Eddie replied. "There's a way out, but you can't ride a horse that way. You have to climb up over a rock ledge where the water comes out of the ground before you come over the back of the hill and down through the trees to that game trail."

Ansel was not happy to hear that, but he decided he would have to take the boy's word for it. He didn't like the idea of losing a lot of time to find out that Eddie was right. That thought triggered a need to hurry now and not waste any more time than he already had. The sun was starting to find its way through the tree branches overhead. "Helluva thing," he muttered, "some hideout with no back door." He climbed up into the saddle and sneered at the two women standing on the porch. "I hope they burn this place to the ground," he said in parting, wheeled the gray horse, and started down the creek to the river.

Elmira and Darlene stood watching until he passed

out of sight. "Well, if that ain't good riddance, I don't know what is," Elmira commented.

"That ol' son of a bitch," Eddie complained. "I laid awake out here on this porch all night and he wouldn't pay me the money he promised me."

"Don't fret over that, son," Elmira said. "While he was peein' on the corner of the house, I went in his saddlebags and got your twenty-five dollars for you. He had so much money in there, he'll never miss it. I got a little extra for what he owes me, while I was at it." Darlene released a howl of laughter and they all joined in. "Come on, let's go inside and cook some breakfast," Elmira said.

Will woke up to the sounds of Buster's snuffling as the buckskin nibbled the grass close to his blanket. Thinking he had slept too late, he bolted upright, only then remembering the wound in his shoulder when he felt a stab of pain shoot through it. Cursing himself again for being careless enough to have let Curry get off the shot, he felt his arm and shoulder for stiffness. To test for mobility, he swung his arm up and down, and while it was uncomfortable, he decided it wouldn't hinder his movements to a great extent. Already having made up his mind that he was going to finish the job he started, he decided he was going into Grassy Creek to get Ansel Beaudry. Riding straight up the creek to the cabin was akin to committing suicide, so he was going to have to go in the back way, and that meant going in on foot. It might not be easy, especially with a tender shoulder—might not be possible at all—but that was what he was going to try. With that settled, he got his horses ready and left the stream where he had spent the night.

Back on the river trail, he followed it to the point where the game trail up from the Washita crossed it. Instead of taking the game trail down to that river, he went the opposite way, as he had on the first day, when he scouted Grassy Creek from above the hideout. His memory was sharp enough to remember the way he had gone to the cabin, even though it took him through a sizable forest of trees on the hillside. Once he reached the rock ledge, he had to leave the horses and proceed on foot. It was time to determine if he had been mistaken in thinking he could climb down the ledge to the back of the cabin. He decided he could, so he checked his rifle to make sure the magazine was fully loaded, then checked his Colt handgun as well. He took a glance up at the sky to judge the time, instead of checking the watch he carried in his pocket, and figured it was getting along to late morning. Then with a little grunt for the pain in his shoulder, he lowered himself over the ledge, hung by his arms for a few seconds, then dropped about three feet to a narrow path below. Before going any farther, he paused there to look and listen, even though he figured it impossible that anyone in the camp below could see him. He stayed where he was for a little longer while he looked for signs of activity around the cluster of outbuildings below. When he was satisfied that there was no one in the barn or the outhouse, he moved down through the trees and bushes to the back of the cabin, where the bedrooms were located. He knew how many people he had to account for because Moon had told him there was no one there except Elmira, her son, Darlene, and now Beaudry.

When there was no sound from inside the bedrooms, he decided everyone was probably in the front somewhere, probably in a kitchen or dining room, wherever everyone met. If he was lucky, he might catch Beaudry sitting at the table eating or drinking, so he moved cautiously around the side of the cabin until he could peek around the corner at the front porch. There was no one there. He stepped up on the porch and moved quietly to the door to listen. He could hear conversation coming from inside, but all of it from women's voices. He looked around him again to make sure Elmira's son wasn't in the yard somewhere before slowly opening the door to a small parlor. With the door only partially open, he could see through the parlor to a large room beyond, where the two women and the boy were sitting at a long table, drinking coffee.

For a moment, he froze until he realized they were not aware of his presence, then when it was obvious they were engrossed in what almost appeared to be a party mood, he walked into the parlor, his rifle ready for Beaudry's sudden appearance. There was no sign of the man. Maybe Will was wrong, maybe Beaudry had not returned to Grassy Creek. In the next moment, the talking stopped as the three at the table discovered the silent figure standing in the doorway. Darlene couldn't suppress a squeal at the sight of the Winchester looking at them. Elmira blurted, "Mr. Walker!"

It was Eddie who declared, "He ain't here, Mr. Walker, I mean Mr. Tanner. He's gone!"

"That's right, Deputy," Elmira said. "You're lookin' for Ansel Beaudry and he ain't here. He took off this mornin' and we're damn glad he did. I wish to hell you coulda caught him."

Will could have doubted her word, but both she

and Eddie had not a hint of deceit in their statements, coming unprepared as they did. He eased the hammer back and lowered the Winchester. "Where did he go?"

"He didn't say," Elmira answered, "and we didn't care, just as long as he went."

"When?" Will asked.

"About two hours ago."

He had missed him. Beaudry had a two-hour start, plus the time it would take Will to climb back up over that ledge where his horses were tied. He had been so certain that Beaudry would be set up in ambush at the top of the creek, never thinking he would leave the protection of the hideout. Now he knew that he could have simply waited for him to come down the creek in an attempt to get away. "Well, I can't seem to keep from losin' that man," he muttered to himself.

"I reckon we oughta be thankin' you for cleanin' out that bunch of snakes," Elmira said, "after what they done to us and all." She paused, waiting to find out how much trouble she was in, since he knew the primary purpose of the cabin built there. Finally she asked, "What are you gonna do about us? I mean, are you fixin' to bring a bunch of lawmen in here to burn my house down and run me outta Oklahoma?"

Lost in his thoughts of what he had to do now that Beaudry was on the run, he had not given her situation any concern at all. "What?" he suddenly blurted when he heard her question. "Oh . . ." He paused. "No, Elmira, I've got no interest in runnin' you out. I've got nothin' against you. I'm interested in one thing only, and that's catchin' Ansel Beaudry." He gave her a faint grin. "Besides, you're a customer of Oscar Moon's, and Moon's the reason I found Grassy

Creek. I tracked him to your place, but I won't be bringin' a posse up here to bother you, and I've got no warrants for Moon."

"Moon's dead," Elmira stated solemnly. "Ansel Beaudry shot him down right out yonder by my front steps."

"For no reason at all," Darlene said. "He's crazy in the head. He just took a notion that Moon mighta told the law where he was hidin'." She shook her head at the memory of the shooting. "Just pulled his pistol out and shot him in the chest. Poor Moon didn't have a chance to protect himself."

Will was stunned, hardly able to believe what he had just heard. Moon was the kind of man you expected to always be there. Moon was a friend of his. More than that, Oscar Moon had saved his life one night in a saloon in Kansas, and for that, he felt always indebted to him. Ansel Beaudry was a marked man from that moment on. No matter how long and how much it took, Will swore a silent oath to his dead friend that he would be avenged—no matter how far Beaudry ran.

It puzzled those watching him that Moon's death appeared to have struck him hard, for it was obvious that the deputy was taken aback. Eddie spoke up then. "We dug him a nice grave on the other side of the barn. Mama and Darlene helped dig it."

All thoughts that Will Tanner was a lawman were forgotten then. Elmira stepped forward and took a look at Will's bloodstained sleeve. "Looks like you got shot," she said. "Take your shirt off and let me see if I can take care of it." When he started to balk, she insisted. "I've took care of a lotta gunshots in my time, so take your shirt off. You've got some fresh bleedin' goin' on." He glanced at his shoulder to see she was right. He had evidently started it again when he dropped over that rock ledge. "Set yourself down at the table," she ordered. "If you're goin' after him, you can't have that bullet festerin' in your shoulder." He hesitated for only a couple of seconds before obeying her. When he did, it served to unite the four of them in a common cause, to bring Ansel Beaudry to justice.

"I'll get you a cup of coffee," Darlene said to him when Elmira went to the kitchen to heat some water to clean his wound. "I'll bring you a biscuit to go with it."

Had it not been for the sorrowful news of Oscar Moon's death, Will might have found the situation amusing. Although never having committed an actual crime, Elmira Tate had always aligned herself and her business with the folks who broke the law. After cleaning the wound, she managed to get the bullet out and bandaged the wound. He knew that every minute he sat there was another minute behind Beaudry, but he thought she was right in saying the wound might give him trouble if it wasn't tended. When she had finished, he thanked her and started out the door, followed by their wishes of good luck in running the murderer to ground. When Eddie offered to get his horses for him, they were surprised to learn that he had walked in from above the creek. "Don't go openin' that wound up when you climb over that ledge," Elmira scolded.

"I won't," Will responded, and started up the back path at a trot.

The three residents of Grassy Creek watched him

until he disappeared into the trees near the base of the ledge. "Ain't that a helluva note?" Darlene muttered. "Looks like we crossed over to the other side of the law."

"Not hardly," Elmira said.

As he climbed back up to his horses, Will's brain was working hard to make the best guess as to where Beaudry would run. Finally, he had to assume that he would probably head to Brinker's first, likely on his way to Kansas. The trading post was in cahoots with the Grassy Creek hideout, and he might be in need of supplies. It was strictly a guess, but if it was the correct one, he would cut into Beaudry's lead a little, since his horses were in the trees above the river trail that led to Brinker's. There were other things on his mind as he rode toward the trading post. When would the posse from Wichita arrive at Camp Supply? He couldn't contact them if he was trying to trail Beaudry. As things stood now, there were only the three prisoners at Camp Supply to escort back for trial. He needed to let his boss, Dan Stone, know what was going on and that he was going to go after Beaudry no matter where he ran. Then another thought entered his mind. *Sophie must think I'm dead.*

The farther he rode, the more concerned he became because he could not see any tracks on the trail that he could say for sure were as recent as that morning, and there should have been. The most recent were some unshod hoofprints. These he could tell for sure, but they were mixed in with tracks left by shod horses, coming and going, over the last few days. Still, he continued on, thinking Brinker's to be the most likely place to start looking for Beaudry.

When he saw the trees that lined the Canadian River, he reined Buster back to a slow walk while he peered ahead to catch first sight of the buildings that were Brinker's. When still at a distance, he stopped and scanned the barnyard and outbuildings carefully. There were no horses tied at the rail in front of the store, but he was looking for something else, too, and in a few minutes, he saw it. He nudged Buster and started again, guiding the horse toward the barn when Brinker's young son, Thomas, walked out. Will figured he was more likely to get truthful answers to his questions from the nine-year-old than he would from his parents.

Thomas looked up when he heard Buster approaching. "Howdy, Thomas," Will greeted him. "I see you're still busy, helpin' your pa take care of the place." Thomas didn't say anything, but continued to stare at him. Will decided that the boy's expression was one of curiosity and not an unfriendly one. That by itself was enough to tell Will what he needed to know, but he decided to ask the question, anyway. "I'm tryin' to catch up with a fellow named Beaudry, who shoulda come by here this mornin'. Did you see him?"

Thomas shook his head. "Ain't been nobody stopped at the store this mornin'," he said, confirming Will's guess. It was disappointing news to hear, and he never doubted the truthfulness of the boy's answer.

Maybe there was the possibility that Beaudry passed by, but didn't stop at the store, so he asked. "He mighta just passed on by without stoppin'. Did you see him

pass by?" Again, Thomas shook his head with the
same puzzled look on his face. "Much obliged,
Thomas," Will said, and turned Buster's head back
toward the trail. There was no need to question Tyler
Brinker—Will already knew what he needed to know.
He had guessed totally wrong in his efforts to catch up
with Ansel Beaudry, and now he was faced with some
difficult decisions. It was important that the Wichita
posse know the status of the Beaudry gang, how many
were dead, and that there was one, Beaudry himself,
still on the loose. To carry that information to Camp
Supply would take a day and a half's ride, in effect,
giving Beaudry more than a three-day head start. And
that was if Will had a trail to follow, which he didn't.
It was not a good position he found himself in, and he
could see only two options: report to Camp Supply
that Beaudry had gotten away or go back to Grassy
Creek and try to pick up a trail. Thinking of Oscar
Moon then, he said, "Well, I reckon I know which one
it's gonna be." He turned Buster's head back toward
Grassy Creek.

While his horses grazed in the small patches of
grass between the cottonwoods beside the Washita
River, Will scouted the riverbank on each side of the
mouth of Grassy Creek. His job was made difficult by
the fact that the creek bed was thick with grass that
was covered with about eight inches of water, which
made for no tracks coming down the creek. There
should have been some tracks, either upstream or
down when Beaudry rode out on the bank of the
river. After searching carefully, with no success, for
some evidence that would show in which direction

Beaudry had fled, Will was about to believe the outlaw had taken wings and flown off the hill. It occurred to him then that maybe Beaudry rode straight across the river when he came down from the cabin that morning, so as to not leave tracks on the riverbank. So he climbed on Buster and drove his horses across to the opposite side, and there on the other bank, he found the tracks he was looking for.

Beaudry had come out of the river on the opposite bank, then followed the river east. Will could plainly see the fresh tracks left by two horses on the narrow trail and he had to wonder if Beaudry had a definite destination in mind, or if he was just running. According to what he had learned about the gang, none of them except Tom Daly really knew the territory they had fled to. As long as Beaudry left tracks to follow, Will figured it was just a question of how long before he could overtake him. If he continued to follow the Washita, he was going to end up in the Cheyenne-Arapaho reservation and Will figured that was not where Beaudry wanted to go. Still, the tracks of the two horses were easy to follow until he came to a sharp bend in the river and saw definite signs that Beaudry had stopped there to rest his horses. "I reckon you could use a little rest right now, too," he said to Buster, and turned the buckskin down toward the water's edge and a grassy bank. Seeing the remains of a recent fire, he stirred the ashes solely by habit to guess how old they were. *Cold*, he thought, not really expecting otherwise, since Beaudry's lead was more than a day at this point. He had wasted a day when he went to Brinker's first, but he had felt sure Beaudry would be heading in that direction, even if he didn't stop at the trading post. It was his impression that Ansel's natural territory was Kansas and Missouri. If he continued in the direction he had started in, he'd end up in Osage territory, or farther on into the Five Nations. *That ain't all bad,* Will thought, *because if he kept going, he'd end up in Fort Smith, and that's where I'm planning to take him, anyway.* "Maybe he'll turn himself in," he japed to Buster as he gathered some small limbs to build a fire.

When his horses were rested, he set out again, following the river trail, but had only ridden about five miles before reaching a heavily traveled Indian trail running north and south. Again, to his surprise, Beaudry fooled him, turning south instead of north, which would have led him toward Kansas. *He's going to Texas,* he thought. He had not traveled far when he felt a definite familiar feeling for the trail and it suddenly struck him why. It had been a good while now, but he remembered it well. This road he followed was tracing the route of the Western Cattle Trail. The last time he had ridden this trail, he was helping to drive a herd of cattle to Dodge City. For the first time since picking up the trail back at Grassy Creek, he wondered if he might be following a trail somebody other than Beaudry had left, but that didn't make any sense. He continued on for another couple of miles when he saw a man on a horse coming toward him, leading a milk cow.

When close enough to tell, he could see that the rider was an Indian, although he was dressed in white man's clothes. Will figured he was probably one of the Indians who was trying his hand at farming. He watched Will carefully as the distance between them closed, and when they were within hailing distance, Will called out a greeting. "Afternoon, friend, you talk white man talk?" The man nodded, still regarding Will with caution. Will pulled his vest aside to expose his badge. "I'm U.S. Deputy Marshal Will Tanner," he said, and as soon as he did, the man was visibly more at ease. "Are you Cheyenne?"

"Arapaho," the man answered. "I am John Little Bear."

"Have you traveled far on this road, John?" Will asked.

"Two days," John answered. "I bought this cow from a man near the Salt Fork of the Red River. I have a paper with his mark on it."

Will realized that John Little Bear was concerned that he might think the cow stolen. "Looks like a fine cow," he said. "Did you meet a white man leading a packhorse, headed the same direction I'm ridin'?"

"Yes, I met a white man, riding a gray horse and leading a sorrel packhorse," John replied. "A big man, with a black beard. Is he an outlaw?"

"Yes, he is," Will said. "He's responsible for a lotta people gettin' killed. Did he say where he was headin'?"

"No, but he asked me if this road went to Texas. I told him that it did. He asked me how far it was to the Red River. I told him two days, unless he was leading a cow. Then it would be longer."

"When was this when you met him?"

"Yesterday, about this time," John said. "So you are three days from the Red River from here," he said, anticipating Will's next question.

"'Preciate it, John," Will said. "Hope your cow gives good milk."

"I hope you catch that man. He looked like an evil man," John said as Will nudged Buster and set out again. With confidence now that the tracks he had been following were, indeed, left by Ansel Beaudry, he pushed Buster into an easy lope, a pace he could maintain for a good distance without tiring.

A day and a half's ride brought him to a point where the winding Salt Fork of the Red changed its more easterly direction to turn south in its journey to flow into the Red River. It was at this point that the common road Will had ridden down through Oklahoma Territory now followed the Salt Fork, headed south to Texas. He knew as well that he was no more than a day's ride from the Red and the Texas border. He also knew that he had been mistaken about Ansel Beaudry. Beaudry was not running aimlessly. He knew where he was going when he fled Grassy Creek. It was Texas for certain, and he picked the quickest trail to get him there. Will racked his brain, trying to recall the name of a man who operated a trading post just over the line in Texas. It was on the Pease River at a spot the Indians called Eagle Springs. The trading post was a favorite place to buy whiskey for those folks living across the Red in Indian Territory. Finally, after a lot of mind searching, it came to him—Cotton was the first name. A minute or two later, the last name surfaced—Poole. The man's name was Cotton Poole. That recovery also served to cause him to remember Cotton as a crooked man who was not above cheating you any way he could.

Chapter 13

It was late in the afternoon when Will reached the Red River at a point where he and the men of the J-Bar-J usually drove their cattle across into Indian Territory. He crossed over to the Texas side before stopping to let his horses drink. While he sat beneath a cottonwood, watching them, he thought to take his deputy's badge off his shirt and put it in his pocket. Whatever happened on this side of the Red was in no way official business, although he fully intended to try to bring Beaudry back to Fort Smith for trial. This in spite of the fact that it would be tempting to shoot him on sight the same way Beaudry had killed Oscar Moon. The thought of it caused the muscles in his arms to tense up, remembering Elmira's accounting of the blatant execution of the unsuspecting old cattle thief.

He figured to let his horses rest for the night when he reached the Pease River, and that was less than ten miles from where he now sat. So he climbed back into the saddle after a short rest and headed for Eagle Springs and Cotton Poole's trading post.

It had been quite a while since he had passed this way, moving a herd of cattle with Shorty Watts and the rest of the J-Bar-J crew, but Poole's store looked the same to him, with the exception of a couple of outbuildings that hadn't been there before. There were a couple of horses tied at the rail in front of the store. Both were saddled, neither was a gray, but he had not expected to have caught up with Beaudry this soon. He rode up to the rail and stepped down, then as a matter of habit, he took a few moments to glance at the barn and the corral beside it. There was no sign of anyone outside the buildings and only a couple of horses in the corral. As a precaution, he drew his rifle from the saddle sling and stepped up on the low porch.

He opened the door and stepped inside the dimly lit room. The only light provided was that from a lamp on the counter and a fireplace on the other side of the room where three men sat at a table. One of them was easily recognized as the owner of the store, Cotton Poole. Will could only speculate that at a younger age Cotton must have had white hair, but for now, his head was barren of any trace of a hair and shiny as a polished doorknob. The two men seated at the table with Cotton looked typical of so many drifters Will had seen in saloons everywhere. Talking raucously before, they all stopped to stare at him when he walked inside.

Cotton got up from the table and came to meet him. "Well, howdy, stranger," he said. "What can I do for ya? You needin' somethin' from the store or lookin' for a drink of whiskey?" He stared openly at Will, as if trying to recall. He didn't wait for Will to answer before continuing. "I swear, I've seen you before, but I can't recollect when."

"A few years ago, I expect," Will said. "I stopped in when I was working cattle, but I ain't been back this way since then."

"What outfit was you ridin' for?" Cotton asked, all the while eyeing the casual way Will carried the Winchester in his hand. When Will answered his question, Cotton looked surprised. "The J-Bar-J?" he echoed. "They came through the first of this summer. Some of the crew was in here, but you wasn't with 'em. I'da remembered."

"No, I wasn't," Will replied. "I don't work cattle anymore."

"Is that a fact? What's your line of work now?" Cotton glanced back at the two men at the table, who were still gaping at Will. All three were curious about the dried bloodstains on his left sleeve, but no one asked about it.

"First one thing and then another," Will answered. "Right now I thought I could use a drink of whiskey to settle some of the dust in my throat." He didn't particularly want a drink, but he thought it might loosen Cotton's tongue if he bought a drink. He hoped to get some information to let him know for sure that Beaudry had passed this way.

"Well, I can sure take care of that," Cotton declared. "Set down at the table with us and I'll pour you one." He glanced at the two men at the table again. "You don't mind, do ya, boys?" They immediately said he was welcome, so Will sat down while Cotton went to the short bar to get another glass. When he returned, he sat down and poured a drink for Will from the half-empty bottle on the table, then refilled the other glasses. "This here's Jack Dunn and Calvin Wallace," he said. "It's easy to tell 'em apart 'cause Calvin's the one wearin' the patch over his eye. Feller tried to cut it outta his head in a bar fight."

"That's a fact," Calvin spoke up then, "but it was the last thing he ever done, and I can see just as good outta one eye as I could with two."

Will couldn't help noticing that Calvin's single eye was still focusing intensely upon him. He tossed his drink back. "Mighty neighborly of you boys," he commented as Cotton refilled his glass, causing him to comment further. "I don't wanna get ahead of you."

"Oh, you've got a long way to go to catch up with us," Jack Dunn said. "Ain't that right, Cotton? This bottle was full fifteen minutes before you walked in."

Will knew for sure that he was sitting in questionable company, well aware he was being sized up by all three of them. "What line of work are you boys in?"

Calvin smirked. "One thing and then another, just like you said. You ain't said where you was headed. You headin' for Injun Territory?" They assumed he was, since they had not seen him ride up, and that was a common destination for outlaws and drifters.

"Nope," Will replied. "I just came down from there and I ain't sure whether I'll go to Fort Worth or somewhere else, depends on the trail I'm followin'." When that brought a puzzled look, he continued, "I'm trailin' a low-down son of a bitch who stole my best horse. He mighta passed through here, ridin' a gray geldin' and trailin' a packhorse, big fellow with a dark black beard. Maybe he stopped here."

"I knew there was somethin' snaky about that feller,"

Cotton said. "He stopped here. I sold him a bottle of whiskey." His comments seemed to be directed toward Jack and Calvin, more so than Will. "Too bad you boys weren't here, you mighta been interested in makin' his acquaintance." He looked quickly back at Will. "If I'd known he stole your horse, maybe I coulda done somethin', but he didn't look like the kind you'd wanna mess with."

"I don't reckon he said where he was headed," Will said.

"No, he didn't," Cotton said, "but he asked me if there was a trail from here to Fort Worth and I told him there was a wagon road headed in that direction about twelve miles south of here."

"Well, I reckon I owe you for two drinks," Will announced, "and it's time for me to get along." He got to his feet and put the money on the table.

"Ain't no need to run off," Cotton said. "It's a little late in the day to start out now, might as well camp here tonight and start out in the mornin'. My woman can fix you some supper, and breakfast, too, if you want it."

"Much obliged," Will said, "but if I stay here much longer, I'm liable to get to drinkin' too much and I won't be worth a damn in the mornin'. I'll find me a good spot up the river a ways and get myself a good night's sleep."

"Sounds like a sensible man," Cotton said. "Hope you catch up with that thief. Maybe we'll see you back this way again." All three got up from the table and walked with him to the door. They followed him out on the porch and stood watching him as he climbed up on Buster.

"That's a fine-lookin' buckskin you're ridin' there," Calvin commented.

"He'll do," Will answered. "He ain't the horse that gray is, though. Been nice drinkin' with you boys." He wheeled Buster away from the rail and started off at an angle that would take him up the river.

"Yes, sir," Jack Dunn remarked as Will rode away. "That is a fine-lookin' buckskin he's ridin'. The pack-horse looks pretty good, too."

"It looks like it might be a good night to pay him a neighborly visit," Calvin said.

"It might at that," Jack agreed.

"Split three ways," Cotton quickly reminded them.

"I don't know about that," Calvin complained, "unless you're gonna strap on your gun belt and ride to his camp with us. Me and Jack do all the work and you don't do nothin' for your share."

"It's just like our regular deal," Cotton claimed. "I line 'em up and send for you. That's my end of the deal. You and Jack handle the rest, just like always."

"That may be so," Calvin said, "but this time you didn't do anythin'. Me and Jack was settin' right here when he came in. We didn't need any word from you."

"Don't make no difference," Cotton insisted. "You got the job because he came in my store, just like all the other times. Maybe you don't want me to send for you next time."

"Nah, Cotton," Jack intervened. "Calvin don't mean nothin' by it. We'll keep workin' like we always have. We'll handle our end of it and you keep settin' 'em up." He was looking at Calvin when he said it. With a slight shifting of his eyes, he directed his partner's attention toward the counter in the store area where Cotton's Comanche wife was listening to their discussion. By her right hand, a twelve-gauge shotgun rested on the countertop.

"Jack's right," Calvin said. "I was just japin' you to get you riled up. I kept winkin' while I was japin' you, but I forgot and was winkin' my left eye. Sometimes I forget that's the eye with the patch over it."

Will guided Buster along the banks of the Pease River, looking for a suitable spot to make his camp. "I apologize for what I said back there," he told the buckskin. "There ain't no way that gray Beaudry's ridin' can stand up to you, but then I reckon you already knew that." Had he not already ridden his horses hard that day, he would have considered moving on to put more distance between himself and the two he met in the store. It was easy for him to make a quick judgment about the two drifters, and he did not rule out the possibility that he might see them again. For that reason, he was looking for a campsite that would afford him the best chance for keeping his horses. He figured them to be no more than horse thieves who might hope for an opportunity to run his horses off while he slept. Consequently, he needed a spot where he could keep the horses close by him, so he kept riding until he came to a small creek that formed a little cove where it emptied into the river. There was grass around the edges of the cove that would afford the horses good grazing without wandering far.

Once his horses were taken care of, he collected enough limbs from the oak trees next to the river to build a fire in a shallow gully that was deep enough to partially hide the flames. The sun was just beginning to sink into the distant horizon when his small coffee-pot began to bubble in time with the sizzle of the bacon in the frying pan. He was more than ready for coffee and food because his empty stomach was complaining about the two shots of whiskey he had swallowed. When his bacon was done, he pulled the pan off the flame and dropped two pieces of hardtack in the hot grease. When that was done, he emptied the grease and ate the bacon and hardtack out of the pan, forgoing the bother of using a plate.

The first shot knocked the frying pan out of his hand. The second one snapped harmlessly over the campfire because when it came, he was already gone, rolling over and over until he dropped into the gully. He lay still, listening to the rifle shots spraying sand around his campfire, silently cursing himself for underestimating the evil intent of the two drifters at Cotton Poole's store. They were not satisfied with stealing his horses, they meant to kill him and take everything he had. At least his reflexes were automatic enough for him to have grabbed his rifle when he rolled away from the fire. And from the pattern of shots that continued to pepper the ground all around his fire, he knew they didn't know he had rolled as far as he did. He was lying in the gully, so they couldn't see him, but if they were to circle around to the bank upstream of the position he was in, he'd be a sitting duck. *So I've got to move out of this gully before they think of that*, he told himself. How to do it without being seen was the problem. His gully was so shallow that he was sure to be seen if he raised up even a few inches. To make matters worse, he couldn't tell where the shooters were, he knew only that they were downstream somewhere. He thought about jumping up suddenly and making a run for the cover of the trees, but when he peeked over the edge of the gully, he realized that it was a sprint of almost ten yards to get to the trees. He had no idea how good his two bushwhackers were, but he knew he wouldn't have any trouble if he was taking the shot. Not only that, but he would be running straight toward his horses. He felt confident that they didn't want to hit the horses, since they most likely figured they were the most valuable things he owned. However, he didn't want to risk a wayward shot hitting one of his horses. *You picked a hell of a spot to camp*, he scolded himself, *hunkered down helpless in this gully. We'll just have to play the hand I dealt myself and trust to luck.* Straining to lie as flat as he possibly could, he edged his rifle over the side of the gully. Then with a long, dead root he had landed on when he rolled into the gully, he carefully pushed the rifle as far away from the edge as the root would take it. It was a hell of a long shot, he had to admit, but he figured it was all he had. Nothing to do now but wait and hope.

"Maybe we shoulda worked our way a little closer before we opened up on him, but I thought I had a pretty good shot," Calvin whispered.

"Yeah," Jack scoffed, "you hit him in the fryin' pan. If either of us hit him, I expect it was my first shot. That's the one that knocked him on the ground. Maybe you've got that patch on the wrong eye."

"Hell," Calvin retorted, "There ain't no tellin' who shot him, we threw so many shots around that fire.

The main thing is he went down and he ain't got up, so I'm bettin' he caught more'n one bullet."

"Maybe so," Jack cautioned, "but I ain't ready to run down there till I know we got him. You go right ahead if you're that anxious."

"Yeah, you'd like me to stick my neck out, wouldn't you?" Calvin said. "We can't even see him from here."

"He's gotta be layin' in that little gully," Jack replied, "and he ain't even fired a shot back at us. He can't be anywhere else. We'da seen him if he tried to run for it."

"I don't know," Calvin responded. "He might be playin' possum, waitin' for us to walk in and get shot. I say let's wait him out. Hell, I ain't in no hurry."

"If we wait too long, that coffee's gonna get cold," Jack japed, "and I was figurin' on havin' myself a cup." His quip brought a chuckle from both of them, but they settled in to wait. They waited for what seemed like a long time, watching the ground around the campfire carefully, lest their victim suddenly jumped up and made a run for it. The flames of the campfire were flickering low before Jack finally declared, "Hell, he's dead, or shot so bad he can't move, I'm goin' in."

"Be careful, I don't trust that son of a bitch," Calvin cautioned as he got up from his position and followed his partner. They made their way upstream, being careful to use the cover of the trees. When they reached a small hummock some twenty yards from the camp, they paused to look the situation over before advancing farther. "Jack, look yonder." He pointed to the rifle lying a couple of feet from the lip of the gully. "We got him! He's layin' in that little gully and he can't reach that rifle from there. If he could, he'd damn sure be holdin' it. He's dead."

"Looks that way," Jack decided. "Let's go see." He left the cover of the trees and walked toward the campfire. When within a few yards of the gully, he could clearly see Will lying there completely still. "Yep," he announced, "he's in there."

"Careful, Jack," Calvin warned, "maybe he ain't dead."

"One way to make sure," Jack replied, and brought his rifle up to his shoulder. That was as far as he got before Will raised the Colt .44, close by his side, and fired a shot that caught Jack in the center of his chest. He staggered backward into Calvin, who was trying to raise his rifle. It was enough to block his shot, and by the time he was able to push Jack aside, it was too late to escape the second shot from Will's .44. He dropped to his knees, still straining to bring his rifle to bear on his executioner, only to feel the impact of another shot in his gut.

Will got up from the gully, his pistol cocked for another shot if necessary, but he saw right away there was no need. He was well aware that the reason he was standing had a lot to do with luck. He knew he had to thank Jack for waiting to shoot until he got closer. Then he was in his debt again for staggering back into Calvin to block his shot. It had been a high-risk defense, but he figured he had no other choice—and it worked out all right. He picked up his rifle and went to check on each of his victims. Checking Jack first, he found him dead, his shot had evidently found his heart. Calvin, although mortally wounded, was still hanging on to life, obviously in great pain. The patch had been shifted to the side, revealing an ugly scar where his eyeball should have been. Unable to talk, he looked up at Will with his good eye, seeming to plea for mercy. It was obvious that he was dying, but it might be a long, painful wait. With the same compassion he felt for any suffering animal, Will cocked his .44 again. When he raised it over Calvin's head, the dying man managed to nod in appreciation. A moment later he was gone.

Finding nothing of value except weapons and ammunition on the two bodies, he left them to be claimed by whatever scavengers happened by after he dragged them away from his camp. "I reckon that's a genuine Texas welcome," he proclaimed.

Then he walked back downstream to find their horses tied near a stand of willows. By this time, it was pretty dark along the river, but he decided the two horses, both sorrels, were fairly good horses. He led them back to his camp, pulled their saddles off, and turned them out to graze with his horses. "I might know where I can sell those horses," he speculated aloud.

Morning found him well rested and ready to get back to the business that had brought him to Texas. He saddled Buster and the two sorrels that had belonged to his visitors of the previous night and loaded his packhorse again. He was pleased to find a coil of new rope on one of the saddles, no doubt to be used to trail Buster and his packhorse, so he used it to lead the two sorrels back down the river.

"That stranger back," Cotton Poole's Comanche wife informed him.

"What?" Cotton blurted. "Where?" She turned from the window to face him, then pointed toward the road. He hurried to the window to see for himself, knowing that if the stranger was back, he must surely be a ghost. What he saw answered a question he had earlier that morning, however. Where were Jack and Calvin? "Uh-oh," he muttered. "This ain't good." He turned to his wife and said, "Get your shotgun and stand over there at the end of the counter where you were last night." He went to a rack of deer antlers on the wall, where a gun and holster were hanging, and strapped the belt on. "We'll just see what he has to say," he told the woman.

"Well, howdy," Cotton called out cheerfully when Will walked in the door. "I thought you were on your way to Fort Worth. What brings you back to see us?"

Will took special note of the Indian woman at the end of the counter and the shotgun lying within easy reach of her right hand. He also noticed that Cotton was wearing a gun, whereas he had not worn one the day before. "Good mornin'," he greeted them cordially. "After I left here yesterday, it struck me that you're in the business of horse tradin', and I remembered that I've got a pair of fairly young sorrels for sale, saddles and bridles included. And I'm willin' to let 'em go at a good price, just because I'd rather not bother with 'em. I ain't likely to give 'em away, mind you, just askin' a fair price. Whaddaya say, are you interested?" He could see that Poole wasn't quite sure what to make of the proposition. Even the Comanche woman had a puzzled look on her face.

Cotton wasn't sure what Will had in mind, but he decided the best course of action was to simply play the game Will had introduced. "Well, I have done some horse tradin' from time to time, although I ain't done much lately. I reckon it would depend on how much you're askin'." Before Will could respond to that, however, Cotton asked, "How'd you come by the horses?" He was reluctant to say he knew the horses well, both their good points and their bad ones.

In answer to his question, Will said, "I reckon you could say they were left to me in the previous owners' wills, so you don't have to worry about 'em bein' stolen. As far as the price, the last time I bought a horse of this quality, it sold for forty-five dollars. Does that sound about right?" When Cotton shrugged, obviously not pleased, Will continued, "So I figure I'll let you have the pair of 'em, includin' tack, for the price of one, forty-five dollars. That way, it's a good deal for both of us."

Cotton could not help smiling. He had to admit that the stranger had a strange sense of humor. He found it ironic that he might pay the man for horses that Jack and Calvin rode to bushwhack him, but he could also see that he was buying two horses for the price of one, so he stood to make a profit. "You've got a deal," he said, and reached in his pocket for the roll of paper money he carried. "Pleasure doin' business with you, stranger. Maybe you'll be back this way sometime."

"Never can tell," Will said as he counted the money, then put it in his pocket. "I'd best be gettin' along now."

"Say, what's your name, stranger?" Cotton asked.

"It don't matter," Will answered, nodded to the Comanche woman, and went out the door. He didn't want his name to get out. There were too many outlaws and Texas Rangers who might find it interesting that a deputy marshal out of Fort Smith was working in Texas. He seriously doubted that his name would be well known here in Texas, but decided that caution was the best policy. Outside, he untied the lead rope and handed it to Cotton. "The rope's yours, too," he said as he stepped up into the saddle. "You say I can strike that wagon road to Fort Worth about twelve miles south of here, right?" Cotton said that was a fact, so Will touched his hat in a farewell gesture and started south. He figured he had been lucky to come out of his encounter with Jack Dunn and Calvin Wallace alive, and he was riding away with a clear forty-five-dollar profit.

Chapter 14

Just as Cotton had told him, he struck a common wagon trail after about twelve miles. It angled off to the southeast in the general direction Will figured Fort Worth should be. For the first time since leaving Oklahoma Territory, he was not sure he was still on Ansel Beaudry's trail. The road he was riding now had tracks of all kinds, showing heavy farm traffic, and there was no way he could pick any tracks out and be sure they were Beaudry's. All he was banking on was Cotton's claim that Beaudry had stopped at his store and asked about the road to Fort Worth. It wasn't much to go on, but that's all he had, so he decided he would trust to luck that he could find some evidence that Ansel had passed this way. His first clue came to him after he had ridden approximately fifteen miles.

He had pushed on a few miles farther than he normally would have before stopping to rest his horses, but there had been no good source of water since taking the road to Fort Worth. When he finally came to a creek, he rode off the road and followed the creek for about thirty yards to a grassy clearing that broke the line of trees bordering the creek. There was a cornfield on the other side of the wide, slow-moving creek, so he figured the creek was probably the property line for somebody's farm. The corn had long since been harvested, leaving the brown, dried-out stalks to await plowing. As he guided Buster into the clearing, he saw right away that he wasn't the first to rest his horses there, for he saw the remains of several campfires. The thought occurred to him that Beaudry might have stopped there, since he had ridden the same distance as he had from Cotton Poole's store. There was no way to tell, however.

After he released the horses to drink and graze, he gathered what wood he could find for a small fire to make some coffee. As he sat there drinking his coffee, he was suddenly aware of some movement in the corn rows on the other side of the creek. The movement was slight, like that caused by a small animal—or an Indian stalking an unsuspecting man drinking a cup of coffee. He chuckled to himself for having such a thought, for the Indians had long ago been moved out of this part of Texas. Even so, he subconsciously reached over and pulled his rifle closer, while keeping his eye on the movement of the corn stalks. Whatever caused it was obviously coming in his direction and was now only a few feet from the end of the row. Finally, the stalker emerged from the cornfield. It was a small boy who looked to be no more than seven or eight. He wore overalls and a straw hat, and was barefooted, even though it was almost fall. Will could not help remembering himself at that age, thinking he must have looked about the same as the boy. The youngster came down to the creek and crossed over, balancing on a couple of logs that served as a bridge. Once across, he came straight toward Will.

"Howdy," Will greeted him when he approached his fire.

"Howdy," the boy returned. "Whatcha doin' settin' there drinkin' coffee?"

Will laughed. "I'm sittin' here drinkin' coffee, just like you said."

"Papa said he wished to hell folks wouldn't stop here to camp. First of the summer some feller went off and didn't put his fire out. Papa said it was lucky I saw it, 'cause the wind blew some skunkweed on it and we had to put it out. Papa's afraid somebody's gonna start a fire in these trees and he won't see it in time to put it out."

"Is that a fact?" Will replied. "Well, I reckon your pa is lucky to have you keep an eye on this spot. I'm glad you told me. You don't have to worry, I'll be sure to bury this fire before I leave here." He could almost feel the boy's eyes as he looked at his simple camp. "You want some coffee?" Will asked, then paused. "Do you drink coffee?"

"Yes, sir," he replied at once. "I drink it, but we don't always have a lotta coffee, so I don't get none too often."

"Well, I've messed around here and made more than I can drink, so I'd consider it a favor if you'd help me out, then I wouldn't have to waste it." He pointed to one of the packs lying near his saddle. "Look in that bag yonder. There's a cup in that bag." The boy went at once to the pack pointed out. "I ain't got any sugar, though," Will said. "Can you drink it black?"

"Yes, sir, that's the way Papa drinks it." He found

the cup and returned. "What's your name?" the boy asked as he watched Will pour his cup of coffee.

"My name's Will," he said. "What's yours?"

"Mark Taylor Thompson," the boy replied, pronouncing each syllable clearly and proudly.

"That's an awful lotta name to carry," Will teased. "Your pa must figure you're man enough to handle it. They call you Mark?"

"No, sir, they call me Skeeter," the boy replied. "That's what Papa said I looked like when I was born."

Will laughed and said, "Well, Skeeter's a good name, too. Do you come over the creek and drink coffee with other people who stop here?"

"No, sir," Skeeter replied. "You're the first one offered me any coffee. One time a man said he'd cut some strips off my behind and use 'em for bacon if he caught me snoopin' around his packs."

"Sounds like he mighta been carryin' something in his packs he didn't want anybody to see," Will said, still just amusing himself making conversation with the boy.

"I bet it weren't nothin' but guns and such, 'cause he talked like a mean man."

Skeeter's comment caused Will to realize he had let his mind go idle. "How long ago was that man campin' here?"

"Yesterday," the boy answered, then changed his mind. "No, day before yesterday. Mama made me take a bath yesterday. She said I'd been playin' with the pigs again."

"Was he a big man with a big black beard, ridin' a gray horse?" Will asked.

"Yes, sir, that's the man. One of his horses was gray. You know him?"

"Yep, I sure do," Will said. "And you were right, he is a mean man." He had the confirmation he needed. He was still on Ansel Beaudry's trail. "How 'bout it, Skeeter? I'll bet you know how far it is from here to Fort Worth. That's where this road goes, ain't it?"

"Yes, sir, this is the Fort Worth road, but it's a long ways from here."

"You ever hear your daddy say how many miles it is?" Will pressed, hoping by chance the boy might have heard him mention it. When Skeeter said he never had, Will shrugged indifferently. He had no idea how far he was from Fort Worth, and he would really like to know. He felt like he was running blind since he hadn't a clue if Beaudry was trying to reach that cattle town, or it was just on the way to his real destination. Where was Beaudry heading in Texas? All he had heard about Ansel Beaudry was that he operated in Missouri and Kansas, and he concentrated on robbing banks. So why didn't he head north to the territory he was familiar with when he ran from Grassy Creek? Once again, Will was prompted to ask himself if he wasn't plum loco, trying to trail Beaudry, instead of turning it over to the Texas Rangers. But he knew it was because he owed Oscar Moon, and he wasn't ready to call off his hunt and leave the cold-blooded killer to disappear into the Texas plains.

He suddenly realized he had let his confusion over Beaudry's flight tie his mind in a knot, and he became aware of the boy's puzzled stare. "I almost went to sleep with my eyes open," Will declared. "I reckon I'd best think about gettin' my horses saddled up and get on the road if I'm ever gonna get to Fort Worth." Feeling the urgency again, he said, "You take your time to drink your coffee while I'm gettin' ready to ride. First thing, I've gotta kill this fire. We don't wanna start any forest fires, right?" He winked at Skeeter and received a wide grin in return.

When he had saddled Buster and loaded his packhorse, he took the coffee cup Skeeter handed him and did a quick rinsing in the creek before returning it to his packs. "Well, it's been a pleasure meetin' you, Skeeter," he declared. "Tell your papa that he doesn't have to worry about the woods catchin' on fire today." Skeeter didn't reply. He stepped back and watched Will wheel the big buckskin and start back toward the road. When he could no longer see him, he crossed back over the creek and ran home to tell his folks about the stranger who shared his coffee. His mother would scold him again for approaching drifters who had stopped by the creek to camp.

Will had ridden for almost fourteen or fifteen miles when he caught first sight of a river. The road he traveled angled toward the river, then turned to follow it. He decided that was a good sign because it meant he didn't have to look for a creek or stream when it was time to camp, as long as the road stayed with the river. He figured he could push on for another ten or twelve miles before the horses would be ready for a rest. That was about as far as he wanted to push himself as well, because his stomach was beginning to remind him that he had had nothing more than a little coffee since starting out that morning. A little over an hour later, he saw what appeared to be a house, or building of some kind, on the bank of the river. The oak trees had been cleared around it to provide a wide yard. When he got a little closer, he decided it was a store or saloon since he saw a couple of horses tied to a hitching rail in front. The sight seemed to trigger an alarm in his empty stomach, for his first thought was the possibility of buying something to eat more satisfying than the bacon and hardtack he planned to fix for himself. "Maybe we can buy some grain for you and your partner," he said to Buster. He had lost the feeling of urgency that had driven him for the past few days. It had been replaced by one of patient determination, for he realized that finding Ansel Beaudry was not going to be quick or easy, with the drab information he had to go on.

He turned Buster off the road when he came to a path leading down into the yard and pulled the buckskin up to one end of the hitching rail. As a matter of habit, he checked the two horses already tied up there and noticed a rifle still in the saddle scabbard on each horse. That usually meant a peaceful customer. When he stepped down, however, he pulled his Winchester, also a matter of habit, and took a look around him at the small barn and corral, before stepping up on the porch. Inside, he found himself in one large room that held a general merchandise store on one side and three small tables set along the wall on the other side. There were two men sitting at one of the tables. Will assumed that side of the room served as a saloon. As he pushed the door open wide, he looked into a stranger's smiling face, beaming pleasantly at him from behind the counter. "Howdy, stranger, welcome," the man greeted him. "What can I do for ya? You needin' supplies or lookin' for a drink of likker? I've got both."

"Tell you the truth," Will answered, "I don't think I

could handle a drink of likker right now—my stomach's flat empty."

"I can take care of that, too," the man announced. "You've come at the right time. My wife's just about ready to put supper on the table. That's what those two fellows over there are waitin' for. Twenty-five cents will get you a solid meal with a cup of coffee. My wife's a mighty good cook. You can't get a better supper anywhere for that price." The two men seated at the table were both staring at him by then.

"You just talked me into it," Will replied at once.

"Won't be but a couple of minutes," the owner assured him. "What's your name, young feller? I believe this is your first time in my store. You from around here?"

"Nope, just passin' through, on the way to Fort Worth," Will answered, hesitated to consider, then decided that it didn't really matter, so he said, "Will Tanner."

"Glad to know you, Will. My name's Sid Worley."

"While we're waitin' for supper, there are a few things I need to buy," Will said. "Some coffee, ten pounds; a sack of flour; about ten pounds of bacon; and some oats for my horses, if you've got any. If you ain't, I'll take whatever kind of grain you've got."

"Yes, sir," Sid replied. "I'll take care of it, but first I'll go tell Bella she's got one more for supper. Why don't you take a seat at one of the tables and supper will be right out in a minute."

Will started to turn away from the counter, but stopped to ask a question. "What river is this you're settin' on?"

"The Brazos," Sid answered.

Will walked across the room and sat down at the

table next to the one where the two men were seated, taking a chair facing them. He was aware of their staring the whole time he was talking with Sid, so he wasn't surprised when they struck up a conversation with him. "You ain't from around these parts," one of them commented. A stocky man with a pudgy face covered with hair from his ears down, he grinned as if he had made a joke. "If you're ridin' the grub line, it's a bad time of year for that. Ain't none of the big outfits hirin' now. Ain't that right, Junior?"

"That's a fact, Rufus," the one called Junior replied. "How long you been lookin'? You didn't even know you was on the Brazos River." Finding that humorous, both men chuckled.

Will smiled. He had hoped the scruffy-looking pair were just cowhands interested in a drink and a good supper, but it now appeared that they were also interested in amusing themselves at his expense. When they had finished laughing, he said, "I ain't ridin' the grub line, I ain't lookin' for work right now. I'm just goin' to Fort Worth."

At that moment, a small boy of about six or seven came out of the kitchen door, carrying a saucer with a cup of coffee on it. He walked very deliberately toward Will, being careful not to spill a drop. "Mama said to bring you this coffee," the boy said, holding the hot liquid with both hands on the saucer, afraid he might tip it to one side or the other. His nervousness did not get unnoticed by Junior.

When Will reached out to take the cup, Junior suddenly blurted, "Boo!" Then both men laughed hilariously when the boy jumped, splashing coffee out of the cup. Quick as a cat, Will took the cup and saucer in his steady hands, preventing any more than a swallow of coffee to spill.

"No problem, son," Will said gently. "The saucer caught all but a few drops of it."

"You might notta spilled much of that coffee, kid, but you better check your britches. The way you jumped, you mighta peed your pants," Junior crowed.

"He mighta peed his pants!" Rufus echoed excitedly.

The boy stood fixed, his eyes wide with fright, so Will took him by the shoulders and turned him around. "Don't pay any attention to that loudmouth," he told him. "Go on back to the kitchen." He gave him a gentle push toward the kitchen door and the boy quickly left the room.

Still laughing over scaring the boy, Junior bellowed, "If she sends that young 'un back here with our plates, I'll bet you a dollar I'll make him dump stew all over the floor."

"The hell you say," his hairy-faced friend said. "You done scared him the first time. If he comes out here again, he'll be ready for you. I'll take that bet."

"He might think he's ready, but I'll make him jump higher'n that counter yonder," Junior boasted confidently. Will didn't say anything for a few moments. The boy's father was behind the counter, collecting from the shelves the items Will had ordered. When it appeared Sid Worley wasn't going to say anything to his unruly customers, Will realized that he was probably afraid to. "You watch him," Junior went on. "I'll make him jump."

"You do and I'll bust your nose for you," Will calmly promised.

There followed a moment of complete silence

before Junior asked the question, his gruff tone menacing now. "What did you say?"

Well past disgust for the simpleminded bully, Will had no patience for the two miscreants. "You heard what I said. Leave the boy alone. Haven't you two got anything better to do than torment little children?"

"Yeah, I got somethin' better to do, big talk, I'm thinkin' I'm fixin' to whip your ass." He pushed his chair back from the table.

"Whip his ass, Junior, whip his ass!" Rufus blurted in childlike excitement, obviously having seen his friend take advantage of his size on many such occasions.

Junior rose to his feet and made a show of rotating his shoulders forward as if loosening them up. "Junior," Will said, "I've got so many things on my mind right now, things a lot more important than a fistfight with you. I just wanna enjoy a good supper without havin' you two spoilin' it, so sit down and let's eat supper."

Neither Junior nor his half-wit friend could believe what they were hearing from the stranger. It stopped Junior for only a moment, however. "Mister, you've been chewin' on loco weed or somethin'. I'm fixin' to break your back."

"I'm askin' you politely this time," Will said. "Sit down and the lady can bring us some supper." He knew it was useless, but he warned him, anyway. "Don't do it, Junior." Junior simply grinned in response and started toward him, his ham-sized fists up before him, ready to throw a punch. He hesitated when Will showed no sign of rising to the bait, then he snorted like a bull and charged. Almost in one swift move, Will came up from his chair, grabbing his rifle as he did. When Junior threw the first haymaker, Will ducked under it and came up inside the brute's arms with his rifle, butt first, with all the force he could muster. His aim was accurate, the butt of his rifle slammed squarely across Junior's nose. It was enough to stagger the big man and before he could regain his senses, Will delivered another blow with the rifle, this time with the barrel against the side of Junior's head. The second blow dropped him to the floor, and before he landed, Will turned to Rufus in anticipation of his reaction, his rifle aimed at the stunned half-wit, the hammer cocked. Rufus immediately had second thoughts and quickly removed his hand from the .44 he had thought to draw.

"Come on," Will said. "I'll help you pick him up and get him on his horse, then you can take him away from here to wherever you're campin' tonight."

Completely subdued now, with no thoughts toward challenging the man who had just destroyed his image of an indestructible man, Rufus meekly did as he was told. "Back to the ranch," he muttered. "I'll take him back to the ranch."

"Good," Will said, and grabbed one of Junior's arms while directing Rufus to take the other one. "All right, pull him up." They got him on his feet long enough to let him drop across Will's shoulder. He couldn't help recalling Lucy Tyler's assailant in the Morning Glory when he loaded him on his shoulder. The difference being Junior felt like a railroad cross-tie, the weight driving his feet into the floor. *At least this one isn't on a staircase*, he thought as he headed quickly for the door, Rufus and Sid following. With help from Sid, Rufus and Will managed to lay Junior across his saddle, then Will and Sid stood by the rail watching Rufus ride out of sight before going back inside.

Inside, Will started to apologize for losing customers for him, but Sid was quick to stop him. "Listen, I wanna thank you for what you did. I thank you for stickin' up for my boy like you did. I always hate to see any of that crew stop in here. It ain't very often, but every time it costs me trouble of some kind—broken glasses, busted chairs, broken window, always something. I need to apologize to you. You just stopped in for a good supper and had to run into some of that sorry crowd." He paused a moment before making another comment. "I heard you tell them you weren't lookin' for work, you were just passin' through. The way you took care of those two, though, I'd figure you for a gunman or a Texas Ranger."

"Neither one," Will replied, and changed the subject. "I take it their ranch is close to here."

"About twenty-five miles east of here," Sid said. "Those two you just met are just cowhands for the big outfit. There's probably fifteen or twenty that work for the Hornet's Nest. That's what folks around here call that ranch, and most of 'em that's been in here was pretty much like Junior and Rufus, troublemakers."

"Must be a sizable ranch, if they've got that many hands workin' for 'em," Will commented.

"About fifteen thousand acres is what I've heard," Sid said. "I don't know anybody that's ever been to the ranch headquarters. Most folks are too scared to go anywhere near the place. In the first of summer, when they drive cattle north, they always have a lot of cows that look like they might be Mexican cattle. Course, you can't really tell, it's just what folks say."

"Hornet's Nest, huh?" Will grunted. "Is it a fairly new outfit?"

"No, it was here before I built this store, and I'll tell you the truth. If I'd known about it before, I'da found me a place somewhere else."

Ready to change the subject to something that was more important to him, Will said, "Well, let's see if your wife thinks it's safe enough to eat whatever it is I smell cookin' back there. I might wanna heat up my coffee, though. I think it's gotten a little cold, what with all the excitement." He hesitated a moment to say one thing more. "If you don't mind, I think I'll pull my horses around back of your store. I don't think we'll see any more of Junior and Rufus tonight, but I'd hate to have one of 'em take a shot at my horses, just outta spite.

Sid went to the kitchen to assure his wife it was safe to bring out a plate of food for their remaining customer. Shortly after, she appeared carrying a plate piled high. Sid introduced her to Will when she placed the plate before him. "I understand your coffee's gotten cold," she commented with a little smile. "I'll get you some hot." He thanked her graciously and dived in without another moment's delay.

A few seconds later, Sid came from the kitchen, carrying a plate of food. "If you don't mind, I'll set down and join you," he said, "since you don't have no more company for supper." He chuckled in appreciation of his humor. "Bella will eat with the boys."

"You've got more than one boy?" Will asked, having seen only the one delivering his coffee.

"That was Sammy. He's eight years old. His brother, Joe, is two years younger almost to the day."

"Sounds like you've got a good start on a nice family," Will said. Even as he said it, he couldn't help but wonder if Sid had enough backbone to defend his family from the likes of the hands from the Hornet's Nest. He silently wished him luck. When Bella came in to refill their cups and see if they needed anything else, he complimented her on her cooking, meaning it sincerely. When he had eaten all he possibly could, he held up his hands in surrender when she came back with the biscuit plate again. "I couldn't possibly eat another bite," he pleaded. "And to be honest, I think I'd best pay you for two suppers 'cause that's what I ate."

"You'll not pay us for any," Sid said. "We owe you for what you did with our friends from the Hornet's Nest." Will insisted that he should pay, but there was no winning that argument, so in the end, he thanked them graciously. They sat and talked for a little while longer, but finally Will declared that it was time he set out to find a spot to camp and take care of his horses. "Why don't you camp here tonight?" Sid asked. "There's a good spot by the river where I graze my horses and you could have breakfast with us before you go in the mornin'." When Will seemed to hesitate, Sid confessed, "Tell you the truth, I wouldn't mind havin' you stay overnight."

He didn't have to say why. Will knew he was concerned that Junior might come back looking for revenge, if he recovered enough tonight. "That's hard to pass up," he said. "Reckon I just might take you up on that." He started to get up to leave, but Bella came in from the kitchen to join them, so he decided it polite to sit a little while longer and visit with her. They talked about the struggle to build their modest business and the promise of more settlers finding the territory. "It's too bad the Hornet's Nest can't help you more," Will said. "A ranch that size could sure need a lot of supplies."

"Yeah, they could," Sid replied, "but they don't. The old man, Mica Beaudry, doesn't buy a nickel's worth of supplies from us. He gets all his supplies packed in from Fort Worth."

His statement stopped Will cold! He wasn't sure he had heard correctly. He had to ask him to repeat it. "Who did you say?"

"Mica Beaudry," Sid said. "He's the man who owns Hornet's Nest, and from what folks tell me, a meaner pirate ain't never been born."

Thoughts were whirling around so fast and furious in Will's brain that he was not sure he could believe what he had just heard. "Beaudry," he repeated, then spelled it out the way he had seen it on Dan Stone's telegram.

"That's right, Beaudry," Sid said, astonished by Will's sudden reaction to the name. "You know him?"

"Has he got a son, or a brother, or some kin named Ansel?" Will asked, ignoring Sid's question.

"I can't rightly say," Sid apologized, recognizing now the urgency his casual mentioning of the name had generated in Will's face. "Like I said, nobody outside that ranch knows what goes on in Hornet's Nest. I think there's a son, but I ain't certain. I'm sorry I can't tell you more about 'em. Is it important?" He couldn't help but ask.

"No, no," Will replied hurriedly, "it's not important." His thoughts were screaming in direct contradiction to his statement. Beaudry did know where he was going! He wasn't just running without a definite destination. He was going home. Consequently, contrary to all the information Will had been given, Beaudry's roots were not all planted in Missouri and Kansas. Hornet's Nest was where he was running to. "You say Hornet's Nest is about twenty-five miles east of here?" Sid nodded. Will continued, "How do I find it?"

"There's a wagon track that runs off the Fort Worth road that's supposed to lead to the ranch headquarters. You won't have no trouble findin' it, there's a sign up that says 'No Trespassing, Violators Will Be Shot.'"

"How far off the Fort Worth road is it to the ranch headquarters?" Will asked.

"I don't have no idea," Sid replied. "Like I said, I ain't never been there." He studied Will's face as the young stranger thought about what he had said. "Will, I don't know what you're thinkin', and it ain't none of my business, anyway, but it ain't healthy to mess with that pack of wolves. About two years back, there was a Texas Ranger rode back on that trail to Hornet's Nest, lookin' for one of their men who killed two fellows outside a church. There ain't been no sign of him since. There was a Texas Ranger posse sent out from Austin to investigate, but they didn't find nothin', no body, no horse, no saddle, and Mica Beaudry claimed no ranger ever showed up at his ranch house. There weren't nothin' the Rangers could do but ride on back to Austin."

"I 'preciate what you're sayin'," Will said. "I'm just curious, that's all. Sounds like this Beaudry family is livin' in a world all their own." He sat with Sid and

Bella for another half hour before excusing himself to set up his camp. Sid got up and went with him to help carry his supplies.

"You're comin' for breakfast in the mornin', ain'tcha?" Sid asked. He thought Will might have changed his mind, based on his reactions after hearing about Mica Beaudry.

"I sure am," Will replied right away. "After seein' how good she can cook stew and biscuits, I've gotta see how she does with breakfast."

Chapter 15

Will slept with his horses close during the night. The grassy clearing Sid Worley used as his pasture was not very big, so there was no temptation for the horses to wander. Will didn't even bother to hobble his pack-horse. For a good part of the night, he kept a close eye on the store and the yard around it. He wasn't sure how badly he had hurt Junior, so he decided it was a good idea to keep alert. It was not hard to do, since he was still rolling the information about Hornet's Nest around in his head. If he could believe Sid, Hornet's Nest was like a fortress, and what was hard to understand was why Ansel Beaudry had not gone to this fortress in the beginning. It sounded like a much better place to hide out than Grassy Creek, and he would not have needed a guide to Hornet's Nest. He knew where that was. Instead, he enlisted Tom Daly to guide him to Grassy Creek. *I don't reckon any of that matters*, he thought to himself. *What matters is that I've got a pretty good idea where Ansel Beaudry is now.* And he had to be at Hornet's Nest—it was too much of a stretch to think it merely a coincidence he had the same name as the owner of Hornet's Nest. So the task now would be to find out just how much of a job it would be to get to Ansel at Hornet's Nest. Judging by what Sid told him about that ranch, it would amount to trying to attack a small army.

With that to challenge his mind, he led his horses up to the store, intending to enjoy a home-cooked breakfast before he set out to invade the pack of wolves, as Sid referred to the men of Hornet's Nest. According to his watch, it was six o'clock on the nose, the hour Bella had said breakfast would be ready. He had been up at first light and saddled Buster, then loaded the packs on the other horse. He planned to eat and leave as soon as he properly could without being rude, since he had twenty-five miles to ride before he struck the trail into Hornet's Nest.

Todd Beaudry stopped short, startled by a man coming out of the parlor, not sure he wasn't seeing things that weren't there. After a few moments, he realized who he was looking at. "Ansel Beaudry," he pronounced first and last names slowly, as if the words left a foul taste in his mouth. "What the hell are you doin' here?"

"Hello, Todd," Ansel replied. "Maybe I came home to see if you're still the same as you were when I left." The two brothers stood glaring at each other in the darkened hallway between the dining room and the parlor.

"Why'd you come crawlin' back here after all this time?" Todd demanded. "How the hell did you get by the lookouts and come walking right in the house, like you were family? Somebody's gonna get his back broke for lettin' you slip in here. What the hell do you want, anyway?"

Ansel sneered to show his contempt for his younger brother. "Why, I just came back to see if you had all dried up and gone to hell. Are you still stealin' Mexican cattle, two or three at a time, thinkin' someday you'll really be cattle rustlers?"

"Get the hell outta here, Ansel. You ain't got no business in this house. Get out!"

"My business is my own," Ansel said, "and it ain't none of yours, so get the hell outta my way." He started to walk toward him and Todd dropped his hand to rest on the handle of his .44. Seeing his threatening move, Ansel smirked and demanded, "Are you fixin' to draw on me, little brother?" He quickly grabbed Todd's arm. "You fixin' to draw on me?" he repeated as he clamped down on Todd's right arm, taking advantage of his superior strength. "I'll bust you up good, little boy," he threatened, and clamped down on Todd's arm while his brother struggled hopelessly to free himself. "You're rememberin' now, ain'tcha, boy? I was always twice as strong as you." He threw him hard against the wall. "Now, get the hell outta my way before I lose my temper." He stalked down the narrow corridor to the kitchen door.

"What is all that racket?" Mae Beaudry complained, and started toward the hallway door to see for herself. When about eight feet from the door, it suddenly opened to present her ex-husband standing, smirking, in the doorway. "Ansel!" she gasped, not sure she wasn't seeing a ghost, and grabbed the corner of the table to keep from falling. Unable to say more, she backed away, steadying herself on the table until she was stopped when she backed into the solid body of her father-in-law. Mica Beaudry did not speak at once. His eyes, still sharp as they were in his youth, were now fixed upon one he had driven from his home six years ago.

In the shocking silence caused by this evil specter's sudden appearance after so long a time, only Ansel had a smile on his face. "Hello, Mae, darlin', ain't you gonna give your ol' husband a kiss?" The frightened woman backed around behind her father-in-law for protection.

"She ain't your wife," Mica said. "You run off and left her, so you ain't got no claim on her. Ain't nothin' else here that belongs to you, neither." He paused for a moment when Todd walked in behind Ansel, prompting him to step aside, so he could keep an eye on his brother until he walked past him. When Todd went to stand beside his father, staring defiantly at their unwelcome guest, Mica demanded, "What did you come back here for? I told you when you left not to come back. What's the matter? They chase you outta Missouri? You runnin' from the law, so now you bring 'em back here to my doorstep?"

"Howdy, Pa," Ansel replied, his smug smile still in place. "I knew you'd be glad to see me again, since I'm the only son you've got that's worth a damn." His sarcastic grin widened when Todd grunted threateningly in response to his remark. He paused to make sure Todd didn't decide to make a move on him, before turning his attention back to his father. "I ain't runnin' from no lawman, I just thought it was time I paid you a visit." He cocked an eye at Mae again. "And

I figured my little wife must be pinin' away, wonderin' if I was ever comin' home again." He chuckled and commented, "Looks like she ain't so little anymore, though. I swear, darlin', you look like you ain't strayed very far from the trough since I've been gone." Her face, a fearful mask, Mae moved from behind Mica and stepped between him and Todd, clutching Todd's arm for support. Her gesture brought a spark of awareness to Ansel's eyes. "Well, I'll be damned," he muttered. "You took up with Todd, didn'tcha?" he accused. "Well, I'll be . . . How long did you wait before you jumped in the bed with him?"

"You were gone two years before me and Todd got married," Mae blurted.

"Married?" Ansel laughed. "How the hell could you get married? You're still married to me."

"No, she ain't," his father said. "They jumped over the broom together when I pronounced you dead. And that ain't changed none, as far as I'm concerned."

"Hah," Ansel snorted, amused. "If that ain't somethin', but I reckon that's the way things are supposed to be, Todd sniffin' around to get my leavings, just like it always was. I don't see no young 'uns runnin' around, though, so I was right when I said she was barren. Ma knew it, too—where is Ma?"

"Your mama died two years ago," his father answered. "Mae's the woman of this house now."

"Is that a fact?" Ansel responded, not really saddened by news of the passing of his mother. "Well, that's good. That's two of us that got out of this rat's nest." He fashioned a contemptuous smile for his father and said, "I forgot, you like to call this place a hornet's nest."

"Damn you," Mica roared, fed up now with his wayward son's insolence. "I don't know how you got the idea you could come back to this ranch anytime you please. Things have changed a helluva lot since you left here. You always had ideas too big for you to handle, so now that I've made somthin' out of this ranch, I'll be damned if you're gonna move back in. I've got a crew of seventeen men workin' this operation in the season, and eight this time of year. And that don't include Todd, who's my foreman. They've got orders to shoot trespassers on sight, and that's what you are, a trespasser. I don't know how you got in here in the first place, but I'm fixin' to have Todd call up a few of the boys to escort your ass right back outta here."

"That was a fine speech," Ansel declared, his smirk replaced by a dead-serious expression. "Now I'll tell you how things are gonna be. In the first place, this damn ranch is the last place I'd wanna be stuck in. I don't want any part of it. I need to be out of sight for a few days and that's all. I've got money and I've got plans. I don't need anything from you except two or three days. I coulda gone somewhere else, but I figure you owe me, since you're my family, and you've got enough men to keep people from snoopin' around." He paused to let that sink in, then continued. "Now, that's all I need from you, but I'll tell you what's gonna happen if I don't get what I want. I'll guarantee you, I'll take down any of your men who come after me. And if it comes down to family, well, we'll just have to see what happens. So how about it, old man? Let me have a bed and three meals a day for two or three days. I'll pay you just like I would in a hotel. You don't bother me and I won't bother you, then when I leave, I won't be comin' back."

Mica thought about his proposal for a few seconds. He had no doubt that Ansel wasn't bluffing. There would be killing, maybe even family members would be among the victims. He knew his son was capable of extreme violence, he seemed to thrive on it. "How do I know you've got money to pay room and board?"

"Because I say I have," Ansel came back. "Have we got a deal or not?"

Both Todd and Mae were staring at the old man, shaking their heads vigorously, trying to influence his decision, while he thought it over. Finally, he gave in. "All right," he said. "Dollar a day for the bed and seventy-five cents for the grub—three days, then you're outta here forever."

"Good, we'll call it a truce. You hate me and I hate you, but if we stay outta each other's way, it'll work all right. I just hope to hell Mae ain't doin' the cookin'. She couldn't fry an egg without it lookin' like a piece of shoe sole." He cut his eyes over toward the mortified woman and grinned when she responded.

"You go to hell," Mae spat. Her obvious anger caused him to chuckle, which served to inflame her more. "Since you left, Todd and Papa have built the ranch up to where I don't have to do the cookin'. We've got a cook to do that, and if you don't like Lorena's cookin', you can take off again."

"You'll not sit at my table with my family," Mica stepped in. "You can eat when we eat, but you'll eat in the kitchen." He turned to address the cook when he noticed she was standing in the doorway listening to the argument. "You hear that, Lorena? He don't eat with the family."

"Yes, sir, Mr. Beaudry," Lorena replied. "No eat in dining room." She turned her gaze back upon the strange man, thinking he didn't look like his father or his brother. He more closely resembled a judge or a preacher, in her opinion. Back to Mica then, she announced, "Breakfast ready, you sit down now while it still hot."

"Good," Ansel sang out before anyone else could respond. "I'll find me a place in the kitchen." He went into the kitchen right behind Lorena, carrying his rifle and saddlebags with him. Behind him the estranged members of his family were left behind, still confused over what had just taken place. A deal with the devil, no less, Todd and Mae decided as they took their usual places at the dining room table and waited for Lorena to bring the platters and bowls. The unassuming Mexican woman was in the process of doing that, but was delayed a few minutes by the menacing stranger. "I'll set myself down right here at the end of this table," Ansel told her. He took a plate from a stack on the table and placed it before him. "What's that on the platter?" he asked. "Looks like pork chops."

"*Sí*, pork chops," she replied.

"Good, I ain't had pork chops in I don't know when. Here, bring that platter over here." When she did as he said, he poked around in the chops with his fork until he decided on the best, then speared two of them for himself. "What's that in the bowl?" When she replied that it was potatoes in that particular bowl, he spooned a sizable portion onto his plate with the chops. "That's fine," he said. "Take 'em on in to the dinin' room, then you can run them other two bowls by me before you take them in." When he was met with a mystified stare from her, he told her that this was to be the standard procedure as long as he was eating in her kitchen. "I'm payin' for my food, so I expect I'd best get served first." After she left to serve the others, he chuckled to himself when he heard the rapid discussion in subdued voices coming from the other room. It was too low, except for an occasional curse word, so he couldn't make it out, but he could pretty well imagine what the discussion was about.

When everyone was finished eating and Mae helped Lorena with the dishes, Ansel remained at his spot at one end of the kitchen table and drank coffee while he watched the women work. It didn't take long before Mae left the kitchen, unnerved by the feeling of Ansel's eyes upon her every move. In a few minutes, she returned with Ansel's father right behind her. "I reckon you've finished up your breakfast by now, ain't you?" Ansel smiled and nodded. His father went on. "Now, I reckon you need to take care of your horses and pack your gear where you're gonna bunk. That will be in the bunkhouse with the rest of the hired hands, so you can be close to the barn and your horses."

Ansel's smile returned. "Maybe so," he drawled, "but I ain't no hired hand. I think the proper thing for your returnin' son would be to stay right here in the house, right back in my old room—lotta memories in that room, right, Mae? Course, if somebody else is sleepin' in there, any other room that's empty will do. I'm willin' to be reasonable. I wouldn't wanna put anybody out." He had an idea that Todd and Mae were occupying his and Mae's old room. It was confirmed by the expression of disgust on Mae's face. She was about to express her disgust openly when Todd walked into the kitchen to see what was going on.

"What's all the talkin' about?" Todd wanted to know, glaring at Ansel, still seated at the table. "What are you gonna do, sit in the kitchen all day? Maybe you'd be best suited to help Lorena in the kitchen."

"Might at that," Ansel replied. "But right now we're decidin' if I move back in my old room, whether Mae wants to stay or move out. I think she's still tryin' to make up her mind."

"Why you low-down son of a bitch," Todd blurted, and started toward Ansel.

Ansel rose quickly to his feet. "Come on, little brother," he taunted. "You deserve a good whippin' for callin' your poor dead mama a bitch."

Mica stepped between them before the fight could start. "By God, that's enough," he swore. "You'll not set foot in my house again!" he railed at Ansel. "You decided six years ago that you ain't no part of this family, so you get your ass out of here. The bunkhouse is half-empty now, so I'll let you stay there for the time we agreed on. Then I want you off my land or I'll shoot you myself."

"Whatever you say, Papa," Ansel responded sarcastically. "I'll go to the bunkhouse, if it'll keep peace in the family." He had never intended to stay in the house from the beginning. There was too great a possibility to get his throat cut while he was asleep, but he had been unable to resist tormenting them with the prospect. "I'll still be takin' my meals here in the kitchen, just like we agreed." He picked up his rifle and saddlebags and walked out the back door.

"We can't let that devil hang around here, Papa," Todd complained. "You know somebody's bound to be chasin' him, and it must be Rangers or somebody to make him scared enough to come back here."

His father thought that over for a few moments before expressing his thoughts. "I'm thinkin' he mighta pulled off a big bank job and ran off with his and his partners' share of the money. That's what he's totin' in his saddlebags, I'll bet, and that's why he's carryin' 'em every step he takes, them and that rifle." He nodded in agreement with his own theory. "I'd like to get a look inside those bags."

"Who the hell is that?" Jim Brady asked Spot Morris when he looked up to see the stranger walking toward the barn, leading his horses. He had seen the two horses tied to a corner post of the front porch earlier that morning, but none of the men knew anything about them.

Spot turned and stared in the direction of the house for only a few seconds before replying, "Well, I'll be go to hell . . . Ansel." When Brady still seemed puzzled, Spot said, "Ansel Beaudry, that's the boss's oldest son."

"His oldest son?" Brady questioned. "I didn't think Boss had any son but Todd."

"I forgot, you ain't been here as long as I have," Spot said.

"Ain't none of us been here as long as you have," Brady replied. "What I can't understand is how come you're still here. I believe you're so good at keepin' out of sight that Boss just forgot you're on the payroll."

His attention back to the man walking toward them then, he asked, "How come we ain't seen this fellow before? Ansel, was that his name?"

"Boss run him off," Spot replied. "It was five or six years ago. Ansel was always in some kinda trouble. I think Boss and Miss Esther was hopin' Ansel would quit tryin' to buck Boss on everythin' when he married Mae."

"Married Mae?" Brady responded. "He was married to Mae?"

"That's a fact," Spot replied. "Then Ansel killed Arthur Goodman, who owned Goodman's Saloon in Fort Worth, in a fight over a whore and that brought the Texas Rangers out here lookin' for him. Ansel got away before they got here, and for a while there, Boss would come down on you if you even mentioned Ansel's name." He paused then as Ansel approached within easy hearing distance, curious to hear the reason for Ansel's reappearance after so many years. "Howdy, Ansel," Spot called out. "Ain't seen you in a coon's age." When Ansel looked surprised, Spot said, "Spot Morris, the cook. What brings you back home after all these years?"

"Spot Morris," Ansel echoed. "I remember you, but if you hadn't said your name, I couldn't have thought of it." He did remember Spot, hired as bunkhouse and chuck wagon cook. "Didn't remember you havin' all those gray whiskers." He took a moment to study the man Spot had been talking to, then asked, "Who's this you're talkin' to?"

"This here's Jim Brady," Spot answered. "He's the top hand, the foreman for your papa's ranch."

"I thought the old man said Todd was the foreman," Ansel said.

Spot cocked an eye at Brady before answering. "Well, that's a fact, I reckon you could say Todd's the official foreman, but Brady, here, is more like the workin' foreman."

A knowing grin broke out on Ansel's face. "So the old man lets Todd tell you what he wants done, and you have the men do it?" he asked Brady.

"That's about the size of it, Mr. Beaudry," Brady replied. "If you don't mind me askin', are you comin' back to take over runnin' this outfit?" His question caused a quick reaction from Spot, who knew very well that Mica had ordered Ansel never to return.

Ansel looked at Spot and grinned, knowing what he was thinking. "Maybe," he answered Brady. "I ain't decided yet. Let's just say I'm visitin' right now, and while I'm here, I'm bunkin' in with you and the men, so I can see how you're runnin' things. If I take over, I'm gonna want a strong top hand that ain't afraid to kick a little ass where it's necessary." Brady cocked his head back like a wild stallion in response, a response that Ansel found appropriate to a challenge. He decided he might be the man he wanted, if he ever contemplated a takeover of the ranch, which he had never considered until that moment. But in the short time he had been back, he had already seen signs of prosperity around the headquarters, and he passed through a great many cows on his ride from the river. His father and Todd had done a hell of a lot better job of building a cattle ranch than he had expected. He was beginning to think that maybe he had landed in the right spot, even though accidentally. If he was figuring things right, the law was looking for him in Kansas or Missouri, or farther west. Nobody should be looking for him in Texas. "Right now, I just wanna turn my horses out in the corral and get my possibles squared away in the bunkhouse," he said to Brady.

"I'll take care of your horses for you," Brady volunteered. "I can take 'em down by the river with the other horses, if you want."

"The corral will be all right for now," Ansel said. "I'll most likely want to saddle the gray up and take a little look around. It's been a long time since I've been on this range."

"I'll help you carry your stuff into the bunkhouse and we'll get you fixed up with a good bunk," Spot offered.

When they started toward the bunkhouse, Brady took the reins and led Ansel's horses to the barn. There were a lot of questions popping up in Brady's mind as he took care of the horses. Aside from the total surprise of Ansel Beaudry's appearance, he had to wonder about Ansel's apparently unnoticed arrival at the ranch house that morning. Sonny Pickens had the job of riding scout on the two-mile trail that led from the Fort Worth road back to the ranch headquarters last night. Sonny never showed up for breakfast this morning, so Brady had sent a couple of the men to look for him.

Ansel had made no mention of having seen Sonny that morning when he rode into the ranch. If Sonny was doing the job he was sent to do, he would have stopped Ansel. He would just have to wait until the men got back. Sonny might have gotten thrown off his horse or something like that. In the meantime, Brady thought it best to take good care of Ansel's horses and the supplies he had on his pack-horse. This Ansel fellow was a hell of a lot different from his brother, Todd, and there just might be a change in the way things were run around here. Even though he still ruled with an iron hand, old man Beaudry wasn't getting any younger. In spite of the bad blood in the past, it might be time for a change, and Brady wasn't convinced that Todd was strong enough to handle it.

Chapter 16

Will paused a good while to study the narrow trail that made its way through a gap in a long ridge that paralleled the road to Fort Worth. By the warning sign, he knew it was the entrance to the Hornet's Nest. Glancing at the hills on each side of the gap, he could imagine it was fairly easy for a lookout to see anyone entering the passage from either side. On the chance there might be a lookout sitting up on the hill now, he decided to backtrack a couple hundred yards, then circle back to climb the ridge short of the trail through the gap. He figured that would give him a better look at the trail beyond the ridge, so he wheeled Buster and started back. *I just hope I haven't picked the side there's a lookout parked on,* he thought.

He rode all the way up the hill to the top, then he dismounted and left Buster and his packhorse while he walked closer to the edge of the gap. As he had suspected, he could see the trail below him from this vantage point, as well as a long straight stretch of it as it led toward the river. He paused to think about what he intended to do and questioned the sensibility of it. It was not his custom to do his job with a sense of vengeance driving him, as it was in this case. His main incentive was to capture the man who had killed Oscar Moon, and he had to admit that he would not hesitate to kill Ansel Beaudry should he resist. Before going forward, he stopped to ask himself if he was letting his personal feelings strangle his common sense. Considering the opposition he was likely to face in an attempt to pluck Beaudry out of the den of wolves that was the Hornet's Nest, the smart thing to do would be to report to the closest Texas Rangers post. After all, the original purpose of this operation was to capture the gang of bank robbers. It mattered not whether it was a deputy marshal or a ranger who made the arrest. To further simplify the decision, he was out of his jurisdiction, and there was no question that it was up to the Rangers to make the arrest. The final point to consider was the odds he was up against. If he reported it to the Rangers, they could authorize a posse of men to storm the ranch. What he was about to do was just plain stupid, he told himself, and not conducive to living a long life. *I'm getting married in a couple of months,* he told himself. *I need to think about making sure I show up for the ceremony.* He started to turn back, but a movement in the trees on the other side of the trail, near the base of the gap, caught his eye.

He froze, waiting to see what or who caused the movement of the bushes below him. He watched as first one man on a horse emerged from the trees beside the trail, then a second rider came behind him. The second man was leading a horse with a body lying across the saddle. They started down the trail toward the ranch, and all thoughts of sensibility disappeared from Will's mind. The trail into the ranch was apparently watched, but there was probably not a better time to follow someone in, because it was doubtful there was anyone left to guard the entrance at this point. Someone, a trespasser, no doubt, had been killed and both men were taking the body back to the ranch. The chance that there was someone else still sitting atop the ridge on the other side of the gap was not likely, so he decided to see if he could get close enough to the ranch headquarters to see the situation he'd have to deal with.

Weaving his way through the trees, he led his horses down the slope to the foot of the hill. He could still see the two riders in the distance, so he waited to give them more time, just to be sure they didn't catch sight of him. "I know you've already done twenty-five miles," he said to Buster. "We oughta strike the river before very long, then I'll let you get some water." The buckskin snorted and the packhorse answered. Even though he reassured his horses, he wasn't sure how he could tarry by the river long enough to properly rest them. Nevertheless, he climbed back into the saddle and started out following the trail the two riders had taken. As he had promised Buster, they traveled a short distance before they struck the Brazos again. He crossed over before turning upstream to find a spot to hide while his horses rested.

Following the river, he kept going until he came to a bend where a grove of oak trees had formed a thick screen. The riverbank was high enough at this point to afford him protection in the event he had to defend himself against attack. He hesitated to decide if he should take the risk of unloading his horses. He might have to leave this riverbank on short notice. It was the packhorse that concerned him the most. He could pull Buster's saddle off very easily and put it back on in a hurry, if he had to. It wasn't that easy with the packhorse. But he wanted to rest them as best he could, so they'd be ready to run if it was called for. Every once in a while, he reminded himself how stupid he was to take the chance he was taking. Sid Worley's remark came to mind about the Texas Ranger who rode into Hornet's Nest and was never seen again. "What the hell," he finally muttered, and pulled the saddle off Buster, then unloaded the packs from Luther's horse and pulled its saddle off. If worse came to worst, he figured he could throw Buster's saddle back on, and if there wasn't enough time, he'd leave the packhorse behind.

While his horses nibbled grass down near the water, Will walked up to the edge of the trees to keep watch. There were a few cattle grazing nearby in small bunches, but no sizable herd, so he figured the most he would have to worry about would be a single cowhand looking for strays to drive back to the main herd. He looked back at his horses grazing and wished that there had been someplace to leave the packhorse before entering Beaudry land. It would be a whole lot easier if he didn't have the extra horse. He and Buster could work much better if it was just the two of them. He couldn't leave the packhorse to graze while he worked in closer to the ranch house— the risk that one of the ranch hands might find him was too great. The more he thought about it, the more convinced he became that it would be best to wait until dark before trying to get close to the ranch headquarters. On this open, rolling range, he would be too easily spotted in broad daylight, even at a distance. If he waited until dark, his horses would be well rested by then, as well, so the decision was easily made.

While Will Tanner waited for darkness on the bank of the Brazos River, the two men who had found the body of Sonny Pickens rode into the barnyard at ranch headquarters. An interested spectator peered out a bunkhouse window, watching as one of the men went straight to the ranch house to report. Ansel saw Brady walk out of the barn to meet the man holding Sonny's horse. In less than a couple of minutes, the other man came back with Mica Beaudry close behind. Ansel smiled to himself and walked out of the bunkhouse to join the small group gathering by the barn. He arrived in time to hear one of them telling his father that they had found Sonny's body where someone had dragged it back in the trees, and his horse was nearby.

"I reckon that explains why nobody tried to stop me when I rode in this mornin'," Ansel remarked as he walked up to join them. "I thought it was mighty damn easy for anybody to ride on our range."

His comment caused the two men who had found the body to pause to take an inquisitive look at the stranger. It also caused Mica to cock a critical eye in Ansel's direction. "Most folks around here know not to ride on *my* range," he said, making a point of emphasizing *my*.

"But he is the lookout, right?" Ansel asked, knowing full well he was the lookout who had made the mistake of trying to stop him that morning. "What's his name?"

"Sonny Ackens," Brady quickly answered.

Before he could say more, Ansel said, "So there's somebody trespassin' on Beaudry range right now," unaware that his statement was, in fact, absolutely true. "Might be a good idea to check on the cattle," he said, looking at Brady. He shifted his gaze to the two cowhands who had brought Sonny's body back. There was a look of total confusion on both faces. "I'm Ansel Beaudry," he said, "Boss's eldest son. I'll be around for a while."

"Maybe you will and maybe you won't," Todd said as he just then joined the gathering.

Ansel grinned and winked at Brady. "That's right, little brother, you never know about me, do ya?"

"How come nobody stopped you from ridin' in here this mornin'?" Todd demanded. "Maybe that's how Sonny got shot."

"That's a good question," Ansel replied at once. "Only anybody with a grain of sense would know, if I'da been stopped, I'da told him who I was, and he'da most likely rode back to headquarters with me to make sure I was who I said I was. I wouldn't have shot him, I didn't have no reason to." He looked at Brady and shook his head as if impatient with his brother. It had been unnecessary to kill Sonny, but he had not hesitated to shoot him for the simple reason he wanted to arrive at his father's house unannounced.

Already getting a strong feeling that there might be changes coming as far as who was going to be running the Hornet's Nest, Brady stepped in to introduce the two cowhands to Ansel. "This is Dan Riley and Junior Hutto, Ansel. They're both permanent hands here, have been for over three years."

Ansel nodded to each one, then commented to Junior, "You look like you got kicked by a mule."

Everyone but Mica and Todd laughed at that, and Brady japed, "That's what he said, but I think him and Rufus got into a little tussle at Worley's store."

"He was lucky he caught me when I warn't lookin'," Junior said, a slight flush now showing on his badly swollen nose.

"Maybe that's the same jasper that shot Sonny," Dan suggested, joking. "Maybe he's lookin' for you, Junior, lookin' to finish the work he started rearrangin' that ugly mug of yours." His comment spurred another wave of chuckles at Junior's expense.

"I don't reckon Sonny Pickens thinks his murder is as funny as some of you do," Mica reminded them. Up to that point, he had been thinking about Todd's suggestion that Sonny might have been shot by Ansel. Ansel was capable of cold-blooded murder, but Mica suspected that Ansel was thinking about taking control of Hornet's Nest. So it didn't make sense that he would kill one of the men he would need to run the ranch. He was disappointed that Todd didn't think of that. Even more, he was disgusted that Todd didn't stand up to Ansel on the matter. "Somebody came on my range and killed one of my men, and that ain't funny to me," Mica finally declared. "Brady, get everybody mounted up and find him." The laughter stopped immediately.

"You're right, Papa," Ansel commented at once.

"Instead of standin' around here jawin', we need to find that jasper fast and see what he's up to. I'll go with the men. Maybe Todd can take care of poor ol' Sonny and watch things here at the house." He turned at once and started toward the corral. Brady and Dan followed right behind him. Junior dropped the reins of the dead man's horse at Todd's feet and hurried after them.

"What the hell . . . ?" Todd growled, not sure what he should do. His father told him.

"Pick 'em up," he ordered, referring to the reins. As he watched Todd bend over to do so, he was unable to resist. He gave his son a firm kick in the butt, causing Todd to take several steps forward to keep from falling on his face.

"What did you do that for?" Todd whined.

"Never mind," Mica said. "Go find Spot and tell him to dig a grave for Sonny." Without another word, he turned and started back toward the house, lacking the patience at that moment to tell Todd of the disgust he felt for him. He was convinced that Ansel was already making moves to take over the operation of his ranch, and Todd was too weak to oppose him. *Ansel's got another think coming, if he thinks I'll roll over for him,* he thought. If Ansel planned a showdown for possession of Hornet's Nest, Mica would be more than ready for it, but for right now, there was a more important issue to face. There was a trespasser on his range for some purpose, and it was serious enough to have caused him to kill one of his men. It was important enough to find that man, or men, who did it. Once that was settled, the issue of his son's ambition would be squashed before it could go any further.

In a matter of minutes, all of the search party were saddled up and mounted. Brady pulled up even with Ansel and waited to see if he was going to give any orders. "How many men have we got?" Ansel asked.

"We've got three men that are roundin' up strays down as far as Coyote Creek," Brady replied. "That's the southern boundary of Beaudry range. They'll work it in three sections and cover our range all the way from east to west."

"So you're sayin' the rest of us need to split up to cover the part north of here, all the way across the river to the road to Fort Worth," Ansel said.

"Yes, sir," Brady replied. "If it was me, I'd send Dan east to Duck Wallow Creek, and Junior west to Possum Run Creek. They can work north from there till they strike the river and work back toward the center. Me and you could ride right up the trail till we hit the river, then split up and work that small section between the river and the road. We oughta all meet up again at the trail back to the house, this side of the river."

"That sounds like the thing to do," Ansel said. "Let's get started." They split up and began a search of the Beaudry range with Ansel the only one thinking there was no trespasser. He was the killer they thought they were looking for, so he found the whole endeavor highly amusing. As he rode beside Brady, he thought he could feel the foreman's total switching of loyalties from Mica and Todd to him. *Strange,* he thought, *that I hadn't even considered taking over control of Hornet's Nest until I came back here.* And now, he felt it was what he was meant to do all along. His father was too old to fight him, and his brother was too weak. He would permit both of them to stay on—he was not an unreasonable man—but if Todd became too much trouble, he wouldn't hesitate to make Mae a widow.

Will tried to pass some of the afternoon by checking and cleaning his weapons, but the time was creeping by as he waited for darkness to descend over the river. It would be some time yet, for the afternoon sun showed no signs of being in a hurry. He took a closer look at the stock of his Winchester and rubbed his finger along the fine crack that ran the length of it. He was going to have to fix that when he got to a carpenter's shop, or cabinetmaker's. He didn't realize at the time that he had struck the oversized bully called Junior hard enough to split his rifle stock. *If I ever see him again,* he said to himself, *maybe I'll tell him he owes me money to fix my rifle.* He held the rifle up to take a final look at the stock before getting to his feet to walk up to the edge of the trees again to make sure he wasn't going to have company.

Almost to the edge of the grove of oaks, he suddenly stepped back and flattened himself against a large tree trunk, not sure if he had been seen or not. Holding the Winchester in front of him, pressed tightly against his body, he slowly eased around the trunk until he could see the lone rider approaching from the west. He immediately thought of his horses back down at the edge of the river and Buster's habit of alerting him whenever other horses were near. The rider was steadily approaching, riding parallel to the line of trees, and showed no signs of riding through them to scout the riverbanks. If he continued along that line, just maybe he would never know the horses were there, but that was hoping for a hell of a lot of luck. Then as the rider came almost opposite the tree Will was hiding behind, Will recognized him. It was Junior! He could see the dull-witted expression, even with the bruised and swollen nose. This was too much of a coincidence. This man was pure bad luck. On the other hand, maybe not, for anyone but Junior would most likely be searching beyond the trees, more inclined to look for a stray cow down by the water. *Now, damn it, Buster,* he thought, *don't you give us away.* He waited, his rifle ready to fire, but there was no signal from Buster, and Junior rode steadily on, along the tree line, until eventually disappearing from sight.

It occurred to him that Junior wasn't searching for strays. Had he been, he would have surely looked down at the river's edge, where cattle might be drinking. In fact, he had paid no attention at all to the few small groups of cows he rode past. Will's thoughts returned to the two men he had seen heading back to the ranch and leading a body on a horse. Maybe the dead man was not a trespasser, as he had assumed, but instead, one of the Beaudry ranch hands. If that was the case, Junior, and probably the other men, were searching for whoever shot one of their crew. *The half-wit,* Will couldn't help thinking. *He still should have searched down along the riverbank.*

He waited a few minutes to make sure there was no one else coming along behind Junior, maybe someone who was searching along the river's edge. If they were trying to cover their whole range, they had likely all split up, and there was the possibility they would all meet at some point. A good spot, if that was the case, was the point where the road to the ranch crossed the river, and there was a chance he might be able to see how many men he would have to deal with. It was still too early to follow Junior on horseback—he might be too easily seen—but it was worth a try to follow him on foot. He had not ridden more than a mile or so from the ranch trail before he came to this bend in the river where he rested his horses. On foot, he could remain in the cover of the trees all the way back to the road. He paused to question his thinking. It was not an easy decision to run off and leave his horses in this situation, especially when there might be a good chance he was going to need them in a hurry if he was discovered. He decided he had to see if his hunch was right, so he loaded his supplies back on the packhorse and saddled Buster. "I might need you in a hurry," he told the horse, "so don't get to wanderin' around." Then he started out through the trees at a trot fast enough to keep pace with Junior on horseback.

It didn't take long to reach the ranch road and he could see another rider already there when Junior arrived. He pulled his horse up beside the other man's and dismounted. Will advanced only a few yards closer to them. The trees thinned out the closer he came to the road to the ranch headquarters, and to try to get any closer would be pushing his luck. Since the two men showed no sign of riding away, Will figured he had been right in his assumption that other riders were searching and Junior and the other man were waiting for someone else to show up.

It was fully twenty-five or thirty minutes before

someone else showed up, time enough for Will to start worrying about his horses and if they might have decided to wander from the river bend. He was just about to retreat to make sure they were all right when two more riders splashed across the river to join Junior and his partner. Will suddenly felt his arm muscles become tense when he saw that one of them was riding a gray horse. Even at that distance, he easily recognized the rider of the gray as Ansel Beaudry, the same man he had seen fleeing the ambush where Luther Curry was killed! After the initial tenseness at suddenly coming upon the man he hunted, Will's next reaction was one of frustration, for there was nothing he could do about it. Kneeling there, no more than forty yards away from Beaudry, he was on foot, a mile or more from his horses, with four mounted men to confront. It was decision time again. He looked back over his shoulder. The sun was rapidly settling down now and the shadows where he knelt watching the four men were beginning to darken the brush under the trees.

Out on the ranch road, the conversation between the four men stopped and they all climbed into their saddles and started for home. Will didn't wait to make sure which way they were going. It was obvious to him that they had been scouting their range, looking for the killer who shot one of their cowhands. And now they were going back to headquarters, having to surmise that whoever the shooter was, he was long gone now. Knowing the kind of killer Ansel Beaudry was, Will figured there was a fair possibility that the killer they searched for might be riding with them back to the ranch. Making his way back through the oaks at a lope, Will intended to get to his horses in time to trail the four men to the ranch house.

"We can send everybody out on another search tomorrow," Ansel said to Brady as he rode along beside him, "but it looks to me like he has cut outta here. Tell you the truth, I was expectin' to find what was left of the cow he was butcherin' when your man Sonny found him."

"You're probably right," Brady said. "That makes sense to me. Mighta been an Injun, I was thinkin', but I didn't see any unshod hoofprints. Maybe some of the other boys did. I reckon we'll see what Boss thinks about it, but I agree with you, the jasper that shot Sonny is most likely halfway to Fort Worth by now."

Ansel smiled to himself, pleased that he had Brady solidly in his camp. The old man was going to be a problem, but he felt confident he could win him over, too. That still left one problem that might be a thorn in his side, so it might be necessary to arrange an accident for his brother, Todd. All things considered, this day had worked out to his advantage, and he was looking forward now to supper. He might have been a bit too hasty in his dealings with Sonny Pickens, however. *It was Sonny's fault,* he told himself. *I should have taken his word for it when he said he was Mica Beaudry's son and let him ride on in unannounced.* Ansel shrugged. He had been in a hurry, and he didn't feel like arguing with him, so he shot him. The way things were working out now, he might wish he hadn't shot one of his cowhands. *What the hell,* he thought, *he got my dander up.* There was one extreme possibility that never entered his mind, and that was the possibility that there might be a U.S. Deputy Marshal approximately one mile behind him in the dusky twilight on the road to Hornet's Nest.

Chapter 17

Holding Buster to a slow walk, Will managed to keep the four riders in sight, just far enough ahead of him so he could barely make out their forms in the growing darkness. After a ride of about four miles, he passed under a high arch that spanned the width of the road, but there was no gate and no fence, nothing but a rough sign nailed to one of the posts. He assumed it was the official gateway to the ranch headquarters, but it was now too dark to read the sign. He continued on, occasionally having to rein Buster back when he began to shorten the distance between himself and the men he followed. After what he figured to be another mile, he saw the lights of the ranch house and a lantern at the barn door. He figured it was dark enough to allow him to continue following them until getting much closer, so he continued until he could see lantern lights shining from what he figured to be the bunkhouse. It was a sizable operation, he declared to himself. He reined Buster to a halt when the men he followed rode into the barnyard and he could clearly see them, so he knew he shouldn't risk coming any closer.

He watched as Ansel and the other three pulled up to a windmill and water trough near the barn and dismounted. Two men came from the barn to meet them, then they were joined by three others. Since they all gathered around the later arrivals, Will figured they were all reporting on the failure of their search to find any trespassers on the Beaudry range. While they talked, Will tried to decide what he should do. *I'm sure as hell not going to ride in to confront eight men and tell them I've come to arrest Ansel Beaudry,* he thought. Eight men, not including Beaudry, were all he was seeing at the moment. There was no telling how many more worked the ranch. His only chance to arrest Beaudry was to catch him alone and preferably far enough away from any help. The odds of that didn't look that good from where he stood right now. This might be one of those situations that was unworkable for one lone lawman, and one with any common sense would back off and go for help. Still, it was hard to ride away before taking a good look at the headquarters' layout, which might be good to know when he came back with reinforcements. There might not be a better opportunity to have that look, since most of the men were gathered at the barn, and he might not have to worry about being discovered by someone riding night herd.

As he faced the headquarters, the barn and corral were across the yard to the left of the ranch house. There appeared to be a smokehouse and an outhouse behind the main house. There was a bunkhouse, another outhouse, and what looked to be a cookshack next to the bunkhouse. He decided his best chance to get in closer would be to circle around to his right and move in behind the smokehouse. That way he could get a better look at the whole layout, including the bunkhouse, so he wheeled Buster and did just that.

As he circled around, he could see a dark line of trees ahead of him that turned out to be a creek behind the smokehouse that ran between the barn and the bunkhouse. He couldn't have asked for a better place to watch the ranch. It afforded him cover and a convenient place to leave his horses in the event he might want to work his way in closer on foot. This close to the barn, he couldn't afford to risk leaving Buster to wander, so he hurriedly tied his reins to the branch of a tree, close enough to the creek to let him reach the water. His packhorse was still tied to his saddle by a lead rope, so there was enough slack to allow that horse to get to water, too.

As soon as his horses were taken care of, he made his way quickly along the creek bank to a point where he could see the group of men still talking beside the water trough. His gaze was naturally fixed upon Ansel. He was not close enough to hear what was said, beyond a loud exclamation or hardy laugh, but he did hear Spot Morris when he came from the cookshack on the other side of the creek and walked as far as the footbridge to call out to them. "I ain't tellin' you this but once 'cause it's already past suppertime. If you're wantin' to eat this chuck before I throw it to the hogs, you'd best get yourselves up here." He promptly turned and went back to the cookshack.

"I believe he means it, boys," Ansel said. "We'd best do what he says." Since he was just meeting some of the men for the first time, he felt it best to eat supper with the crew, even though he had made it plain to his father that he intended to take his meals at the house. He decided that they had likely already finished supper at the house by then, anyway, so he followed the men into the bunkhouse.

Back in the cover of the creek, Will watched as the men hurriedly pulled their saddles off their horses and turned them out into the corral. He noticed that Ansel handed his reins to one of the men, who promptly took care of his horse. Thinking it a sign that Ansel was already well on his way to taking over as boss, Will couldn't help a cynical grin. It might be near impossible to ride out of here with Ansel his prisoner. It was hard to fight the frustration he felt for his helplessness to do anything but sit and watch. Retreat now, while it was safe to do so, would surely be the only rational thing to do. Ride out while he still could, then go to Fort Worth on the chance there might be a Ranger post there—he could do that. But what if there was no Ranger there? How far to Austin, and how long would it take to assemble a posse sizable enough to take on the Hornet's Nest? There are some battles you just can't win, he tried to tell himself, but the thought of Oscar Moon brutally murdered by Ansel Beaudry came back to him. *I can't let the son of a bitch get away,* he told himself.

"Hold on there a minute, Papa." Ansel stepped quickly to catch up to his father before he returned to the house.

Mica turned to glare at him. "I've got nothin' to say to you," he said.

"Well, I've got somethin' to say to you," Ansel responded. "I've gotta say you've done a pretty good job with the ranch, seein' as how you didn't have much help. I've changed my mind about movin' on in a couple of days 'cause it looks to me like I could build this ranch into the biggest in Texas. All we need is somebody who knows how to build it and a little cash to do it with. Just so happens I'm the man to take care of that." He saw an instant look of anger on his father's face, so he hastened to continue. "Your men are already thinkin' I'm gettin' ready to take over, and I'm holdin' six thousand dollars to use for stock. So you think that over before you decide you still wanna kick me out."

Mica's immediate reaction was one of hostility for Ansel's brash proposal, but also one of surprise at the mention of the six thousand dollars. He was at once reminded of Ansel's tendency never to have his saddlebags out of his sight. It caused him to hesitate to tell him to go to hell, and instead he said, "I'll think about it." He turned then and headed for the house, thinking of how best to take possession of the money.

Will remained where he was until Mica and his son parted with Ansel, who was following the men to the bunkhouse. Since Will saw little chance that he would be discovered, he decided to cross over to the other side of the creek, where he would get a better look at the bunkhouse. The cookshack was a small cabin and used only to prepare the food and clean up the dishes. It was obvious that the men ate in the bunkhouse. *I could use a little grub, myself,* he thought, since he had had nothing since breakfast. *At least my horses are getting some grass.*

He waited out the supper hour, thinking that maybe Ansel would be coming out of the bunkhouse to go to the ranch house. *Surely he would be sleeping in the house,* he thought, but as the evening wore on, there was no sign of him. At first he thought that he had somehow missed him, but then he saw him step outside the bunkhouse. He paused for only a moment before walking a short distance to join a couple of men who were draining some of the coffee they had consumed at supper. There was an outhouse only a little farther away, but that was typically used only in cases of more serious business. Will stared at the man who had cold-bloodedly murdered Oscar Moon and thoughts of him escaping his just deserts for his blatant act began to eat away at Will's conscience. He slowly raised his rifle to his shoulder. Very deliberately, he laid the front sight on Ansel's back, between the shoulder blades. Holding his breath to maintain a steady aim, he gently squeezed the trigger until hearing the click of the hammer on the empty chamber. He exhaled gently and lowered the Winchester. It was tempting, even easy, but it was not in the rules he played by. If at all possible, he would try to take Ansel back for trial and afterward take a front-row seat at his hanging. In the meantime, he would just have to hope for an opportunity to catch him without any of his men around.

He was surprised when Ansel finished and went back inside the bunkhouse instead of going to the

main house as Will had assumed he would. Curious
now, he waited until the bunkhouse eventually qui-
eted down and the cook had finished cleaning up the
cookshack. Still no Ansel Beaudry. Evidently he was
not living in the main house after all, preferring to
bunk in with the crew. He waited a while longer, until
it seemed certain Beaudry was not leaving the bunkhouse. Will thought maybe he had taken a hand in a
card game or something, but when the lamps went
out, he had to conclude Ansel wasn't coming out.
It was a walk of forty yards or more from the bunkhouse to the main house, and Will was thinking he
might have had a chance to jump him, although it
would have been difficult to do it without Ansel
shouting an alarm. It had little chance of success,
he decided. He was probably lucky Ansel stayed in the
bunkhouse. His best hope was to try to keep an eye on
the ranch and maybe see where Ansel went the next
day. If he was lucky, maybe Ansel might ride off to
some part of the range by himself. It was a lot to hope
for, but that's all he had.

He got up from his position on the creek bank and
went back the way he had come. As he walked, he
took a good look at the area surrounding the creek
and the number of trees and bushes growing close by.
Just having discovered that he was in no danger of
being seen in the dark of night, he now decided there
was enough cover close to the bunkhouse to make the
odds good that he could escape detection even in
the light of day. He decided it worth the risk of
coming back to the same spot early in the morning to
watch the ranch wake up.

When he got back to his horses, he was greeted by

a soft nicker from Buster. "At least you had some grass to eat," he said to the horse. "As soon as we get to someplace to camp, I'll get some grain for you outta the packs." He climbed up into the saddle and guided the buckskin across the creek. Coming up out of the trees on the other bank, he looked out across the dark prairie to the west, then gently gave Buster his heels. With the line of trees between him and the ranch headquarters, he rode until he came to a tiny stream that flowed between two low hills. "This'll do," he announced, and reined Buster to a stop. Freeing his horses of their burdens, he then fed them some grain before he dug in his packs for some jerky for his supper. Far enough from the ranch for a fire not to be seen, he built one just big enough to heat up some water for coffee. He spread his bedroll and set his mind to wake up at first light, then went to sleep.

As was his usual habit when in the field, he awoke sometime just before first light and promptly packed up and readied his horses to ride. He climbed aboard Buster and rode back across the prairie toward the line of trees bordering the creek in the distance. When he reached the spot where he had tied his horses the night before, he rode into the trees and dismounted. With his rifle ready to fire, he crossed over the creek and walked up into the trees on the other side in order to take a precautionary look toward the house and the barn. After a few minutes' watch, he was satisfied the ranch had not roused itself for the day as yet. The only sign of life came from the cookshack beside the bunkhouse.

He returned to his horses then and moved them slightly closer to the bunkhouse, thinking the cover better, now that the sun was threatening. As before, he tied his horses close to the water, then made his way through the grove of trees, more carefully than he had before, since the chance of being seen was greater. When he settled into the best spot he could find to stay hidden as well as for cover in the event he was spotted, he waited. Before long he saw the cook starting up his stove to begin cooking breakfast. There were soon noises that announced the men in the bunkhouse were rousing themselves out of bed.

In a short while, there was a fire belching smoke out of the stovepipe in the bunkhouse, and shortly after that, the chuckwagon cook came from the cookshack carrying a large coffeepot and a large iron pot. He would make two more trips carrying pans and trays before breakfast was officially under way. Will sat patiently as every man inside hurried outside to the convenience of the laurel bushes to make room for the cook's coffee. He counted nine men, including Ansel Beaudry and the cook. Now he knew for sure that he had eight men to account for, since nature's call went out to every man upon first waking up in the morning. In addition to the men in the bunkhouse, he also had to account for whoever might be in the house. Based on what he had learned from Sid Worley, that would be old man Mica Beaudry and one other son. Thoughts he had had earlier of brazenly walking into their midst and arresting Ansel were now out of the question. In all likelihood, he would be the second lawman to disappear in the Hornet's Nest. He had to keep reminding himself that the crew of this particular cattle ranch was more akin to an outlaw gang. These were the troubling thoughts that cluttered his mind as he remained in his hiding place long enough to see the men file out of the bunkhouse and head for the barn—all except the cook and Ansel.

Still, he waited to see what Ansel was going to do. He figured he would soon come out and head straight for the house, thinking surely he would make some connection with the family. A few more minutes passed before Ansel finally showed in the doorway of the bunkhouse, but instead of heading for the house or the barn, he paused on the steps of the bunkhouse, as if making up his mind. In one hand, he held what appeared to be a canvas sack. Eventually, he made his decision, walked around behind the bunkhouse, and headed for the outhouse. Not anticipating this move by Ansel, Will hesitated, rose to his feet, and looked in all directions around him. The cook was busy inside the cookshack and none of the other men were anywhere close. Had he taken the time to think what he was about to do, he might not have done it, but in the moment, he saw a chance to get to Ansel when he was alone. He didn't hesitate.

He decided that he might attract attention to himself if he ran to the outhouse, so he attempted to walk as casually as he could while still hurrying to reach the outhouse before Ansel completed his toilet. The most critical point was when he passed the open door of the cookshack, but when he glanced inside, he could see Spot bent over a washtub, his back to the door. Once he was behind the cookshack, Will levered a cartridge into the chamber and clutched his rifle, ready to shoot his way back to his horses, if necessary. At any rate, he was fully committed at this point, so he strode right up to the outhouse and knocked on the door. "Hold your horses," Ansel bellowed from inside. "I'll be done in a minute."

Will didn't answer. He took another look behind him before planting himself solidly with his back against the outhouse wall, right beside the edge of the door. He held his rifle in both hands, level with his shoulders. In another minute, he heard Ansel throw the latch back on the door. Will braced himself, certain that if he missed, the whole attempt would blow up in his face. The door opened and Ansel started to make some remark, but was stopped stone cold by Will's rifle butt when it struck his forehead with the force of a battering ram. Stunned, he was knocked backward into the outhouse. He was not unconscious, but helpless and confused as he struggled to get up, but Will was on him like an angry wolf, stuffing his bandanna into Ansel's mouth, then yanking Ansel's bandanna from around his neck and using it to tie the gag in place. Next, he rolled him over, pulled his arms behind him, and clamped his handcuffs around Ansel's wrists. With Ansel still unable to gather his wits, Will pulled him up on his feet and got a shoulder under him. The only sound to that point was a low grunt from Will when he straightened up under the weight of Ansel's sizable body.

Once he was sure he had the big man's body balanced as well as he could, he started to turn around to face the door, pausing a moment when he saw the canvas sack beside the toilet seat. The thought occurred to him that there must have been a reason to take it to the outhouse with him. Not likely hand soap or shaving mug, since there was no wash room in the outhouse, it had to be something Ansel wouldn't leave unguarded. Will picked it up, managing to grasp it in his hand with his rifle, needing to keep one hand free to help steady his load. He made his way awkwardly through the outhouse door then, with his cumbersome burden across his shoulder. Once outside, he stepped as quickly as he could toward the cover of the trees by the creek. Clutching his rifle in one hand along with the canvas bag, he knew he would be hard put to use it, impaired as he was under the load on his shoulder. His only chance was to cross over the open area between the bunkhouse and the trees without being seen. All it would take would be for the cook to happen to look out the cookshack door. Luck was with Will and he reached the cover of the trees just moments before Ansel began to recover and started trying to yell. His efforts only added to his confusion, causing him to panic when he realized what had happened to him. Before Will reached his horses, his captive started kicking his feet in an effort to free himself, causing Will to stagger drunkenly under his load. At this point, however, he had no choice but to persevere to finish what he had started, as unlikely as it was to succeed.

Although it seemed much longer, he reached his horses after a few minutes and dumped his burden on the ground. Ansel landed hard, causing him to emit a heavy grunt, blunted considerably by the gag in his mouth. Will stood over him, gazing intently at his dazed prisoner, staring, wide-eyed back at him, the two men confronting each other face-to-face. *Now that I caught him,* Will was thinking, *what the hell am I going to do with him?* Someone was bound to wonder where Ansel was, then it would be only a matter of time before they looked for him. *If I was fishing, I think I'd throw this one back,* he couldn't help thinking. It would have helped his situation if he also had Ansel's horse. He was going to have to put him on his packhorse, although he would have to rearrange the supplies he was carrying, especially the extra weapons he had confiscated. The big problem, however, was whether or not he could ride out of there with his prisoner without being seen. The only possibility for that would be to ride back to the west, the way he had come that morning, so there was no sense in trying to think of other options. That was the only direction that would utilize the line of trees along the creek, keeping them between him and the house. Unfortunately, someone at the back of the bunkhouse, or at the door of the cookhouse, could see him should they happen to look toward the prairie to the west. He was going to need a hell of a lot of luck. *Might as well get on with it,* he told himself.

He left Ansel to struggle against his chains for a few minutes while he made a place for him on his pack-horse by shifting much of the load to Buster. When he was ready, he led the sorrel gelding up beside Ansel. By that time, his prisoner's brain was beginning to function more normally and he was glaring up at Will, trying to shout at him, but the gag muffled his every angry curse. Even with the gag, Will could still understand what Ansel was trying to demand answers for. "Let me spell it out for you," Will said to him. "You're under arrest for murder and bank robbery. We're fixin' to ride outta here as soon as I get you up on this horse." His announcement brought a new tirade of muffled threats too garbled for Will to understand. "It's up to you how hard this is gonna be," Will continued. "If you don't give me any trouble, I'll treat you as fair as I can and take you back for trial. But I'll be honest with you, I had just as soon shoot you, if you give me the slightest reason to. And that goes for anybody that comes after us, tryin' to save your worthless ass. If at any time I have to run for it to save my life, I'll guarantee you I'll shoot you before I take off." He paused to make sure Ansel understood him. There was no sound from the infuriated prisoner, so Will said, "All right, let's get started."

At first, Beaudry resisted when Will took hold of one of his arms and started to pull him to his feet, but Will stomped his boot down hard on the arch of Ansel's foot. Then he grabbed him by his shirt collar and jerked him to his feet, his body like a lever with his foot anchored as the base. Ansel seemed surprised to find himself on his feet. "Now, you've got a choice," Will said. "You can sit up on the horse and ride, or I'll lay you across him and you can ride on your belly. If you'd rather ride sittin' up, give me your foot and I'll boost you up on the horse." Ansel thought about it for only a moment, but the look on Will's face implied that he would just as soon throw him across the horse on his belly, so he submitted to being hoisted up on the horse. Since his hands were locked behind his back, he landed awkwardly on the sorrel's back, but Will kept him from falling off the other side. Once his prisoner was settled on the horse, Will cut off a short piece of rope, made a loop, and dropped it over Ansel's head. Pulling the loop up tight around Ansel's neck, he tied the other end around the horse's neck. "That's just a safety device in case you happen to fall off the horse," Will said. "That way, the horse can't run off and leave you. Best try to hold on with your knees, though, 'cause it looks like I didn't take enough slack outta that rope. I expect there's enough rope to let you land on the ground." It was obvious by the scowl on Ansel's face that he got the picture. With his prisoner mounted, Will picked up the canvas sack and looked inside. As he had expected, it was filled with money, Ansel's share of the bank holdups. "I expect I'd best carry this in my saddlebags," he said to Ansel. He placed the sack in one of the pockets of his saddlebags. The other pocket already held Luther Curry's share.

Although seemingly cocksure when he spelled everything out to Ansel, there was a great cloud of doubt over Will's head when it came to riding away from the Hornet's Nest with his prisoner intact. He stepped up on Buster and guided the buckskin out through the oaks lining the creek and started out to the west across the rolling prairie with the early morning sun on his back. Looking back over his shoulder, he could not see the ranch house or the barn, since they were hidden behind the trees by the creek. He could clearly see the bunkhouse and the cookshack, consequently he was depending on nothing but blind luck that there was no one there who would catch sight of the two of them riding away. He was pretty sure the bunkhouse was empty when he had walked past the cookshack on his way to the outhouse, but there was the cook to worry about.

Back at the cookshack, Spot Morris poured himself another cup of coffee, picked up a biscuit he had saved to eat when he had finished cleaning up after breakfast, and walked out of the cookshack. He sat himself down on the step and studied the clouds overhead and the possibility of rain, never turning to notice the two riders gradually disappearing into the vast prairie. "Things are gonna change around here," Spot said to a chicken that came to scout for biscuit crumbs, knowing the gray-whiskered little man's habits. "Yes, sir, Todd better watch out 'cause big brother Ansel's come home to run the show."

Chapter 18

Will held Buster to a steady pace for what he figured to be about eight to ten miles, when he came to a sizable creek running north and south. He was unaware that it was called Possum Run and was the western boundary of the Beaudry range. He decided it served his immediate purpose, which was to put distance between himself and any possible pursuit from Hornet's Nest, so he followed the creek north for another ten miles or so until he came to a place that looked familiar to him. A well-traveled road crossed the creek at that point and he realized that it was the Fort Worth road, so now he was no longer on Beaudry land. He also knew that his horses were in need of rest, so he crossed over the road and followed the creek for another fifty yards until coming to a good spot to build a fire out of sight of the road.

When he went to help his prisoner off his horse, Ansel looked as if the ride had been pretty hard on him. The cut across his forehead, where Will struck him, had bled a great deal, although it had now stopped, but it had left Ansel with dried blood all over his face and a dazed expression. Will speculated that Ansel hadn't spent a great deal of time riding a horse with the added incentive of staying on the horse with his hands behind his back and a rope around his neck. He figured that contributed to the dazed expression as well. When he was on his feet on the ground, Ansel found it hard to remain steady, so Will said, "Get on your knees." Ansel made no show of defiance and did as he was told. Will walked behind him. "I'm gonna unlock your cuffs, so you can take that bandanna out of your mouth, and I expect you'd like a drink of water."

He must have been parched, for as soon as Will pulled the gag out of his mouth, he crawled straight to the creek and dropped his face in the water. Will picked up the bandanna that had been used to secure the gag and pitched it to him when he pulled his face out of the water. "Here, use this to wipe some of that blood off your face." Ansel looked at Will, standing behind him with his .44 leveled at him, as if still dazed, but he took the bandanna and started cleaning his face. When he had finished, Will explained the practice of tree hugging, just as he had with Ansel's former partners and every other prisoner when he didn't have a jail wagon with him. He picked out a tree for him, and Ansel went to it without a word. He held his hands out on either side of the tree trunk and waited. "You know," Will informed him as a precaution, "your old partner Bo Hagen—maybe you noticed that's his saddle you're ridin' on—anyway, Bo was standin' just like you're standin' there now, with one handcuff on his wrist and the other one hangin' free. He got the bright idea to take a swing at me with that chain and

I put a bullet in his leg, so you ain't the first one that's thought of it."

Ansel scowled in response and uttered the first words since the gag had been removed. "Damn you, Will Tanner." He had at first figured he might be a Texas Ranger, which he would have preferred to the deputy marshal who never cared if he was in his legal territory or not. The way Tanner had destroyed his gang, one and two at a time, seeming to be unstoppable, had served to work on Ansel's mind to the point where he had fled to escape his vengeance. To have the menace come onto his father's ranch and blatantly pluck him right out of the outhouse, no less, was enough to convince Ansel that the deputy was crazy, so he held his arms steady while Will locked them around the tree. "You've got my share of the money now," Ansel suddenly suggested, "so I reckon you oughta have everybody's shares. That's what you've been after, ain't it? So why don't you let me go? You've got the money." He found it hard to believe that Will really intended to take him back to Fort Smith. He didn't understand why Will hadn't killed him and left with the money.

"All the money you and your gang stole has to go back to the banks you stole it from," Will replied.

"You tryin' to tell me you're gonna give the money back to the bank, all of it?" When Will nodded, Ansel said, "Then you're crazier than hell."

"You may be right," Will said, and left to take care of his horses, then went about the business of building a fire and preparing a meager meal of bacon and hardtack. "You're lucky you had a good breakfast for yourself," he said to Ansel. "Maybe a little bacon and coffee will do you some good, though, 'cause we're

gonna ride a ways before we camp for the night. I
need to put a little more country between us and your
daddy's men." Although he was not really familiar
with the part of Texas he was now in, he had a general
idea of the direction he needed to head out to get to
where he wanted. His plans were not that firm for the
simple reason he hadn't known he was going to
kidnap Ansel Beaudry until he found himself in the
midst of doing it. He considered turning Beaudry
over to the Texas Rangers if he encountered one on
his way back to Oklahoma. If not, he was prepared to
transport him all the way to Fort Smith. As near as he
could guess, and it was a guess, he figured he must
be at least six or seven days from there, and what he
hoped to do was find his way to Durant, across the Red,
then Fort Smith from there.

When the coffee was ready, Will unlocked Ansel's
cuffs to free his hands, so he could eat. And while he
ate, Will sat a few yards in front of him with his Colt
.44 drawn and lying on his lap, while he sipped from
a cup of coffee. His prisoner showed very little enthu-
siasm for the breakfast of bacon and hardtack soaked
in the grease, but he consumed it anyway.

While he waited for Ansel to finish, Will glanced at
his Winchester on the ground beside him and
frowned when he saw the crack running the length of
the stock. The fine-line that had resulted from the
collision with Junior Hutto's nose was now a good bit
wider, thanks to Ansel's hard head. Studying his prisoner, he couldn't help but wonder how much trouble
he was going to be to transport. As docile as he seemed
to be so far, Will could not believe he would remain
that way. It was not the impression of the man he had
gotten from the threats and comments he'd heard

from Ansel's gang members. He had formed an image of a cruel and powerful felon with a gift for presenting himself as otherwise, until he struck his victim, whether it was robbery or murder, or both. Whatever, Will cautioned himself to expect the worst.

"Damned if I know," Spot Morris replied when Brady came to the bunkhouse, looking for Ansel. "I saw him go to the outhouse after all you boys finished breakfast, but I never did see him come out. Course, I weren't payin' no attention to whether he did or not. Hell, maybe he's still in there. We can go look, but if he's still in there after all this time, there musta been somethin' he et that upset his stomach or somethin'. Ain't none of the other boys complained, have they?"

"No," Brady said, "ain't nobody else complained." He stood there a few moments, trying to decide whether to look in the outhouse or not. "I was fixin' to ask him if he wanted me to saddle his horse, but maybe he's thinkin' about gettin' together with Boss and Todd this mornin'. He didn't say at breakfast what he was gonna do." He hesitated a moment longer before announcing, "I'll go check the outhouse, just to be sure." He started toward the door and called back over his shoulder, "Hell, with your cookin', it's a wonder we ain't all sick half the time. He just ain't been back long enough to get used to it."

"I'll go with you," Spot said, ignoring the sarcasm concerning his cooking. He'd heard enough of that to dismiss the comments as common complaints when there wasn't anything else to complain about. He went out the door after Brady.

When they reached the outhouse, they stopped

and listened for any sounds that might tell them the outhouse was in use. When there were none, Brady knocked politely on the door. When there was still no response, he looked at Spot and shrugged, then asked, "Mr. Beaudry, you in there?" After waiting another few moments, he opened the door to find the outhouse unoccupied.

"Well, I reckon that means there weren't nothin' wrong with the cookin'," Spot declared. "I'da heard a lot more bellyachin' if there had been. He musta gone up to the house."

"I reckon so," Brady agreed. "I'd best go check on the men. It's about time Boss and Todd showed up to see what's goin' on."

Brady and Spot weren't the only two who were curious about the whereabouts of Ansel Beaudry. Todd Beaudry stood in the kitchen, questioning Lorena when breakfast was long over. "He made a lotta talk about how he was gonna eat all his meals here in the kitchen," Todd said, "and you say he didn't show up here this mornin'?"

"*Sí*, he no show up," Lorena answered.

Mica Beaudry walked into the kitchen, and Todd promptly informed him that his brother had not eaten in the kitchen that morning. Mica thought about that for a moment before replying, "He ate supper with the men last night and he's had breakfast with them again this mornin'." To the rugged old owner of the Hornet's Nest, that was a definite sign of trouble brewing, and he made his thoughts known to his younger son. "I shoulda run him outta here the minute he showed up again. I reckon he thinks I'm gettin' soft in my old age, but I'm fixin' to show him how soft I am. He's tryin' to get my own men to back him while he tries to take over my ranch. I ain't so old I can't see that." He glared at his younger son. "It's about time you stepped up to protect this ranch, too, else you ain't gonna last a day after I'm in the grave. Let's go find your brother." He had not told Todd about the offer his brother had made.

"Where's Ansel?" Mica demanded when he found Brady in the barn.

Surprised, as well as aware of the anger in the old man's tone, Brady blurted, "I don't know, Boss, I thought he was up at the house with you." He looked from Todd's concerned expression back to his father's dark countenance. "I ain't seen him since breakfast." When Mica asked if Ansel was out with the cattle, Brady answered, "I don't think so. He wasn't with any of the boys I sent out." He turned and pointed to the gray gelding in the corral. "Yonder's his horse. It's been there ever since yesterday, and his saddle's still layin' where I left it." He told him then about looking for Ansel in the outhouse, only to find it empty.

"He's up to somethin', Papa," Todd said. "Maybe he's layin' up in the bunkhouse."

"He weren't there after breakfast," Brady said, shaking his head. "He's just by God disappeared."

"That ain't hardly likely," Mica retorted. "I want him found and I want him brought to me. Do I make myself clear?" Brady was quick to answer that he did. Mica turned to Todd and said, "Go up to the bunkhouse and make sure he ain't there. If he ain't maybe Spot knows where he went." Todd immediately headed for the bunkhouse at a trot.

Unaware of the excitement down at the barn over

the missing Beaudry brother, Spot was just then in the process of answering a distress call from the lower regions of his bowels. At the moment Todd started up the path that led to the bunkhouse, Spot opened the outhouse door and proceeded to unbuckle his belt. It was then that he noticed a couple of drops of blood, now dried, on the boards of the single-hole facility. It puzzled him, but not to the point where he could deter the urgency of his reason for visiting the outhouse. It was only after he had dropped his trousers around his boots and settled down to answer the call that he noticed the .44 in the holster on the gun belt hanging on a peg beside the door. Initially puzzled, he wondered who could have walked off and left their sidearm hanging in the toilet. He didn't think it was in there earlier when he and Brady were looking for Ansel. But thinking back, he realized that neither he nor Brady went into the outhouse, they had just looked in. They would have had to look closely to see the tiny drops of blood on the board, but they had no reason to inspect the inside. Consequently, the bloodstains and the weapon could have been there when they looked inside. He was trying to decide if his findings meant something important, or not, when he heard Todd yelling his name. "Hell," he muttered, his mood having been compromised and his feeling of urgency lost. "I'm in the outhouse," he yelled back. "I'll be out in a minute." He pulled his trousers back up and went out to see what Todd wanted.

"Have you seen Ansel?" Todd asked when Spot came out.

"Not since this mornin'," Spot answered, "but come see what I found in the outhouse." Todd wasn't very enthusiastic about seeing what Spot might have found in the outhouse, but the cook remained at the door, holding it open, a look of amusement on his chubby, round face, so Todd walked up to see. When Todd was also puzzled by the firearm hanging by the outhouse door, Spot offered his opinion. "It's Ansel's," he said with a chuckle. "He came in to crap and went off without his gun." He found the situation amusing, especially after the sinister impression the older Beaudry brother had made upon the whole crew.

Perplexed, but finding the sudden disappearance of his brother less than amusing, Todd said, "Ansel's missin'. He's up to somethin' and we can't find him anywhere on the ranch. You let me know if he shows up here." He took the gun and holster from the peg and hurried back to the barn to tell his father. Caught up in Todd's reaction to his find, Spot ran behind him.

With the mysterious circumstances surrounding the missing brother and the firearm left behind, a sense that something disastrous was about to happen descended upon the Hornet's Nest at first. So strongly convinced that his evil son had come back to destroy him and take over the ranch, Mica Beaudry was desperate to defend against him. He sent Todd back to the house with orders to search it thoroughly to make doubly certain that Ansel was not hiding there. Then he and Brady, with Spot following along behind, searched the smokehouse and the outhouse behind the main house. They were back at the barn when Todd returned from the house with a report that Ansel was definitely not hiding there.

With no knowledge of Ansel's flight from authorities in Missouri, Kansas, and Oklahoma, Mica could not know about the relentless deputy marshal who caused him to run and the fact that he was desperately trying to find a haven anywhere. It was from the unlikely council of his younger son that a reasonable explanation came forth. "He ain't takin' over nothin'," Todd said. "He's on the run from the Rangers, and he came here to hide. He mighta had ideas about takin' over the ranch, but the Rangers snuck in here and got him, got him while he was takin' a crap." His statement was not his own, but a repetition of his wife, Mae's theory, word for word. His speculation was not taken seriously at first, but his father humored him when he suggested they should scout the creek that ran between the barn and the bunkhouse for signs of trespassers. Along with Brady and Spot, Mica and Todd went to the creek to search.

"Look here!" Brady cried out, and stood up to signal the others. When they caught up to him, he pointed to tracks in the trees along the creek. "Somebody was walkin' through here."

"Follow them to see where they came from," Mica ordered, and they hurried back along the creek, picking up tracks every so often until they led them to the place the trespasser had left his horses. It was obvious that there had been two horses. There were plenty of tracks as well as fresh droppings. "What do you make of it, Brady?" Mica asked, not completely sure, himself.

"Looks to me like Todd's right," Brady answered. "The way I see it is, the lawman hid his horses right here and walked up there to the edge of the clearin' where the bunkhouse sets. He waited till he saw his chance when Ansel went to use the outhouse, went in, and knocked him in the head, and carried him back here. That's the reason he had two horses—he brought an extra one for Ansel, since he couldn't go down to the barn to get Ansel's horse. Hell, with everybody gone down to the barn there weren't nobody to see him while he was doin' all that."

"Damn," Spot swore. "I was right there in the cookhouse. It's a wonder I didn't see him."

"I bet, if we was to look around a little, we might find which way he rode outta here," Brady continued. To confirm it, they all started following any tracks that left the creek and readily found the tracks of Will Tanner's horses. None of the four spoke for a few moments, as they all stared out to the west where the tracks led from the creek. "I'll be damned," Brady started. "Todd's right, somebody snuck in here and grabbed him, right under our noses."

Mica considered the possibility for a few moments longer, but finally agreed with Brady and Todd. "Well, it's a helluva day when I can say the Texas Rangers have done me a favor, or whoever it was that took him. As mean a snake as Ansel is, it coulda been somebody else that got him." He pulled Todd aside, so Brady and Spot couldn't hear what he said. "Go find his saddlebags. I got a feelin' there might be a good bit of money in 'em. Could be that's the reason somebody came to get him."

In spite of Mica's attempt to tell only Todd, Spot overheard his remark. "Ansel's saddlebags is on his bunk," he volunteered. "I seen 'em there this mornin'."

All four started immediately toward the bunkhouse. As they walked, Mica issued an order to Brady. "I want you to set some of the men to work clearin' out some of these trees on this creek bank. I don't want anybody else ridin' in here without us seein' 'em." When Brady asked if he wanted all the trees down, Mica answered, "No, just the ones that keep us from seein' from the house and the barn." When they reached the bunkhouse, Spot hustled ahead, picked up the saddlebags from Ansel's bunk, and handed them to Mica. He searched the bags, but there was no money inside. "I reckon that's the reason he didn't take 'em to the outhouse with him," Mica concluded. "'Cause there was money in 'em when he got here, he musta took it out of 'em." His comment served to instill Todd with a feeling of satisfaction that the problem of the prodigal son had solved itself. The feeling lasted only until his father ordered the men to prepare to ride.

Mica turned to Brady. "Looks to me like there was one man that came here to get Ansel, right?" When Brady confirmed that to be his opinion, Mica issued his orders. "Whoever it was that grabbed Ansel, maybe a lawman, maybe not, he didn't come here just to get Ansel. Ansel had about six thousand dollars in his saddlebags, and I suspect that's what whoever took him really came for. That money belongs to me and I aim to get it back." His statement brought a look of surprise to all their faces. "Brady," Mica went on, "get the men on their horses, we're goin' after them."

"Everybody's out with the cattle but Junior and Rufus," Brady responded. "You want me to send them out to find them?"

Mica hesitated for only a moment. "No, we ain't got time. We'll be enough. Saddle my horse and get Junior and Rufus saddled up. Spot, you stay here and let the men know what's goin' on when they come in, and we'd best take a packhorse with us with some supplies, in case it takes us a while to catch up with this bastard." He turned to Brady again. "I'm goin' to the house to let the women know we're goin' and we'll get started as soon as we can." He started for the house and Todd followed him.

When all was ready, Mica Beaudry led the posse of five out across the prairie, following the tracks left by Will and Ansel, already several hours behind, according to the best they could figure.

When Ansel had finished the meager meal Will had prepared, Will locked his arms around the tree again while he ate. When he finished, he rinsed his pan and the plates in the creek and put them back in his packs. While he was doing that, he shifted his gaze toward his prisoner and noticed the cut on Ansel's forehead was still bleeding, so he decided to clean it up a little and bandage it. Digging into his packs again, he pulled out the remains of the old bedsheet that had been used for bandages before. He ripped off one small strip to use for a washcloth and wet it in the creek. Then he approached his sullen prisoner embracing the tree. "If you'll hold still, I'll do a little doctorin' on that cut," he said. Ansel stared at him as if he suspected something other than tender care, but he had no choice other than to submit. "Ain't much I can do, but maybe it'll keep the blood outta your eyes." Will cleaned the blood away, then from the strip of bedsheet fashioned a bandage to tie around Ansel's head. "Maybe that'll hold you for a while. It needs stitchin' up, but I ain't got nothin' to do that with."

When Will sat down with his back against a tree eight or ten yards away, Ansel continued to study him, trying to figure him out. He had an impression of the relentless lawman as one of single-minded purpose, with no regard for human life, not a lot unlike himself. Now he was not sure, after no show of abuse and some concern for the wound on his forehead. Maybe Tanner was not the merciless hunter he had envisioned. The thought of that tended to make him think there might be a better possibility of escape, if he convinced him that he was not going to cause trouble. He considered Will's remark about shooting Bo Hagen in the leg, but that might have simply been a bluff. There was a question of how much time he might have to work on Will's sense of alertness, since he had not said where he intended to take him. Will worked out of Fort Smith, Arkansas, and that was a hell of a long ride from where they now sat. Ansel hoped he planned to take him there, for the longer the trip, the more opportunities for escape. He relaxed his position with his arms and legs on either side of the tree, feeling more of his old confidence returning. This deputy was no invincible lawman and should prove to be no match for him.

The man being judged by his prisoner was also considering the long journey ahead of him and reminding himself of his decision to treat Ansel Beaudry as he would treat any felon he was transporting to Fort Smith. The cruel execution of Oscar Moon, as described by Elmira Tate, was difficult to remove from Will's memory, however. The temptation to make himself judge, jury, and executioner was ever present in the back of his mind. It would be so much simpler to put a bullet in Ansel's brain and be done with it. He was bound to hang, anyway, so where was the sin in that? He cursed when the same answer always came back, telling him he was no better than the Ansel Beaudrys in the world if he was to yield to that temptation.

When he was satisfied that the horses were rested and ready to go again, Will saddled and loaded them. He decided to handcuff Ansel with his hands in front, instead of behind him as he had started out from Hornet's Nest, so he let Ansel climb on the sorrel without his help. Now that they were away from the ranch, he also let Ansel ride without the noose around his neck. The packhorse's reins were tied to a lead rope that Will held, so he was not concerned that his prisoner might make a run for it. As a precaution against the possibility that Mica Beaudry might have his men watching the Fort Worth road, Will did not return to it. Instead, with no trail to follow, he set out from the creek on a heading to the northeast across the open plains, planning to swing wide of Fort Worth. Behind him, Ansel rode more comfortably now that he could hold on with his hands and not just his knees.

Not certain where he was exactly, Will was confident that he was heading in the right direction to eventually strike the main road that ran along the MKT Railroad, leading up through Sherman, Texas, into Oklahoma Indian Territory. As he held Buster to a working pace, he passed several trails, but none that seemed to head in the direction he was heading in. As the morning turned to noontime, and the afternoon began to turn toward evening, he started looking for a place to camp for the night. A couple of miles farther, he came upon a well-traveled road that looked to be headed in his direction. Still not certain, he was about to cross it when he saw a man driving a wagon approaching, so he pulled up and waited for him.

More than a little concerned, the man driving his

wagon home from town was uneasy when he saw the two riders waiting for him, one of them with what looked like a bandage wrapped around his head. He reached behind the wagon seat and dragged his shotgun closer, thinking he might be about to face the danger of being robbed. Knowing he couldn't outrun them, he continued on toward them. "How do?" he greeted them when he pulled up even with them.

"Howdy," Will returned. "Where does this road go?"

"Goes to town," the man replied. "Denton." He turned and pointed back the way he had come. "I just came from there, spent all the money I had."

Will almost smiled. "How far?" The farmer said it was two miles. Then thinking he should do the right thing for his prisoner, he asked, "Is there a doctor in Denton?"

"Sure is, Doc Slaughter, on the right as you ride into town."

"Much obliged," Will said, and turned Buster's head toward town, leaving a relieved farmer to continue on home with his wagon to tell his wife about the strange man leading a handcuffed man with a bandage on his head.

"Boss!" Jim Brady called out, and signaled with a wave of his hand. When Mica and the others caught up with him, Brady pointed to some tracks on the other side of the Fort Worth road. "We don't have to guess if he headed to Fort Worth or not. He went on across the road, followed the creek right on north."

"You sure they're the same tracks we've been followin'?" Mica asked. "I figured he'd take the road and head for Fort Worth."

"I'm pretty sure, Boss, and these tracks are fresh, so it ain't likely somebody else came along and turned off the road right here. I wouldn't be surprised if we found a spot where he stopped to rest his horses, 'cause ours are gonna need some rest pretty soon."

"I reckon you're right," Mica reluctantly agreed. They had driven the horses hard in an effort to catch up with Ansel and his abductor. "We'll ride on a little farther and see if you're right about him stopping a little farther on."

With Brady scouting the creek bank ahead of them, they soon found the place where Will had stopped. The ashes of his fire were still warm, according to Brady.

Chapter 19

Will rode the two miles to Denton, and as the farmer had said, one of the first houses he came to had a sign on a post by the road saying it was the office of Dr. John B. Slaughter. He turned Buster onto the lane leading up to the house and tied the horses at the rail. With his rifle in hand, he stepped up on the porch and knocked on the door, then turned to keep his eye on Ansel while he waited. Ansel sat patiently waiting, willing to cooperate in getting his forehead stitched up. Will rapped again and in a few minutes the door opened and a bewhiskered little man peered out at him through the screen door. "Reckon you could stitch up a man's forehead?" Will asked.

"You're late," Doc Slaughter replied, noticing Will's bloodstained sleeve, then looking around Will at Ansel astride the sorrel.

"I am?" Will responded, thinking he must mean his office hours were over.

"Yeah," Doc said. "I've already finished my supper." Then he broke out a hearty chuckle in appreciation for his humor. When Will appeared not to understand,

Doc explained, "Usually you fellows with cuts and gunshot wounds come dragging in here just when I'm sitting down to eat my supper, but I've already eaten." He laughed again. "Bring him on in." He turned back from the door and yelled, "Martha! I'm gonna need some hot water."

Will went back to the horses and told Ansel to get down. "I sure am surprised you're takin' me to the doctor," Ansel said. "I figured you didn't care if I bled to death."

"You figured right," Will said, and walked him in the door, his .44 pressing against Ansel's back.

"Whoa!" Slaughter exclaimed when they walked in. He had not noticed that Ansel's hands were in hand-cuffs when he was outside sitting on the horse. "What have we got here? Are you a lawman?"

"That's right, Doc," Will answered, "and we've got a man with a split forehead that needs some doctorin'."

"How about that arm?" Slaughter asked when he saw Will's bloodstained sleeve. "Is there a bullet in it?"

"Not anymore," Will answered. "Just need his forehead stitched up."

"Are you gonna pay for it?" Doc asked. He stepped up to Ansel, pulled the bandage off, and took a closer look at the wound. "Three dollars," he said. "Who's gonna pay for it?"

"I am," Will replied. He reached in his pocket for some money, peeled off three dollars, then asked, "Can we get started? I'd like to find a place to camp tonight."

"Bring him in here and set him down on that chair," Doc said as he picked up the three dollars and put them in his pocket. He got some instruments ready to do the stitching and by the time he looked about ready to start, his wife walked in, carrying a kettle of boiling water. She poured some of the water into a basin beside the table, then stepped back behind her husband. Well accustomed to seeing all manner of patients who came to see the doctor, she nevertheless eyed Will and his prisoner carefully. When she locked eyes with Will, he smiled politely and nodded, causing her to quickly shift her gaze back to focus on her husband. Will decided neither she nor her husband were convinced that he was a lawman. "Will you be talking with Sheriff McCauley after you leave here?" Doc asked casually as he pulled his needle through Beaudry's forehead.

"Hadn't planned on it," Will answered. "Why?"

"Just wondered," Doc replied. "I thought maybe you might be takin' your prisoner to jail after I sewed him up."

"Never been to Denton before," Will said, and took a couple of steps to the side when Doc moved and momentarily blocked his view of Ansel. "I didn't know you had a sheriff. Maybe I'll stop by to see him before I leave town."

"He's easy to find, office is right in the middle of town," Doc said. In a matter of minutes, he snipped the end of his thread and paused to take a quick look at his work. "That oughta do it. Nice job of stitching, even if I do say so myself. Martha, put a bandage on that, please." He stepped out of the way and his wife promptly took over.

"'Preciate it, Doc," Will said, and started Ansel toward the door. The doctor and his wife both walked them out and stood in the door until they were on their horses and rode away.

"There's something that doesn't look exactly right

about that pair," Doc commented to his wife. "Did you send Jimmy to tell Joe McCauley about them?"

"Yes, I sent him as soon as I set the kettle on the stove," she said. "I wouldn't be surprised if their next stop is at the blacksmith to get those handcuffs off that one fellow."

Denton, Texas, proved to be a thriving little town. Will hesitated when he came to the square in the center of town, then decided to skirt the main street and led a freshly bandaged Ansel Beaudry up the alley behind the stores. He thought it best not to parade his handcuffed prisoner past the people on the street. Coming out on the upper end of the street, he continued on a road that led north out of town, hoping to find a good spot to camp for the night. In less than a mile, he crossed a wide creek that made its way through a grove of oak trees. Thinking that was just what he was looking for, he turned Buster off the road and followed the creek for about fifty yards when he came to a small clearing. Judging by the remains of a couple of old fires, it had been used for camping before, so he dismounted and secured his prisoner to one of the many trees available. He went about his usual routine then, taking care of his horses first, then gathering wood for a fire, and before long he had coffee boiling and bacon in the pan.

He drank coffee while he watched Ansel eat, and when he had finished, he chained him back up to the tree. "How the hell am I supposed to sleep, handcuffed to a tree like this?" Ansel finally complained.

"You've just got to learn to relax," Will said. "You'll be surprised how soon you get used to it. Hell, after we've been ridin' a couple of days, you won't wanna sleep in a bed again. I'll find some bigger limbs, so I can build the fire up and you'll stay warm all night." He walked back in the trees then to leave Ansel uttering a string of profanities.

"All right!" The voice came suddenly from the edge of the clearing. "I'm holdin' a twelve-gauge shotgun on you right now, so s'pose you move away from that tree."

"Fair enough," another voice a little deeper in the darkness of the trees called clearly then. "I've got a Winchester 73 aimed at your back, and he can't move from that tree. So you'd best lay that shotgun on the ground and walk on out in the clearing by the fire."

Sheriff Joe McCauley froze for just a second, then carefully laid his shotgun on the ground and walked over by the fire, his hands raised shoulder high. Will walked out of the trees behind him, his rifle leveled at the sheriff. "Now," he asked, "just who might you be?"

"Joe McCauley. I'm the sheriff."

"What is your business with us?" Will asked. "Is it against the law to camp here?"

"No, it ain't against the law, but it's my job to find out what a man's intentions are when he leads another man through town handcuffed. When our citizens complain about somethin', it's my job to look into it."

"The doctor?" Will asked.

"It don't matter who," McCauley replied. "I get a complaint and I have to check it out. So who are you and what is your business in Denton?"

"You're makin' a helluva lot of demands, seein' as how you're the one with your hands in the air," Will said. He reached down and picked up the shotgun. "You can turn around now." When he did, Will released the hammers on the shotgun and handed it to him. "My business in your town is to get through it as fast as I can and be on my way toward Sherman. I'm a U.S. Deputy Marshal, transporting one of a gang of bank robbers back to Fort Smith, Arkansas, for trial. He pulled his badge out of his pocket and showed it to him. My name's Will Tanner, and I wanted to get outta your town without causing any trouble for anybody. My prisoner needed a doctor, or I woulda rode around Denton."

McCauley studied Will carefully while he was talking and when Will paused for his response, he asked a question. "You do know you're in Texas, don't you? It's about fifty miles from here to Oklahoma Territory, dependin' on which way you go."

"Yeah, I know," Will said.

"Seems to me, if you were chasin' this fellow, and he crossed over the Red, you'da got in touch with the Texas Rangers to go after him."

"That is the way we'd usually handle it," Will conceded, "but I've been on this outlaw's trail for a helluva long time, and I couldn't just let him go because he crossed the river." McCauley shrugged and considered that. Will continued, "Besides, this is a personal matter. He killed a friend of mine, so I'm determined to see him stand trial."

After a few more moments' consideration, McCauley decided Will was who he said he was and figured there was no threat to him or his town. "You wanna keep him in my jail tonight, instead of chainin' him to a tree?"

"No, thanks just the same, Sheriff, but I don't want him to get too comfortable sleepin' on a bed, and I ain't worried about him yankin' up that tree and runnin' off on me. At sunup in the mornin', I'll be on my way, and you won't have to worry about us."

"All right, Will Tanner," McCauley said. "I reckon that would save you some time, so good luck with your prisoner. I hope you don't have any trouble."

"Much obliged, Sheriff," Will said. McCauley turned to go back the way he had come, thinking it was a hell of a long way for a man to hug trees all the way to Fort Smith. He hadn't taken more than a few steps when Will called after him, "Did you track me in here to this clearin'?" It occurred to him that he must have been careless about leaving a trail to follow.

"Nope," McCauley answered. "I just looked here first. Everybody knows about this spot. Seems like it's everybody's favorite place to camp."

That was not especially good news to Will. If he had known that before, he would have ridden on farther to find a place that wasn't so well known. It was a little late for that now that he had Ansel locked away for the night. He walked back into the trees after a few seconds to follow the sheriff, and when he saw him get on his horse and leave, he went back to pick up the wood he had gathered. After a final nature call for Ansel, he locked him back around his tree. Then he suggested to him that he should lie on his side. That way, he could stretch his legs out on one side of the tree. When Ansel took his advice and settled himself to sleep, Will laid his extra blanket over him.

Much to Will's surprise, Ansel fell asleep and was soon snoring. He figured the stress of his capture and the uncomfortable ride had contributed to his need for sleep. *I wish I had the urge to sleep,* Will thought, for he was wide-awake and his mind was still working on the fact that he had chosen this spot to camp in. *Might*

as well have camped in a public park, he chided himself.
As the night crept by, he could not rid his mind of the
sensing that his camp and his prisoner were vulnerable. He didn't know for sure if he had been followed
from the Hornet's Nest, but if he had, he had given
them a lot of time to catch up while he was in the
doctor's office. As long as he was awake, he kept the fire
stoked up. *Might as well keep ol' Ansel warm*, he thought
after placing a few more pieces of wood on the fire.
That done, he laid back down on his blanket with serious intentions to go to sleep. He had not lain there
for more than five minutes when he heard Buster
nicker. With a thought that something might be both-
ering his horses, he got up to check on them. He found
Buster by the edge of the creek and the big buckskin
nickered again in greeting when he saw him. In a few
seconds, he heard his packhorse answer Buster. Nothing seemed amiss with the horses, so he took a minute
to rub the buckskin's face and neck. He turned when
he heard the sorrel come up from the trees behind
him and started to give him some attention, too, when
he suddenly realized that the nickering he had heard
did not come from that direction. He was at once
alert! There was somebody else in the trees with him.
Sheriff McCauley? Maybe the sheriff had not bought
his claim as to who he was. Then while he stood between his two horses, he caught a glimpse of a figure
no more than twenty yards from him, darting through
the dark forest toward his camp. Once again, he
owed the buckskin for warning him. If Buster hadn't
tried to alert him to the presence of other horses, he
would undoubtedly be a sleeping target by his big
campfire.

Without knowing who, or how many, he decided to

get behind the figure he had seen slipping through the trees bordering the clearing. Until he knew what he was facing, he was reluctant to take any action. His immediate concern was Ansel Beaudry lying helpless near the fire. Whoever was advancing upon his camp, lone robber or Beaudry men, might not realize he was chained to the tree, and open fire. Driven by his intent to see Beaudry executed by rope on the gallows in Fort Smith, he quickly pushed through the bushes where he had seen the figure disappear. He came upon the stalker almost immediately, lying on his stomach, his rifle before him, aimed at the sleeping figure lying beside the tree. Unaware of Will behind him, the man reached up and levered a cartridge into the chamber, then put his finger on the trigger. With no time for conscious thought, Will fired, no more than a split second before Junior Hutto squeezed the trigger. His shot was high and wide of the target, while Will's struck dead center between Junior's shoulder blades.

On the other side of the clearing, Mica Beaudry cursed. "That damn fool," he hissed to Todd kneeling beside him, "I said nobody shoot, until I shoot." His plan to walk right in to surprise the sleeping pair was now destroyed with more reports of gunfire from Brady and Rufus. He raised his Colt handgun and fired, concentrating his aim on what appeared to be a sleeping man several yards away from the one by the tree, thinking that to be the lawman. It mattered little, because there were enough pistol and rifle shots fired at the camp to hit both targets a dozen times over. Finally, the shooting stopped, there being no return fire from either form lying in the camp. A long moment of silence followed until Mica suddenly appeared at the edge of the clearing with Todd a step behind him. Soon, Brady and Rufus left their ambush positions and they all advanced cautiously toward the campfire.

Back on the far side of the clearing, Will moved up to the body lying still in the bushes before him. Kneeling beside him, he rolled the body over to make sure he was dead. Even in the darkness, he recognized the battered face of Junior Hutto. His shot to prevent Ansel from being executed was unsuccessful, but at the time, he didn't know there was a firing squad getting set to murder anything living in the camp. He knew now that he was up against four men, as they closed in on the campfire. Then he heard one call out.

"Where's Junior?" Brady asked, then yelled, "Hey, Junior, come on out. We got 'em."

When Junior failed to come out or respond to Brady's call, Mica said, "Better go see about him. He mighta got hit by one of our shots."

Brady started to do as he said, but was stopped when Todd blurted, "That ain't nothin' but an empty blanket." He followed that with, "Ansel's chained to the tree! Where the hell's the other one?"

"I'm right here," Will announced from the edge of the clearing. "You can drop your weapons on the ground and get on your knees. I'll shoot the first one that tries anything."

There was a moment of hesitation on the part of all four, then Mica, infuriated to have succeeded only in the death of his son, shouted back, "The hell we will. You're by yourself, so maybe you'd best come outta there and maybe I'll let you live."

"I'll shoot the first one that tries anything," Will repeated, "so drop the weapons."

"Maybe we'd better do as he says, Papa," Todd said,

not willing to chance a wild gunfight that was bound to result in some of them getting shot before the lawman was dead.

"The hell we will," replied the stubborn old man. "You'd best run if you wanna live 'cause we're comin' after you." He started toward Will. "Come on, boys, he can't fight all of us. Spread out!"

With only a small tree for cover, Will had hoped they wouldn't follow the old man's orders to charge him, but caught between their reluctance to attack and their fear of Mica Beaudry, they spread out and came at him in a line. He did the only thing he could think of to stop the assault. He fired at Rufus on the left, hitting him in the leg, and as he went down, Will reloaded, turned to the right and put a bullet in Brady's shoulder. It effectively stopped the charge. "The next one's for you, old man," Will warned. "Stop right there and drop your weapons."

"To hell with you!" Mica shouted, and started to come forward again, firing at the tree where Will was kneeling. Then suddenly Todd staggered and fell to his knees, clutching his side, leaving his father to face the lawman alone. Mica stopped and looked at his son as if angry that he let himself get hit. "Now, by God," Mica roared, "you've killed my family, but you'll by God face me."

"Let that be the end of it," a voice from behind Mica advised, "or I'll cut you down with this shotgun." Sheriff Joe McCauley appeared at the edge of the clearing and walked up behind the fallen men. "There's enough dead and wounded here already. If there's another one, it's gonna be you, old man." Finally seeing the hopelessness of his situation, Mica cursed and threw his gun on the ground and stood there scowling as Will stepped out into the clearing. Mica turned to glare at McCauley then before merely glancing at his wounded crew, with no more compassion for his son than for the other men. "Rusty!" McCauley yelled. "Bring them horses up here and bring some rope. We've got some prisoners to tie up." He looked at Will. "Good evenin', Deputy, looks like you were havin' quite a party here. I don't think it turned out the way your guests were plannin' it, though. Hope you don't mind me bargin' in, but it looked like you had more'n you could handle."

Will smiled. "Sheriff, you're welcome to any of these parties I have." He took a close look at Mica then, thinking he was looking evil right in the face. "So you'd be Mica Beaudry," he said to him, then nodded toward the body lying chained to the tree. "You sure as hell killed your son dead enough. I reckon you're proud of that."

"I was aimin' to kill him, anyway," Mica claimed, with no show of remorse. "And I was damn sure gonna kill you." With the guns of two lawmen trained on him, he finally accepted the fact that he was finished.

Rusty Dale entered the clearing at that moment, leading all of the horses that the Hornet's Nest gang had left by the creek. McCauley introduced him to Will and the three of them decided what to do with the prisoners. Much to Will's relief, the sheriff was willing to put the lot of them in his jail and send word to the Texas Rangers. "They can decide how to charge them and what happens after that," McCauley said. "I'll get Doc Slaughter to patch up their wounds, but he'll wanna be paid to do it. It'll be like any arrest we have. The town will have to pay to treat 'em and feed 'em till the Rangers take possession."

"I've got a better idea," Will said, "that'll save your town a little money. I've got Ansel Beaudry's share of some money from bank robberies in Kansas and Missouri. I've never counted it, but it's a helluva lot of money. I think it should be turned over to the Rangers and the Texas courts, less your expenses for taking care of the prisoners. Course, all these gentlemen didn't take part in those robberies, but the dead one chained to that tree was the leader of the gang that stole it."

It took a while, but they finally took charge of the prisoners and got them on their horses for the short ride back to town. Will helped with the jailing of them and left Ansel's share of the bank money with McCauley. After Mica and his men were locked up, Will accepted the sheriff's invitation to have a drink at the saloon across from the jail. After the evening just past, he felt like he needed one. It wasn't until the drinks were poured that Will thought to ask a question. "Like I already told you, I was sure happy to see you when you showed up back there by the creek. But how'd you happen to come, anyway?"

"I've got special mental powers that tell me when a lawman is in trouble," McCauley said, paused to watch Will's reaction, then laughed. "Nah, Rusty was here in the saloon when that fellow and his men rode into town. The old man came in here askin' if anybody saw a man ridin' a buckskin horse and leadin' another man in handcuffs ride through town. Rusty told me and we decided to see if you might be needin' some help." He chuckled again. "We were almost too late for the party, weren't we?"

"I ain't complainin'," Will answered. With Ansel off his hands, and his father no longer chasing him, he couldn't help having a great feeling of relief.

When he thought about it later, he would feel a certain regret for not transporting Ansel back to the gallows. He didn't even take the body back, since he and McCauley decided it best to leave it there to verify Ansel's death for the Texas Rangers. He had planned to watch Ansel hang to fulfill the promise he had made to Oscar Moon's memory. All things considered, however, Ansel suffered a fitting execution at the hands of his father.

Chapter 20

After a couple of drinks with McCauley, Will decided it was time to try once again to bed down for the night. When the sheriff suggested he should stay at the hotel that night and breakfast there in the morning, Will had to remind himself that his job was finished and there was no longer a threat upon his life. "I'll join you there for breakfast," McCauley said.

Will thought about it for a couple of moments before deciding. "Hell, why not? But I think I'll put my horses in the stable and sleep in there with 'em, if the owner will let me. Then I'll be glad to take you up on that breakfast. I've eaten so much sowbelly and hardtack lately till I feel like I'm part hog."

When they left the saloon, McCauley walked down to the stable with him and introduced him to Lamar Morgan, who owned it. Morgan was happy to accommodate Will's horses and charged nothing extra for Will to sleep with them. McCauley left then with the promise to meet him for breakfast in the hotel dining room at six the next morning. Will agreed, even though it would mean a late start for him, but he reminded himself once again that it didn't matter now. After giving his horses a portion of oats, he made his bed in the fresh hay Morgan had tossed down for that purpose.

With no reason to sleep with one eye open, he took advantage of his soft bed and awakened only when Lamar Morgan opened the stable at five-thirty. After Will saddled Buster and rearranged his packs on the packhorse, since there was no longer a rider on the sorrel, he paid Morgan and climbed up into the saddle. There was a dun gelding tied up at the hitching rail in front of the hotel, so he figured McCauley was already there. He grabbed his rifle as a matter of habit, and his saddlebags because they still held Luther Curry's share of the bank money, and went inside. McCauley, seated at a table near the kitchen door, signaled him with a wave of his arm.

The breakfast was as good as McCauley had promised it would be, and Mary Bea, the lady who ran the dining room, was quick to keep the coffee cups filled. When Will decided it was time for him to get started home, he thanked McCauley again for his help with the Hornet's Nest crew. As he got up to leave, the sheriff asked, "You mean to tell me you rode all that time with that big mess of money, and you never counted it?"

"That's a fact," Will answered. "Never had a reason to. It didn't belong to me." He thought he could almost hear the wheels turning in Joe McCauley's brain, so he couldn't resist adding something else. "That money was from at least two different banks, and there ain't no tellin' how much of it Ansel Beaudry has already spent." McCauley did not reply, but nodded as if seriously considering that fact. "Well,

I'd best be on my way," Will said, extended his hand, and got to his feet. He guessed that McCauley, unlike himself, had already counted the money in the sack he had given him and couldn't keep his mind from speculating. Will had to admit that he didn't care what he did with the money. He said good-bye and left McCauley seated at the table, drinking coffee.

In the saddle again, he set Buster on the road to Sherman at a pace comfortable for his horses, with only a glance at the spot where he had turned off the road to follow the creek up to make camp. *That could have turned out a hell of a lot different,* he thought, *if Joe McCauley hadn't shown up when he did.* He shook his head when he considered what might have been. *Sophie might have been a widow before she even got married.* That, in turn, opened the floodgates in his mind to thoughts of his upcoming wedding. These were the thoughts that he had constantly struggled to suppress while he was in the midst of trying to bring Ansel Beaudry's gang to justice. As he rode along, following the road to Sherman, Texas, he thought about that last morning at Bennett House, when he had left before breakfast without smoothing things over with Sophie. She had refused to see him the night before when she found out he was planning to leave again. He had discovered that she was possessed of a hot temper when sufficiently aroused, and he seemed to arouse it every time he left town on an assignment. Sophie's mother was not very talented at hiding her opposition to the marriage, although she never openly said as much to him. Maybe Ruth was right in trying to save her daughter the same heartbreak she had suffered with the death of Fletcher Pride. Maybe it would be the honorable thing for him to break off the relationship for Sophie's sake. It would be a hard thing for him to do, because he knew he genuinely loved her. He had made a promise to her to leave the Marshals Service and take her back to the J-Bar-J in Texas, and he was sincere in that promise. The thing that was difficult to explain to her was the loyalty he owed to Dan Stone to at least stay until there was not such a shortage of deputy marshals. "Hell," he muttered to Buster, "I told her we'd ride down here to see the ranch, so, damn it, that's what I'll do. I'll tell Dan he's just gonna have to do without me for a while." The decision made, he tried to put it out of his mind, else he was afraid he was going to drive himself crazy.

Anxious to get back home now, he did not stop in Sherman and rode into the little town of Durant, Oklahoma Territory, in a day and a half from Denton. It was late afternoon when he reined Buster to a halt at the railroad depot, where he dismounted and walked into the telegraph office. "Will Tanner!" Wilford Leach exclaimed when he opened the door. "It's been a while since you've been to Durant."

"I reckon it has, at that," Will returned.

"What brings you down our way?"

"I've been down in Texas," Will replied. "I'm on my way back to Fort Smith and I need to send a telegram to my boss and let him know I'm still alive." Although it was a casual remark, Dan Stone was not at all sure if his best deputy was alive or not. He had not heard from Will in quite some time. Will wrote the message for Wilford to send, telling Dan where he was and that he expected to be back in Fort Smith in three and a half days.

When the message was sent, Will paid for it, and Wilford commented, "So you ain't gonna be stayin' in town."

"That's right," Will said. "I'm gonna stop at the store and get a few things. I'm about out of supplies. Then I'll be on my way." He said so long to Wilford then and headed for Dixon Durant's general merchandise store.

"Howdy, Will," Leon Shipley greeted him when he walked into the store. "You just get into town?"

"Yep," Will answered, "about twenty minutes ago, and I'll be ridin' out in about that long, if I can get a few things I'm short on."

"Yes, sir, I'll see if I can fix you up," Leon said. "First thing is some coffee. You ain't ever come in here without buyin' some more coffee."

"That's a fact," Will said with a chuckle, "so gimme two pounds of it. That oughta see me to Fort Smith. I need some flour, some sugar, and some dried apples, if you've got any. Wouldn't hurt to throw in a box of .44 cartridges, too, and about five pounds of bacon. I think I'm gonna have to throw out the last of mine, it's gone rancid on me." *At least, that's what Ansel Beaudry said*, he thought.

Once he had packed up his supplies, he left town, heading for the Jack Fork Mountains and the Sans Bois Mountains beyond. It was a familiar trail and one which in years past sometimes found him stopping overnight in the Sans Bois for a visit with an old friend. But Perley Gates was long gone from his crude shack built in the side of a mountain, headed west, so he heard. He wouldn't be riding that far today, anyway. His horses were already tired, so he'd stop as soon as he found a place that suited him.

* * *

True to his word in the telegram to Dan Stone, he rode into Fort Smith at three o'clock in the afternoon, according to his railroad pocket watch, on the fourth day after leaving Durant. His first stop, as usual, was at the stable, where Vern Tuttle welcomed him back. "I was startin' to wonder when I was gonna see you again," Vern said. "You musta been on a long trip."

"You could say that," Will responded as he pulled Buster's saddle off and placed it in his customary spot on the rail of one of the back stalls while Vern pulled the saddle off the sorrel. "Near 'bout every time you come home, you're leadin' a different packhorse," Vern couldn't resist commenting. "And half the time they're totin' a saddle instead of a pack saddle."

"Reckon so," Will said. "Buster and the sorrel have been workin' hard, so they need a portion of grain. After I report in, I expect I'll be back today or tomorrow and take both of 'em over to see Fred Waits to have him put new shoes on 'em." He said so long to Vern then, threw his saddlebags over his shoulder, pulled his rifle from the saddle sling, and walked up the street in the direction of the courthouse.

"Well, I'll be damned," U.S. Marshal Daniel Stone proclaimed, "if it ain't my missin' deputy."

"Howdy, Dan," Will returned. When his boss appeared to be genuinely surprised to see him, he asked, "Did you get my telegram from Durant?"

"Yes, I got it," Dan replied. "I got that telegram and the one you sent from Camp Supply. What I'm wonderin' is what the hell were you doin' between those two wires? It was a mighty long time between."

"Well, like I said in the telegram, I arrested the last one of that gang, and I started back here with him, but we were jumped by his daddy and four of his men. Ansel Beaudry didn't make it through the attack, and I reckon I might not have made it, either, if it hadn't been for Sheriff Joe McCauley and his deputy."

"So you had to shoot Beaudry?" Stone asked.

"Well, I didn't shoot him, his daddy did," Will replied.

Stone hesitated, confused, then asked, "Where is this Sheriff McCauley?"

"Denton," Will answered.

"Denton?" Stone recoiled. "I don't know as I recall a town in Oklahoma Territory named Denton."

Stone was playing a game of cat and mouse with him, and Will knew it, but he persevered. "Denton, Texas," he stated simply.

Stone paused, pursed his lips, and frowned as if admonishing a child. "There, you see, you're operatin' all over the map, anywhere you take a notion to go. I gave you a direct order not to follow those outlaws out of Oklahoma Territory, didn't I?"

Will shrugged and hesitated before answering. "Well, sir, what you said was not to follow 'em into Kansas. You never said anything about Texas." In an effort to cut Stone's intention to reprimand him for crossing borders, Will took the money out of his saddlebags and placed it on Dan's desk. "Here's what I brought back. It was in the possession of a fellow named Luther Curry. I had to shoot him when he and Beaudry tried to ambush me. Beaudry's share of the bank's money was left with Sheriff McCauley, along with his body. McCauley's turnin' the body and the money over to the Texas Rangers. The rest of what's left of the money is in a safe at Camp Supply."

Finding it difficult to reprimand Will for disregarding his orders, especially when he considered Will Tanner the best deputy he had, Stone gave up. He sighed and shook his head, then said he was glad to see Will safely back home. To bring him up to date, he told Will that the prisoners, along with the stolen money, had been taken into custody and they would go to trial shortly. Will felt obligated to offer his opinion that, of the three, only Bo Hagen should be tried for murder. "You know Tom Daly," he said. "He ain't really done much more than steal cattle and act as a guide for Beaudry. And Cecil Cox wasn't a gunman, either. He just ended up with the wrong folks at the wrong time."

"I'd like you to write it all down, everything you can remember," Stone said. "Then I guess you'd like to get on home to see that little lady of yours. When you see her, tell her you did a job single-handedly that two companies of deputy marshals in Missouri and Kansas couldn't get done. Then you'd best take a couple of days off to take care of that business with her." Pointing to Will's left sleeve, he asked, "Is that something Doc Peters needs to look at?"

"No," Will said. "It's already been doctored." He declined to say by whom, and he wasn't planning to say anything about Elmira Tate and her cabin on Grassy Creek in his written report. He started to leave, but thought of one more thing. "Was there any mention in the report from that posse about some horses the army was holding for me at Camp Supply?"

"Yes, there was, as I recall, there was a number of horses the army had been holding that went back with

the posse. I forget the number, but I can find it for you."
He made a motion to leaf through a stack of papers on
his desk.

"No need to bother," Will said. "It ain't important."
Damn, he thought, *I was planning to sell those horses.*

He was torn between two emotions as he walked
down the street toward Bennett House, eager to see
Sophie, yet not sure what his reception might be. She
was pretty hot under the collar when he left, even to
the point of refusing to see him when he knocked on
her door. Consequently, he wasn't sure if he would be
welcomed back. He made it a point to quicken his
pace when he passed by the Morning Glory Saloon,
lest someone might hail him. The last time he stopped
in there for supper on his way home didn't turn out
too well for him.

Once he was past the saloon, he slowed his pace
again in order to give himself more time to think
about what he was going to do. It was past time to
decide if he wanted to marry Sophie or not. That was
already a commitment, and one he wanted to honor.
He had already popped the question, and she had
accepted his proposal. He had also told her he would
turn in his badge and return to the J-Bar-J. He decided
he could honor that commitment as well. Sophie was
worth it. With those thoughts settled in his mind, he
opened the gate in the picket fence before Bennett
House and followed the path to the porch.

Neither Ron Sample nor Leonard Dickens was on
the front porch, so he figured supper must be ready.
When he walked in the front door, he found the
parlor empty as well, but he could hear the sounds of

suppertime coming from the dining room. He took a glance at the clock on the parlor wall and decided he had time to do a quick cleanup before he surprised everyone, at least a quick shave and wash his face and hands, maybe a clean shirt from his room. He was sure he must look pretty woolly, but he didn't want to miss supper, so he went down the hall and took the back stairs up to his room.

Startled when he suddenly appeared in the doorway of his room, Sophie jumped when she saw him. Startled as well to find her in his room, he wasn't sure what to say, so they stood frozen for a long moment before she finally spoke. "We heard you were back, so I was just checking to make sure your room didn't need dusting or anything."

"How'd you know I was back?"

"Vern Tuttle sent word that Fred Waits came in the stable after you left. He wanted to tell you that he told Fred to shoe your horses."

"Oh." Will nodded, then after a moment, said, "At least that was better than stoppin' at the Mornin' Glory before I came home."

She couldn't help laughing. "I guess it is," she said. Then she realized that the brown stains on his sleeve were dried blood. "Oh, Will," she cried.

"It's nothin'," he quickly explained. "A little bullet wound, but it's all fixed, bullet's out, and it's already halfway healed." She shook her head impatiently. "I guess I look pretty rough," he said. "I was gonna try to clean up a little bit before I scared everybody at the supper table."

She placed her hands on her hips and fashioned a pretty little pout. "Oh, you did, did you? What makes you think there's a place set at the table for you?"

Will wasn't sure if she was serious or not. She had indicated that she was all but finished with him when he had left. "Well, I thought I'd paid Ruth for my room and board through the first of the year," he said, then grinned.

She shook her head and sighed a weary sigh. "Will Tanner, I wish to heaven I didn't love you so much."

**Keep reading for a special preview
of the next Johnstone epic!**

SPRINGFIELD 1880
by William W. Johnstone and J. A. Johnstone

*From the greatest western writers of our time comes a
blazing epic adventure inspired by a weapon from
America's past—and dedicated to those who
used it to forge America's future . . .*

Captain Jed Foster is more than a thief. He's a traitor.
With a handful of murderous rogues, he's run off
with four wagons containing new Springfield rifles,
bayonets, and ammunition meant to resupply the
troops at Fort Bowie in Arizona Territory. Foster plans
to sell the weapons to the highest bidder—whether it's
Apaches, Mexican revolutionaries, or Confederate
veterans who still dream of destroying the Union.
But that's the least of Foster's problems . . .

His junior officer, Lieutenant Grat Holden, is coming
after him. If Holden can't bring the renegade to justice,
he'll face court-martial for losing the wagons. If he's
caught crossing the Mexican border, the U.S. Army will
deny knowledge of the mission. Holden can't do it
alone. With the help of an ornery ex-sergeant known
as "Hard Rock" Masterson and the fiery guerilla fighter
Soledad, the young lieutenant will have to face off with
war chiefs, banditos, and cutthroat outlaws.
That's just for starters. Then he's got to take down a
man with enough guns for a small army . . .

*So begins the biggest, bloodiest manhunt south of the border—
and the only way out is to go down fighting . . .*

**Look for SPRINGFIELD 1880
coming in May 2019 wherever books are sold.**

Prologue

In 1880, the Springfield Armory of Springfield, Massachusetts, sent roughly one thousand new Model 1880 trapdoor .45-70-caliber rifles to Army troops stationed on the American frontier for testing in the field. The factory and the US Army hoped the new rifles would be an improvement over Springfield's Model 1873 rifle.

This is the story of two hundred and fifty of those Springfield 1880s.

Chapter 1

The last thing Second Lieutenant Grat Holden wanted to see was the dust he just spotted. It drifted in the cloudless sky beyond the "Two Heads," the outcropping of rocks that topped the Dos Cabezas, which was how the mountains got their name. He had seen dust earlier, too, on the other side of the trail and had shrugged that off as a dust devil. Now, he unfastened the flap that protected the Schofield .45-caliber revolver on his left hip.

Hooves beat toward him. Sergeant Byron Lusk reined in his dun gelding and turned his head to water a rock with tobacco juice. "Beggin' yer pardon, suh, but—"

"I see it, Sergeant," Holden said.

"Figured you would, sir. Almost didn't even ride up to tell you."

"Be glad you did, Sergeant. I don't see everything."

"Like that, suh?"

Holden followed the gray-haired sergeant's crooked finger, which pointed southeast, toward the pass they found themselves bound to pass in a few minutes. The lieutenant, however, saw only Arizona rocks, Arizona sky, and felt the Arizona heat. He was soaked with sweat beneath his dark tunic, but it wasn't just the heat that caused him to sweat.

"What was it, Sergeant?" Holden asked.

"Looked like the sun reflectin' off somethin'. Rifle. Knife. Pretty brass concha." He chuckled. "Maybe gold. Wouldn't that be somethin'?"

Pulling the reins up on his bay gelding, Holden raised his right hand and heard the command called out from the first wagon behind him down to the fourth. As soon as the horse stopped, he turned to his saddlebags and found the pair of binoculars, which he brought to his face after pushing up the brim of his battered slouch hat and studied the trail, the hills above the trail, and the split between the "Two Heads."

"More dust, suh," Lusk said.

Without lowering the binoculars, Holden asked, "Where?"

"On the trail. Somewhere between the hills."

The lieutenant swept another look through his glasses, but, seeing nothing, lowered them in his left hand and studied the road before him. "On the trail?"

"Yes, suh. But if it's a rider, he ain't come out yet."

"Unless he's riding toward Dos Cabezas, Apache Pass, or Fort Bowie," Holden said. Dos Cabezas wasn't much of a town to be riding to at a pace fast enough to raise dust seen by the naked eye from that distance.

"He ain't, suh." Lusk pointed to the road. "Rained yesterday. Good soaker."

Holden nodded. "I know, Sergeant. No tracks. Maybe he sees our dust, though."

More tobacco juice splattered the road. Sergeant Lusk wiped his mustache, beard, and lips with the brown-stained end of one of his gauntlets. "We are close to Bowie, suh."

"Close to Apache country, too, Sergeant."

The noncommissioned officer chuckled. "Hell, suh, we're surrounded by Apache country."

Holden looked back at his command. He was twenty-seven years old. The men behind him made him feel ancient. Five years out of West Point, five years in Arizona Territory, and he was a battle-hardened veteran of the frontier. The men he commanded, with the exception of his sergeant, were as new as what they were hauling in four government freight wagons.

Brand-spanking new Springfield trapdoor rifles, fresh from the armory in Springfield, Massachusetts. Crates of them, not to mention the new triangular bayonets that could be affixed underneath the barrel and enough .45-70-caliber cartridges to start a war. The Army didn't need to start another war. They had a good one going on with the Apaches. Sometimes, Holden thought the Apaches might win.

Back at Fort Bowie, Colonel Carlton Smythe didn't think much of sending experimental Springfield rifles to be tested by troops, most still wet behind the ears, against veteran Apache guerrillas. Nor did Colonel Smythe like rifles. The cavalry used shorter carbines, easier to maneuver on horseback. And he despised bayonets. Shoot, Holden hadn't even seen one saber carried by an officer in that desert country except during parades.

So Colonel Smythe had sent Lieutenant Holden to Fort Lowell in Tucson to fetch the weapons, the ammunition, and some new green troops, and bring them back to Fort Bowie.

Rubbing the beard stubble on his cheeks and jaw,

Holden tried to figure out his best course. Make it through the little pass, and they would be a few miles from the village of Dos Cabezas. Another twenty-five miles, through Apache Pass, and they would be home safe at Fort Bowie.

It was just getting there . . . alive . . . that troubled him.

"You know what the colonel says." Sergeant Lusk shifted his chaw to another cheek.

"Yeah." Holden leaned back in the saddle. "But he hasn't fired a Springfield or any rifle in the five years I've been here. He leaves that to his junior officers and their men. He hasn't led anything but Fourth of July parades and courts-martial."

"That's one reason I like you, suh. You speak your mind. You tell the truth. And you fight, suh. You fight alongside the rest of us. I figure you ain't no officer at all."

That led Holden to grin . . . till the sergeant said, "Just gettin' kilt over weapons that might not be worth spit . . . I dunno, suh."

"Want to leave the wagons behind?"

"No. Don't reckon we should do that, suh."

Again, Holden looked back. He had eight troopers on four wagons. Ten men.

"Maybe the Apaches heard the same Colonel Smythe heard, suh. That these weapons ain't worth spit."

Holden shook his head. "I've seen Apaches armed with a blunderbuss that likely hadn't been fired since the Revolution. I've seen them throw rocks. And, begging the colonel's pardon, I don't think the Springfield Armory would send us a rifle that will blow up in our faces. Might not be better than what we have now, but an Apache or some Mexican bandit would likely sell his soul to have one. Especially as many as we're carrying."

"Lieutenant!" Sergeant Lusk pointed to the opening of the passage.

A rider came loping out. He was raising a lot of dust.

Chapter 2

Holden let out a curse, wheeled his horse around, and loped back to the first wagon where he barked orders at the two blond-headed troopers, one pudgy, the other weighing about as much as a cholla cactus.

The troopers—he couldn't remember their names—stared at him blankly.

"Ich verstehe nicht."

The other said, *"Ich Rann Sie nicht verstehen."*

Then both said, shrugging, *"Nein."*

Holden cursed the two Germans probably just off the boat. He cursed the recruiters who sent those two pilgrims to Arizona. He cursed his father for sending him to the United States Military Academy, and he cursed his commanding officer. Then he yelled at the two men, both Americans, in the next wagon.

"Set the brakes to the wagon and crawl into the back. Cock your weapons and wait for me. But if somebody shoots me off my horse, do your best to stay alive. And pass the word down!"

It was a silly order. He'd shouted so loud the men in the last wagon understood, and maybe even the two

Germans got an idea about what he wanted because both took their Springfield carbines.

Those were 1873 trapdoor models with twenty-two-inch barrels, and they fired the same caliber as the ones in the crates they had been hauling for close to a hundred miles. He doubted if the recruits with him had fired a weapon since Jefferson Barracks, and if shooting started . . . *God help the mules pulling our freight.*

The bay gelding carried Holden back to Sergeant Lusk, who had brought up his Springfield, also a carbine, and rested the butt against his right thigh while keeping the reins in his left hand.

Holden reined up and studied the dust and the rider. "Still just one?"

"Yes, suh. Ain't slowed down."

"Watch the hills, Sergeant, especially where you saw dust earlier."

"You are somethin' cautious, Lieutenant."

Holden grinned. "I'm alive, Byron. I'm alive."

He found the binoculars again, and brought them to his face. It took him just moments to find the rider and bring him and the horse into focus. What he first saw, at least clearly, were the spurs. Brass. Army-issue. On black boots, also provided by Uncle Sam. He saw blue pants.

The horse was steel dust. He saw the beaded gauntlets gripping the rein, the posture that told him the rider had likely been born in the saddle. The saddle seemed to be a McClellan. By then Holden's heartbeat had steadied and his lungs had stopped heaving. He still sweated. He figured he would always sweat. But he was about to think that he had worked his men up, his horse up, and himself up for nothing.

The binoculars raised, and he saw the rider's face.

The damned prankster seemed to be smiling, and his eyes, though squinting from the pounding in the saddle and the wind and the dust, might have been staring all the way across the remaining three hundred yards at Lieutenant Grat Holden. Laughing.

"Sergeant Lusk." Holden lowered the binoculars and shook his head.

Lusk turned toward him.

"Have the men stand down," Holden said. "It's the captain."

The noncommissioned officer stood in his stirrups and trained his bare eyes on the approaching galloper.

"You sure, Lieutenant?"

"I'm sure."

"What's Captain Foster doin', suh, ridin' a horse like that?"

"Other than acting like one son of a bitch, Sergeant, I don't have a clue. But I'm sure he'll tell us directly."

Captain Jed Foster's cackles could be heard over the pounding of the steel dust's hooves. An expert rider, Foster pulled on the reins and the gelding slid to a stop in front of Holden and Lusk. By the time the dust cloud had settled, Foster was removing his buckskin gauntlets and shoving them into the deep pockets of his golden buckskin jacket with fringes longer than eight inches on the sleeves.

"Hello, Mr. Holden." Jed Foster was forty years old, and after close to twenty years in the service—the first four with the Seventh Michigan Cavalry during the War of the Rebellion, and the last decade and a half in the regular Army—he looked no older than Holden.

Foster had a golden mustache with the ends twisted, a pointed goatee, and hair that fell to his shoulders.

"Captain," Holden said, offering a salute that was not returned, "you're looking a lot like Custer today, sir."

"I sure hope not." Foster pulled at the stampede string securing his white hat dangling on his back and set the hat on his curly blond hair. "He is dead, you know, Mr. Holden. I'm very much alive."

"Yes, sir." Holden had to smile. *Very much alive* described Jed Foster to a T. Tall, muscular, athletic, Foster was the envy of practically every junior officer at Fort Bowie . . . and quite a few of the married officers looked upon the dashing figure with a good amount of jealousy. He could waltz. He could do everything from the French contra dance to the mazurka or the galop or the quadrille.

Holden noticed the bedroll and grip strapped behind Foster's saddle.

"Are you going somewhere, Captain?"

"Taking a leave, Mr. Foster. The Army owes me six months. They're giving me one."

"Where to, sir . . . if I may ask?"

"I think Mexico, Mr. Holden. There's nothing like celebrating Independence Day on the Fourth of July in Mexico."

"I don't believe Mexico celebrates our independence, Captain."

Mexico. Jed Foster belonged in a place like San Francisco or New Orleans. Maybe the new mining metropolis just south of there called Tombstone. Chicago, New York, Boston, Charleston, or even Washington City.

"Then I'll celebrate her. By myself if I have to."

"Why Mexico, sir?"

Foster grinned. He had perfect teeth, too, and dark blue eyes. "Mr. Holden, have you ever heard of tequila and señoritas?"

"I have met tequila on two occasions and have conceded that he is the better man."

Foster laughed his thick laugh, shook his head, and beat the dust off his clothes. "And what about señoritas?"

"I don't get out of Bowie much, sir."

"You were just in Tucson."

"Only saw Fort Lowell, sir."

Foster's tongue clucked. "One day, Grat, you and I will need to take us a trip. I can show you some fine places. Let you grow up some."

"Thank you, sir."

Foster looked at the wagons, the men, and then turned around in his saddle to stare at the road to Fort Bowie.

"You nervous, Lieutenant?"

"Cautious, sir."

"Want some company?"

"You have Mexico, sir."

"Well, the canyon you cut through is shady, and it is a trifle warm today. And my horse here"—he patted the neck—"seems a bit winded. I could at least get you to the other side of the canyon. Maybe even all the way to Dos Cabezas. There's a saloon there. You can reacquaint yourself with your old nemesis, tequila."

Holden's head shook good-naturedly.

"Well . . . let's just say that I might not make it to Mexico. Dos Cabezas might do me fine. I'll ride along with you, Lieutenant, if you have no objections."

"I always enjoy your company, sir."

"Very good." Foster raised his hand and turned his horse. "Forward, yo-oo."

Connect with Us

Visit us online at
KensingtonBooks.com
to read more from your favorite authors, see books
by series, view reading group guides, and more.